# The
# Impossible
# Lover

BOOK ONE

OF

THE GRAILCHASE CHRONICLES

BY
DARA FOGEL

Copyright © 2014 Dara Fogel
All rights reserved.
ISBN: 0985926163
ISBN-13: 978-0-9859261-6-8

To My Infinite Beloved

*Ire fortiter quo nemo ante iit*

# CONTENTS

# ACKNOWLEDGMENTS

Special thanks to my husband, Richard, my mother, Joane',
and my son, Julian, for putting up with me. I am
eternally indebted to Kevin Mathe'
and to my father, Norman Fogel

# Chapter One

"So, my friends, it is decided," Don Alessandro Eduardo D'Amici told his guests as he ushered them through the secret doorway and into the wood-paneled library. Once all were inside, he said, "Sergio Aldo must be stopped, and it has fallen to we three to do it… we three and my Telepathon device!"

Don Alessandro, the twenty-third Marquis of Perego, pivoted closed and secured the two doors to a large enclosed bookcase, concealing the hidden stairway to the underground. The muffled click of a heavy bolt sounded as he turned the two keys simultaneously in their holes. He removed the keys from the thick, glass-paned doors and placed them into a small silver box, which he slipped into the pocket of his charcoal grey frock coat.

"Aldo cannot be allowed any further influence in the politics and governance of Europe," Don Alessandro continued, turning to the others, determination hardening his kind features. He was the smallest of the trio, a pudgy man in his mid-seventies, bearded, with a white curly mane and the bearing of an indulgent grandfather. A sweet-acrid whiff of frankincense still clung to the spry Don, lingering evidence of nocturnal activities below.

He made his way to a large, carved mahogany desk, while his two comrades sank into deep red tufted leather armchairs. Behind the desk, a fire roared upon the large hearth, warmth seeping into joints still aching from subterranean cold, despite the moderate summer night outside. Over the mantle, beneath a peak-arched ceiling, hung a fantastical life-size portrait, in which a beautiful young woman in black and blue gazed serenely over the three from her nest of stars.

"Once more, the Dark Brotherhood rises up to threaten the world with violence and tyranny. We thought we had taught them decades past to keep to Bavaria. But like the hydra, they keep returning with a new face. Aldo and his old *Carbonari* 'cousins' are using the unification of Italy to usurp the will of the people. The Carbonari have put their corrupt puppets in high political offices, and are bleeding the nobility and merchants dry. They make themselves rich whilst the people suffer deprivations and tragedy in the wake of civil war. The blackguards are writing this new constitution to favor themselves and their bootlickers, whilst bewitching the foolish masses with talk of 'One Italia!' and false promises of security and prosperity."

"But these Dark Ones are not content with taking over only Italy," the old Don went on, punctuating his words with broad gestures. "No, they threaten the liberty of all peoples, not only in Italy, but also in Spain, Prussia, France, even the Baltic kingdoms. Under the guise of nationalism, the Dark Ones seek to sow the seeds of anarchy and seize the levers of power for themselves. Crying 'Unity,' they seek to divide and conquer. Promising sovereignty, they dominate and rule like despots... They are fomenting rebellion and all over the Continent. And this is their most insidious goal, for they are reshaping of the minds of the masses by enticing them with the newest shiny toys. They convince the people to sell their life's efforts and passions to purchase shoddy manufactured goods, losing their craftsmanship skills to become factory workers, wage slaves afraid to lose their positions, to think only what thoughts the Illuminati would have them think... rendering them incapable of free thought and higher perceptions. The intellectual and spiritual freedom of the world is threatened."

"It is our duty to fight these forces of entropy and devolution," D'Amici continued, urgency raising his voice. "If we, the Grail Guardians fail, then many of the other traditions will also fall, and our ancient wisdom will no longer be used to guide humanity – it will vanish from the world, or worse, instead be turned to selfish purposes, and God help us then. All of Europe - perhaps the world, depends on stopping the advance of the Dark Ones, and the soul-destroying greed and materialism they bring. Now, they have sent Aldo to wrest this stronghold from us. I have sworn to defend this repository with my life." D'Amici slammed his fist on the leather desk pad. "I will destroy the Villa D'Amici and all the knowledge it contains before I will allow the Dark Ones to take it! ...However, I am confident that it won't come to that. I know it has been a long time, but we are now summoned us back into action, my brothers.

I stand ready to take up my ancient duty. I now call upon your support to help stop Aldo – we three, just like the old days."

"Yes, it is decided," said a stern, spindly man, his long legs folded up beneath him. Giuseppe Calyx, Don Alessandro's compatriot, was a Milanese judge with silvered hair and wire-rimmed spectacles poised on his hawk-like roman nose. A slight accent of Naples blurred his consonants. "But it is no longer the old days, 'Sandro. Now, it is a new day…" He stopped to take a deep breath before continuing. "The Matriarch has requested I relay that, after much debate and meditation on the matter, she has approved your plan." He bowed his head to the aging Don. "She orders you to stop work on developing the war machines for the time being and devote yourself to this matter.

"However, she cautions extreme care," Calyx went on. "Aldo was one of the most influential members of the *Carbonari* during the wars and now he has allied himself with outliers from the Germanic wing of the Dark Ones. If he can make these two branches of the Dark Brotherhood to put aside their historical differences and work together... The Illuminati and the Carbonari allied." He fought an unbidden shudder, and leaned forward to underscore the seriousness of his words. "Heavens defend us... There would be no end to the evil and death unleashed. Yes, we must stop Aldo before it is too late, before he is able to unite these diabolical influences."

Don Alessandro bowed his white head in mute acknowledgement, hiding the twinkle in his eye.

"What concerns the Matriarch the most about your plan is granting Aldo *any* access to the villa," Calyx reported. "We can't risk losing the Archives, as well as your workshop. If something were to go amiss and Aldo were to gain control of this stronghold..." His pause allowed the implied catastrophe to dawn upon the others. "Aldo and his friends have manipulated the tax laws and will legally seize the Villa if we do nothing. We *must* act, but is this the best way? It is the ancient trust of your ancestors to hold and protect the library and the accumulated wisdom of our brotherhood that it contains, Alessandro. Under no circumstances can we allow Aldo and his minions to discover how much of the old knowledge we still possess. The disaster that could result if the Archives or the Genealogies fell into the wrong hands would be unlike any previously faced in Europe. It carries the potential to destroy all Christendom, to undermine the very fabric of our civilization. And what of your contrivances? If they managed to seize just one of your Phlogiston devices Aldo could subjugate any army practically single-handed. The only way he could penetrate this fortress' defenses are from inside, by admitting him. Are you absolutely sure you can manage Aldo alone?"

The third member of the trio, a tall, man of late middling years, rose unbidden, went to a side table containing a large cut-glass cruet of Napoleon brandy and began pouring three stiff drinks.

"They didn't make me Defender of the Ages for nothing, Giuseppe," Don Alessandro retorted. "Aldo doesn't yet know we are onto him. I shall lure him here under the pretense of developing some mineral deposits up in the north quadrant, and then use the Telepathon to capture his mind. Once our trap is sprung, you and Delacroix will step in. Aldo won't know what hit him," Don Alessandro said with relish. "Over twenty-one years of working with the blasted thing, but finally, I have it. The Telepathon is my greatest achievement! With it, we cannot only manipulate Aldo's will, we can also peer into the contents of his very mind. But, you are right - Aldo *is* coming for Villa D'Amici, whether we stop him or no is up to us. Yes, the risk is great," Don Alessandro answered the lanky Neapolitan with a reassuring smile, "but I think you give Aldo too much credit. I have dealt with the man, you have not. Aldo is just a glorified errand-boy. I'll allow that he is cunning after a brutish fashion - but he is not that clever. Most of his success is due to blind luck and intimidation, not guile. You and I handled much worse than he, back in the old days, my friend. Aldo is nowhere near as wily as our old nemesis, Wittgenstein. Thank the heavens that devil Wittgenstein is long since dead and buried! Never fear, we three can easily dispatch the likes of Aldo. He will not have the opportunity to find the Archives.

The aging Don dismissed his companion's fears with a wave of his hand, as he continued.

"Even if Aldo does gain access to the villa, he is too lumpen to discover where Sangraal truly lies. Old Wittgenstein was a much subtler man than Signor Aldo. If I were up against Wittgenstein, then, yes, I would need all the help I could get. But Aldo... pah! The secrets of the Holy Grail are well hidden from the eyes of the profane. Don't let your new title of Counsel to the Matriarch go to your head, Giuseppe," he admonished Calyx with a wagging finger. "As well you know, my dear friend and partner, we D'Amici's have been guardians of the Archives for over thirty generations. We have learned a thing or two about dealing with megalomaniacs bent on twisting our sacred heritage to their own advantage. " Don Alessandro sat in the high-backed chair, with banked excitement.

He picked up a round brass clockwork device roughly the size of a grapefruit from his desk and waved it before his friends with bravado.

"Once I get the final adjustments completed on my Telepathon, Aldo will become *our* willing servant. I just need a little more time to calibrate the aetheric resonator with the new power source. The preliminary results are very promising… very promising indeed! Then, I will be able to impress upon Aldo that he has pursued the wrong path by directly accessing the inner recesses of his mind. I can use the Telepathon to learn from Aldo the Dark Brotherhoods' future intention, and determine if the Matriarch's suspicions are justified. The intelligences we access should prove extremely valuable. Once Aldo steps into range, boom! My Telepathon will ensnare him, whether he will it or no… We may then hold him for as long as necessary for the Matriarch to complete preparations for her campaign with our main forces, while we squeeze Aldo for information to help our brethren fighting so hard throughout Europe."

"I hope so, Sandro, I certainly hope so…" replied Calyx. "No one doubts your genius or your invention. However, I must confess to some ethical misgivings about mentally entrapping our enemies… Isn't that precisely why we condemn them – for enslaving the minds of the masses? I know what you are going to say, Sandro… they do it through deception for diabolical motives, and we are using your mind machine to protect the future of humanity… But does the end justify the means? Does resorting to their level, even if it is to defeat them – doesn't that corrupt the morality of our efforts…?"

"I can understand your scruples, Peppe," Don Alessandro said. "But the harsher truth is, if we do not change Aldo's mind, the only other alternative is to kill him. He is too dangerous to allow his blundering schemes to continue. We must protect this keep. I doubt he would find a nice philosophical conversation sufficiently persuasive."

Calyx's dark eyes took on a faraway stare and he considered the conundrum. Then, shaking his head and his doubt, he continued. "But, yes, you are right. The Matriarch agrees with your assessment. We must protect this stronghold. The greater good demands that we use all means at our disposal to stop our enemies. We don't have the resources for a frontal attack, and therefore needs must use subterfuge before it is too late," Calyx agreed thoughtfully, rubbing his temple with one hand as he accepted with the other a proffered crystal snifter of brandy from the third, silent member of the trio. "We may not get a second chance. But we must be sure. Remember, it is not only we Guardians whose fortunes are at stake, this has much broader implications. Mater Magda was very clear on that… What about your neighbor?"

Don Alessandro cracked a crooked grin.

"Old Stephano Calendri? He's in," the Marquis declared with satisfaction. "He doesn't like the new regime any more than we do. Calendri knows what is at risk and is willing to buy us all the time we need. Our old 'feud' has proven a very helpful camouflage, in that regard. Don't worry, Peppe. You'll see… It will be just like that time in Budapest."

Calyx glanced sidelong at Don Alessandro, as he muttered, "I think we remember Budapest differently." Removing his spectacles, he wiped them with a monogrammed linen handkerchief before returning them to their craggy perch. He then turned to the other member of their trio. "But what about you, Anton? You haven't said a word."

The silent man cleared his throat, uncomfortably on the spot, as he handed a fine crystal snifter to the Don, before taking a swig from his own glass.

"Well, I can see no way around it," he sighed at last.

Of the three men, Anton Delacroix was the youngest, being in his late fifties, yet easily the most imposing, even compared to the tall Neapolitan Calyx. Powerful, yet leanly built, Delacroix was in the last flush of robust middle age, with an easy agility that once fluttered many a young lady's heart. His shoulders were still broad and strong, but his narrow waist thickened. His handsomely weathered features twisted into a scowl above his salt-and-pepper beard, as his quick, perceptive eyes moved between his two companions.

"Obviously, Aldo must be stopped before he can gain a foothold. He cannot be allowed to take Villa D'Amici," Delacroix said, his deep resonant voice carrying a note of concern. "But, I don't understand why such a delicate job is left to us. We are all well past our prime. Why doesn't the Matriarch get some younger men to take down Aldo?"

"Because there are no young men available," Don Alessandro scowled. "You know as well as I that we lost the flower of our warriors in the wars, the remainders are either in Prussia or Spain, like Diego, preparing for the next campaign. Without sons and grandsons, all that is left is old men and babes."

"Yes, yes, I know all that. But what of that Haldane fellow?" Delacroix argued impatiently, as he retook his seat facing Don Alessandro. Calyx looked over sharply at the name. "Aldo plans to include him in his plot, already. Perhaps Haldane could be convinced to help from inside Aldo's camp as a double agent. Even if his mother did go renegade, he's still in the Lineage, and the lad shows promise. I've been keeping tabs on him, you know, despite what the Registrar might say about the official purity of his blood. I suspect that he might even carry some of the Delivier gifts, from his mother's line, of course."

"Yes, I've heard that too," Don Alessandro agreed, rubbing his chin thoughtfully. "He's certainly got the kind of tactical expertise we sorely need. We might approach him and see where he stands."

"I suggested as much to the Matriarch, but she said absolutely not," Calyx said with cautious regret. "Haldane's too unpredictable, just like his mother. Four decades later and we are still reeling from the blow she dealt us. She set back the Program for generations to come." Delacroix looked away at Calyx's words. The judge continued, "The Matriarch knows how gifted his line is, but that branch of the Delivier bloodline has become unstable, too adulterated with outsider blood. Besides, he is completely untrained, and well past the usual age of training. He has already developed bad habits that he likely could not unlearn. Haldane is unsuitable for our purposes. If the British Royal Army is unable to control him, what makes you think we could do any better? ...No, we cannot involve Haldane in this deeper than Aldo intends. The Mater forbids Haldane's involvement in this scheme of yours, Sandro. If Aldo suspected that Haldane knew the secret of his own heritage, Aldo would kill him without a second thought. As it is, Haldane is all too prone to Aldo's manipulations. For his own safety and ours, Haldane must never learn of our existence or his own hidden inheritance. We might be able to retrieve his bloodline in a generation or two, once the fires of rebellion have burnt out. But it is best that more experienced heads handle this. It is therefore up to us alone, we cannot trust Haldane."

The other men nodded in grudging agreement.

"Pity to waste all that potential," Delacroix murmured. "But I suppose you're right, Calyx."

Behind the reflective glass of his wire-rim spectacles, Calyx's eyes flashed relief at Delacroix's capitulation. He stood abruptly.

"I must be getting back to Milano – I'm expected at court in the morning. I trust you will notify both Delacroix and I when the time comes?"

"Of course, Giuseppe," the Don muttered, his white goatee twisted in a thoughtful frown, as he stood up. "I hope that you will be able to get some rest on your long ride back to town."

"Oh... and one more thing" Calyx paused, peering at the large painting of the ebony and cream young woman dominating the mantle. "A caution to you, Alessandro – keep your daughters well away from Haldane, should he ever have occasion to visit the villa. Remember the prophecy - and his reputation with the fairer sex."

# Chapter Two

## 13 September, 1872   Geneva, Switzerland  5:37 a.m.

Lieutenant Colonel Christopher Jordan Haldane, of Her Majesty, Queen Victoria's Royal Army Diplomatic Corps, snapped to consciousness. In the pre-dawn gray, he did not recognize the elegant bedroom in which he found himself. With accustomed volition, his hand slid under his pillow to touch the small revolver he had placed there the night before. Its hard, smooth surface assured him that he must be there of his own choosing, and he relaxed against the down pillows.

In the scant light, Haldane could almost make out the dark shadows and gold braid of his dress uniform sprawled across the thick Persian rug. Next to his hastily discarded clothes, he saw the folds of an abandoned ball gown.

*Ah, yes. Now it all comes back...* The formal reception he had attended last night at the British Embassy in the thriving financial center of Geneva, and the willowy young wife of a Swiss banker he escorted home.

*What's her name again? I know it begins with a G... Gretchen? No, that doesn't quite seem right. Greta, maybe... no, I remember now – Gretel.* He recalled teasing her by asking if she had a brother named Hansel lurking about. That was it, Haldane was sure. *Gretel... something.*

That established, he rolled over to see if his memory served. The pearl gray light revealed the expected white shoulder and masses of golden hair. A slow smile curled his dark mustache as he remembered the pleasures of the night before.

*Beautiful girl,* he thought, *but sadly, she has not been at all initiated in the ways of love. Why, she's absolutely inept.*

He had dutifully accepted it as his responsibility to be her tutor, and remedy the situation as best he could. Memories of the night before piqued his desire. Haldane rose onto one elbow and reached out to her smooth shoulder, glowing silver in the early morning light.

Gretel rolled onto her back. Smiling, she looked up at her lover. In the shadowed bedchamber, his eyes looked dark, but she remembered their smoldering green intensity, fringed in thick dark lashes any woman would kill to own. She had been attracted at once to the tall, dashing British officer and the forbidden adventure he offered. His fluid grace seemed exotic compared to the fat financiers and politicians with whom she was accustomed to socializing. Her station in life as the obligatory young and beautiful domestic accessory bound her to the powerful man she had married some four years before, and constrained her to the dull company of his investment banker friends and associates. She had almost decided not to go alone to the tedious reception the night before, when her husband was unexpectedly called away to Zurich. She was glad she changed her mind.

"Bonjour, mon cherie," Haldane murmured, with flawless Parisian inflection as he bent down to kiss her.

Gretel responded to his early morning kisses with passion. Haldane's hands slid over her smooth skin. A small sigh escaped her lips as he expertly teased and probed her body. Giving in to the growing excitement his attentions were eliciting, he brought her to the very edge of ecstasy. Then, as she thought she could stand no more, he moved in. Within moments both were caught up in an exploding whirlwind of passion.

At the peak of her fervor, Haldane studied her face as it contorted in pleasure in the scant light of dawn, felt her held breath and the arch of her back in sweet spasms. This gratified him more than the pleasant sensations of sex ever could. He craved to see the abandon on his lover's face and know he was the cause and creator of her ardor. The rush of her surrender far exceeded what any momentary seizure of carnal pleasure could provide him. In both love and war, Haldane demanded and usually achieved total victory. Only after Gretel's climax subsided did Haldane allow himself sweet release.

They held one another in the languid afterglow of their lovemaking. Outside, in the cold, steely dawn, a clock tower rang out the hour.

*Bloody Hell! Six already!*

Haldane began to disentangle himself from Gretel's embrace. She resisted, pulling him on top of her once more. He allowed himself to

9

be drawn down by Gretel, even as he whispered, "I must go, love."

But to linger a few moments wouldn't cause any harm.

After several more minutes of savoring her warm kisses, Haldane again moved to extricate himself. "This time, I really must be going...I have a train to catch."

Gretel released him with regret, feeling the sudden coldness of the room rushing in to fill the void created by his absence. She shivered under the thick satin duvet while Haldane quickly dressed.

"Jordan...Will I see you again?" Hope shined in her pale eyes.

"Oh, I do hope so, love," he replied lightly, checking his panther lean, uniformed reflection in the gilded mirror before sitting on the edge of her bed to pull on his boots.

He took her in his arms once more, deftly sliding his left hand under the pillow to retrieve his derringer. He concealed the tiny gun in the palm of his hand. Distracted, Gretel did not notice his actions, just as she had not noticed when he had slipped the pistol under the pillow the night before. Realizing that he did not know when this enchanting young woman's husband was expected home, Haldane decided it was best to leave at once.

*But one more kiss...*

This time, Gretel broke their embrace.

"When?" she demanded. "When will I see you again, Christopher Jordan Haldane?"

He thought a moment.

"Well...if I come back from Milan the same way I came, I shall have a layover here in Geneva. I could come along and look you up then," he told her breezily.

"And when will that be?"

"I-I really can't say, for I don't know how long it will take to conclude my business in Italy. It could be days or even weeks before I am to return, but I promise to find you again, love."

Gretel reluctantly recognized the outer boundaries of his commitment. Still, she was glad to have spent the night with this dashing British officer who had found her charms irresistible, even if she did suffer the occasional twinge of guilt.

"My dear, sweet Gretel," Haldane murmured into her fine, flower-scented hair. One final kiss, then he was up and headed for the bedroom door.

"Don't you even want breakfast?" she asked, her voice rising.

"Haven't time, love. I'll see myself out, you stay warm," he said as he slipped through the door.

Gretel snuggled back into the warmth of her bed and smiled as she remembered his touch. Her lips and chin were chafed from his mustache and overnight growth of beard, but she didn't mind having this tactile souvenir of their night of stolen passion for a while.

In the hallway, Haldane concealed the pistol into the breast pocket of his uniform tunic with practiced ease. The serviceable little gun had gotten him out of more tight squeezes than he cared to recall. He then followed his nose to the kitchen, choosing to make his exit from the more discreet servants' entrance than the ostentatious front door of the fine mansion.

Passing through the kitchen, he nodded amiably to three women busy preparing the household's morning meal.

"Bonjour, madams," he said with the most charming grin he could muster at that early hour of the day, as he snatched up a hot croissant from steaming pile as he went by.

He slipped through the back door, as the three women stared gape-mouthed after him. They looked at one another askance, then as one, turned their astonished gaze in the direction of the lady of the house's boudoir.

A cold northern wind whipped through the fine wool of his midnight blue dress uniform as Haldane left the grand mansion, frosting his breath. He stuffed the flaky roll in his mouth, savoring the buttery warmth. He regretted that he had not taken the time last night to fetch his greatcoat from his room before leaving the nearby embassy compound with Gretel.

*Ah, fall in the Alps,* he thought ruefully, as he relieved himself behind a sculpted juniper tree in the wide, dew-soaked lawn. He hurried down the tree-lined avenue, his long legs eating up the distance between himself and the front gate of the estate. Brilliant red, yellow and orange leaves filled the trees above him, scattering colorful showers in the wind.

*This is always the least pleasurable part of this sort of liaison,* he thought with a shiver, *and the chill only makes it worse.*

Now that he had granted his desires full sway, his tardy conscience eventually caught up with him. He had no intention of returning to Geneva any time soon. He planned to travel to Milan, Italy by train, conduct his business there, then another train south to Naples, where he could use his influence to catch a ride back home to London with one of the many British military ships that were always coming and going.

*But, I never really lied to her. I will look her up the next time I'm here and have some free time. Oh, bugger! What's her last name? I'll have to ask someone at the embassy before I go.*

Walking in the pink, early light, the old familiar pangs of disappointment and guilt engulfed him. Gretel was a delicious creature, but it had been all too easy to seduce her. He saw at once that she was brimming over with unsatisfied passion. He enjoyed releasing her pent-up sexuality, but now wondered why he had bothered, when he could have saved himself a cold morning hike back to the embassy.

Emptiness filled him, as he realized the experience failed to move him. He was even somewhat bored with it, in a strange, impersonal way. And now he could add another sin to the long list that had accumulated in the many years since his last confession, not that he actually bothered to keep count anymore. He snorted in derision at his religious reflex, long since having abandoned the faith of his childhood. But, he supposed, the habit was too deeply ingrained to be completely forgotten.

His mind turned to its usual ruminations, as he dissected his life for the millionth time in search of a glimmer of understanding what motivated his behavior and feelings. After tremendous focus and utilization of every means at his disposal (both honorable and not), he had managed to get everything he had always wanted from life. Every component that was supposed to make his life complete was in place. He had wealth, status and an adoring family. But somehow, instead of the anticipated satisfaction, he still felt a longing in his soul like an itch he could not quite reach. It was as if a hidden part of himself was actively preventing his fulfillment, spoiling his victories and draining away his joy.

He suffered the guilt of a life that never seemed enough to content, no matter how hard he tried. Not his meteoric rise through the Royal Army Diplomatic Corps as a young noble officer, not the near hero-worship accorded him amongst the elites of the British Empire as a top military negotiator and cryptologist, and especially not his home life.

Haldane never really intended to be unfaithful to his third wife and mother of two of his three children – *Soon to be four,* he thought with a wan smile – it just kept happening. He didn't regret the acts of betrayal as much as he regretted his culpability afterwards. Although he knew he really had no valid grounds for complaint, he felt stifled by his socialite wife of seven years, Elizabeth, and the stuffy, aristocratic society that encompassed both his professional and personal life. The happiness that was promised to result from professional success and private accomplishment had failed to appear on schedule. All turned to ashes on his tongue.

At thirty-two, Haldane's driving ambition assured that he was the second youngest to ever hold the high rank of Lieutenant Colonel in the Corps. Yet even this achievement did not fulfill.

*Always second...*

*My whole life's a sham.* He turned bleak eyes to the north horizon, as the rising sun revealed pink-and-purple-hued storm clouds moving in. *I think I've been dead for a few years now and never knew it. Or maybe it's just the weather,* he mused with a humorless smile as he rounded a corner. *What's wrong with me? Will I ever be satisfied?*

The gabled British embassy loomed ahead, and he hastening his pace to reach its warmth. He nodded curt acknowledgment to the saluting military guards at the gatehouse as he approached. The embassy guards were accustomed to all manner of personnel arriving at any hour of the day and night, in diverse manners of conveyance. Haldane's early morning return raised no eyebrows.

Two hours later found the elegant young colonel bathed, shaved, packed and boarding the southbound train to Milan. He had an appointment to keep with a certain Signor Sergio Aldo, a rich Sicilian lawyer of questionable morals and dubious practices, with whom he had some dealings in the past.

Haldane regarded Aldo as something akin to a tick that had attached itself to the soft underbelly of Europe's ancient nobility and was steadily sucking the lifeblood out of them. But Aldo had an uncanny business sense and was often called upon by panicked aristocrats in financial difficulties.

Haldane had agreed to meet Aldo in Milan to discuss how he could aid in Aldo's current project. He sincerely hoped nothing too vile would be expected of him. Not that he was squeamish; rather he knew that blatant abuse of power decreased its effectiveness. He desired to retain the reputation of *wunderkind* he had worked so hard to build in the Royal Army. Yet he was obliged to help Aldo, against his inclinations.

Unfamiliar with either of the two great Italian households involved in Aldo's latest scheme, the D'Amici's and the Calendris, he sympathized with their plight, nonetheless.

*Nothing in the aristocracy's long history could have prepared them for the likes of Aldo,* Haldane thought as he watched distant mountains and forest-lined valleys slip past the train window, mixed with dark smoke and sparks from the chimney of the train's engine. As the train steamed its way south through the high Alpine passes, Haldane considered the current unkind state of nobility.

Many of the old families had to sell off vast portions of their holdings when the peasants, who had always worked the lands, left their sharecrop fields for higher paying work in the new factories that mushroomed across the Continent. Former farmers poured into the burgeoning urban centers, lured by a steady income unaffected by storm and season. Once living in the cities, the farmers-turned-laborers created the demand for more manufactured goods. This, in turn, swelled the purses of *nouveau riche* factory owners, merchants, bankers, barristers and similar forms of low life.

Without the income from crops or rent, many of the old noble houses tottered on the edge of bankruptcy. Haldane's own family had not been immune to the consequences of the move from an agrarian to an industrial economy, tottering on the brink of annihilation. Their name survived with relative grace only through Haldane's heroic, if distasteful, efforts to save it, with Aldo's eager assistance. He hated the thought of helping Aldo inflict that same fate on another house. Yet, if the truth of Haldane's own financial success were publically known, he and his family would be ruined in the ensuing scandal.

This was not the first time the Sicilian had called on him to assist in contractual negotiations between houses of Europe's landed gentry, as they tried to evade legal entail, which restricted what lands the nobility could sell or develop. While once vast estates were a guarantee of perpetual income, in these turbulent times, without enough sharecroppers to work the land, the large estates of the aristocracy became an expensive but unavoidable liability. Aldo had found rich feeding grounds in the nobility's need to wring income from their lands, in order to maintain the expensive lifestyle expected of their status. Aldo ruthlessly used Haldane's skills as a military negotiator.

By the time his train pulled into Milan, a decidedly foul mood settled about Haldane. He resolved to end his obligation to Aldo once and for all.

*Aldo uses me the same way he uses all the nobles of Europe,* Haldane thought with fermenting rancor, as he made his way through the noisy marble halls of the burgeoning Stazione d Milano Centrale transit station, with its great glass-arched ceiling some four stories above. *Oh yes, he helps us maintain the way of life we are accustomed to, while he slices a healthy percentage off the top of all future earnings, the bloody leach.*

Haldane's family, the Haldanes of Malwick, as old and proud a family as any in Europe, had been careening towards that same fate under the close-fisted rule of the Baron Malwick, Sir Charles Haldane IV, Haldane's father. After his father's death eight years before, Haldane's older brother and heir to the Barony, Richard, was bound by the law not to sell off any more of the family holdings, despite the ever increasing debts owed to discrete London bankers.

*The same kind of banker as the husband of my dear Gretel,* Haldane thought with vengeful satisfaction, weaving through the crowds outside the station in the warm afternoon. A brilliant blue sky spanned over the ancient city, but Haldane was too steeped in his brooding to notice.

These bankers and lawyers, such as Gretel's husband and Aldo's sort, were more than willing to loan exorbitant sums to desperate peers. Eventually, they would force the families to sell off their remaining assets or pressure them into harmful exploitation of their lands when their debts became insupportable.

Haldane narrowly spared his family that same humiliation only through Aldo. Haldane invested money he borrowed from the Sicilian lawyer-entrepreneur in Europe's booming railroads and new telegraph systems, based on Aldo's inside information of new technologies in those fields, months before the advances were made public. And of course, Aldo always "reimbursed" Haldane generously for his negotiating help. But Haldane wondered if the price he'd personally paid for the family's security wasn't too high. Now he relied on Aldo's constant good will, lest some untoward tidbit of information find its way to the scandal-hungry London tabloids.

*I'll make it clear to him that this is the absolute last time, no matter how much he offers,* Haldane vowed. *I wish to God I hadn't agreed to this, but I still owe him twenty thousand pounds. I can't break my word or he'll have me flayed out in the press, and then have a go at Richard. I'll just have to ride this one through and see if maybe there isn't some way I might help mitigate the damage.*

As Haldane stepped into a tall handsome cab and directed the driver to his hotel, he realized that he had neglected to ask anyone at the Geneva embassy Gretel's last name.

# Chapter Three

**13 September, 1872   Villa D'Amici, Northern Italy   4:15 p.m.**

The high Romanesque castle known as La Villa D'Amici glistened apricot and cream in the early autumn Lombardi sun. Nestled for five centuries atop a low peak in the foothills of the Italian Alps, at the elevation of some seven thousand feet, it seemed an organic part of the mountainous terrain. Generations of vegetation covered the outer fortifications, silent witnesses to the long history of the D'Amici family and Northern Italy. Tall towers, constructed during the Renaissance, aspired to the heavens. Flying buttresses joined the two tallest towers, providing a high, covered walkway between them. From their vantage point, the terraced vineyards were visible, where the D'Amici's had produced some of the finest wines of the area for generations. The main structure served as the ancestral home, fortress and place of business for the D'Amici's since the late thirteenth century.

The Don of the family, Marquis Alessandro Eduardo D'Amici, had added the great glass-enclosed arbor to the back of the main villa as a wedding gift to his dear departed wife, back when palmhouses were all the rage. The Glass Arbor of the Villa D'Amici gained a regional reputation a few short years after its completion in 1854. Visitors once came by the score to see this tropical paradise that flourished in the midst of the rugged mountains.

It was here that the eldest child of that great family now sought solitude. Marquessa Sophia Dominica Maria D'Amici paced down the cobblestone path that bisected her beloved arbor, a rumpled, earth-stained apron hastily tied over her fine lace ruffles and flounces.

She had retired from the game of croquette which she, her

younger sister, Gemma, and her new brother-in-law, Roberto, had been playing on the inner courtyard, before the newlyweds of six weeks switched their attention to another, more interesting game.

Light filtered through the green leaves and bounced off the colorful flowers planted in raised beds. The earthen bricks of the path were mopped daily, lest La Donna Sophia's palest pink satin slippers and gown become soiled with dirt from the growing beds.

Artificial heat and humidity in the glass arbor was maintained by volcanic steam through an elaborate system of ingenious ductworks, which also served to heat the villa in winter. Thousands of yards of ceramic pipe served to maintain a consistent, comfortable temperature inside despite any external conditions, an ancient wonder of Romanesque plumbing. The lifeblood of the Alps steamed through the veins of the villa, drawing on a natural hot springs for heat and power deep underneath in the bowels of an old caldera. Inside this bell jar grew rare and delicate things, unable to survive unaided in the mountain extremes found outside its enclosure.

The arbor was a place of sanctuary for Sophia since childhood. Often, she went there to read the ancient classics she so adored, to gather flowers or to simply to drink in the natural beauty. Other times, like today, she sought solace from the unwanted thoughts that plagued her.

At the ripe old age of twenty-six, Sophia was a confirmed spinster. After the death of her mother ten years before, Sophia took up the role of family matriarch along with her high title of Marquessa, a role which her effervescent charm and quick mind made easy, bolstered and educated by a doting father. She had chosen against all convention not to marry, devoting her time and love to her father, her siblings and her studies.

When at the age at which most young girls discover romance and seek the most advantageous match, Sophia was discovering the likes of Socrates, Caesar, Plato, Alexander and Herodotus, preferring the vibrant company of ancient heroes and philosophers to the vapid aristocrats who sought to woo her. In her teen years, she trained for the opera, channeling her adolescent passion into exquisite music. But only as a lark, for all knew Marquessas do not perform on the stage.

Petite, with long dark curls and large dark eyes, Sophia puttered about the garden, tending the plants as she absently moved amidst them. Raised in the style of a grand lady, Sophia was something of a dreamer, with ample time to let her fertile imagination full play, as she was rarely required to do anything for herself. Yet, she delighted in the task of tending and nurturing her mother's garden – in keeping her mother's image alive for her aging father. At least, that was what she always told herself and all others who might inquire.

Passing a tall date palm, Sophia ruminated how her sister, Gemma, and her new groom's amorous games recalled sensations from a disturbing dream early that morning.

Once, when Sophia was a child, her father had received a mysterious visitor from overseas who brought botanical specimens from America. He was dark and handsome in his uniform, a champion in Union blue for her girlish adoration. He gave the young Sophia candy, and held her hand. He told her of his daring adventures in the American Wild West, fighting the cunning Rebels and fierce Red Indians. He promised that one day, he would return when she was grown to womanhood, and would take her away to see the wonders of the world.

As a young girl, the image of this mysterious soldier had sunk into her psyche. In her mind, she created a perfect dream lover based on the child's memory of an irresistibly charming man, and then added on the qualities of the men of history that she found most fascinating. She fashioned herself into the kind of woman she fancied her dream lover would desire. Now in her mid-twenties, Sophia had long since given up her adolescent fantasies of romantic rescues by her dashing hero come to life. Yet, this imaginary model was still the measure by which she judged all suitors, and no flesh and blood man could ever measure up.

This morning, her fantasy had invaded her dreams. Long ago she dubbed this fantasy-hero *Alcibiades,* after the infamous rogue warrior of the Peloponnesian War and close friend of Socrates, whose convoluted story intrigued her no end. Sophia pondered the strange imagery of her dream and the disquiet it evoked.

In her dream, she watched her fantasy lover scale a high cliff on a dangerous mission. She had watched him planting explosives in a cave on the craggy peak, aroused as always by the sensuality her dream lover exuded.

Then as her Alcibiades climbed down to a safe distance, she saw the mountain as if from a great distance. As Alcibiades prepared to hit the plunger to detonate the dynamite, Sophia now discerned a gigantic face carved upon side of the mountain. To her horror, she recognized the face as her own, just as it exploded and she jerked awake.

Any dream appearance of Alcibiades was rare enough to excite Sophia. He had done no less this time. But now, she felt both aroused and disturbed. Gemma and Roberto's display of affection had stirred her animal longings. Yet, she now found no solace in her usual protective fantasies.

Confused, Sophia meandered up one side of the arbor and then down the other. Brilliant colors and rich textures and fragrances invited her, filling her senses, yet she did not acknowledge them.

She felt somehow betrayed by her Alcibiades.

*What was he trying to do?*

Was a creation of her own imagination and unfulfilled desires threatening to destroy her?

*But he is just a dream.... He has no real power over me,* she thought, all the while knowing by the pleasant tightenings in her groin that this dream did indeed exercise a strong effect upon her, even though none knew of his existence but her. *But, if he* is *my enemy, why am I so attracted,* she wondered.

All day, Sophia had been unable to dismiss the lingering feeling of dread fascination with her dream images. The mood pervaded her inner landscape and forbade distraction.

"Oh, this is so ridiculous!" she abruptly cried aloud, and marched back to the entrance to the house, yanking the apron from her waist and depositing it on a table near the door, her heels clicking on the brick walkway.


As she entered the villa and strode down the twisting corridors, she could hear the voices of her father and some business associate talking in the library. Her father's voice seemed agitated and he coughed between sentences. The acrid smell of cigars wafted from the library.

Concern filled Sophia. Cigars meant business, and business meant trouble for her ailing father. She forgot her complaint of the moment and moved closer to the dark wood doors of the masculine domain to listen.

"I realize it is quite a task, Don Alessandro," came the nasal voice of her father's guest. "That is why I want to include this Haldane fellow."

"You said *you* could handle all the business transactions," countered her father's voice, in obvious distress.

"The business transactions, yes," continued the unseen voice, "but the negotiations with Calendri are another matter. Haldane is a nobleman, like you. Though I have some social standing, being one of Garibaldi's Thousand, I am not recognized in certain circles... I am sure that Don Stephano will respond to him much more agreeably than he has to me."

"But, Signor... The British government –"

The stranger cut his words short.

"He is attached to the British army, it is true, but we would be hiring him simply to serve as a mediator and witness for the contracts – no more. The British government will have nothing to do with our dealings. If we are to complete the plans, we must have Don Stephano's cooperation."

The stranger's voice died away to an intent whisper Sophia could not make out. She crept closer to the partially open door.

"Very well, Signor Aldo," her father's tense voice relented. "Do what you must to finalize the negotiations. You have served the D'Amici family well in the short time you have been in our employ. Thank you again for the cigars, but really, this is all I should enjoy, as much as I adore a good smoke."

"Nonsense, my good Don Alessandro," spoke the visiting intruder. "Those are the finest cigars from Cuba. They are fresh off the boat just two days ago. You keep them and enjoy them with my compliments. After all, there will soon be occasion for great celebrating."

"That is my constant hope, Signor Aldo." The voice of Don Alessandro seemed tired, and by the distant tone, Sophia knew he must be worried as well.

"Until then," spoke the guest, "I will be in contact with Colonel Haldane to establish the proper place and time for the negotiations." Then, a different tone came to the guest's voice. "Don Alessandro... I could not help but notice the most striking woman I have ever had the pleasure to behold as I arrived for our meeting this afternoon." His speech was smooth and polished, like gilded honey. "She was on the lawn, playing croquette with a young couple. I believe she was wearing a pink gown. I see this lovely painting hanging over your fireplace. Could this be the same lady I saw outside?"

Sophia stifled a gasp of surprise.

"If you mean to ask who she is, I shall tell you," Don Alessandro's voice said with a hint of amusement. "That is my Sophia, my eldest and dearest child. And yes, the portrait over the fire is hers. The other lady was her sister, Gemma, and her new husband."

She strained to hear the visitor's reply over her pounding heart.

"Never have I seen such a lovely lady."

"Lovely," Don Alessandro told him, "and kind, and intelligent... yet strong and sometimes quite willful and stubborn."

"Pardon, Don Alessandro," said Aldo. "I wonder, might I be so bold as to ask, is the Donna Sophia yet married?"

Sophia held her breath as she awaited her father's response. She had noticed the heavy set, balding man as he had entered the villa, but she paid him no mind. Now, she wondered if her father would encourage this unwanted suitor.

"She is not," Don Alessandro sighed at last, "much against my wishes."

"Then, Don Alessandro," Aldo's voice oozed through the doors, "Might I ask your permission to seek the pleasure of Donna Sophia's company... after the negotiations are settled, of course."

"You, Signor, are not the first to seek the company of my daughter. She is her own mistress. If you have the intention to try to court her, then I suggest you take that question directly to her for consideration."

Dread filled Sophia as she realized that, some time soon, this bourgeoisie Signor Aldo would seek her out, and she would be forced to show him the door, as she had countless others. She could not fathom why her father did not outright reprimand this forward commoner for his unseemly presumption, and spare her the nuisance.

"I thank you for your advice," came the simpering reply.

"Now, you thank me, perhaps later, you will curse me, no?... I will ring for your carriage to be brought to the front court." Don Alessandro's voice became louder as he neared the door, and Sophia's position.

She had heard enough. Fear of imminent discovery sent her dashing down the twisting corridor and into the main kitchen. Here, she hid under the pretense of seeking a cool glass of water from the cook.

After a sufficient amount of time passed for the visitor to be far gone, Sophia sought out her father in his library. He sat at his large mahogany desk, dismantling a small clockwork device in his palm with a screwdriver, when a harsh cough forced him to stop and put down his project. He rested his head in his hand for several moments before picking up his tools again.

"Damn thing was working fine this morning... I don't understand..." he muttered as he removed the filigree shell and a large gear from the ailing mechanism, tossing the parts onto his desk. "What the devil happened to make it stop? Don't suppose Aldo could have some kind of shielding agent... But how could he even know...?"

"Papa?" Sophia called from the thick, carved door to the library.

"Yes, my daughter," he answered. "Come in, child, come in." He waved at her, screwdriver in hand.

"Papa, who was that man who just left?"

Don Alessandro looked up at his daughter's query, then deliberately turned his attention to the disassembled device before him. "No one of any importance, Sophie. I can't fathom why this piece of ... equipment quit operating properly."

"Papa, do you owe this man money?" she asked, with sharp

candor.

Gales of laughter spilled out of Don Alessandro until he began to cough again. Sophia hurried to his side to pour a glass of water for him, and extinguished the smoldering cigar in the ashtray. As he drained the glass, Sophia scolded.

"Papa, you are not supposed to smoke cigars. Remember what the doctor told you last winter when you were so sick. My fingers are numb just from touching the vile thing. Imagine what that must be doing to your lungs."

"There is no reason to think that a fine cigar could cause any harm," objected Don Alessandro.

"But look," insisted Sophia as she placed her hand on his cheek. "My fingers are cold to the touch just from handling it. Please, Papa. Those horrible things will be the death of you! You promised me before that you would only smoke your pipe, and that only in the evening when I am with you."

"You just want to make sure I do not inhale the smoke," said Don Alessandro with a raised eyebrow.

Sophia met his eye with defiance.

"Yes, you are right," Sophia finally allowed, with a hint of a smile.

"The man who came visiting is a lawyer. He is part of a project that hopefully will prove vital to our future. He offered me a cigar and -"

"And naturally, you accepted and smoked the evil thing, in breach of your promise to me." At last, her eyes softened. "Papa," she began. "I heard you discussing me with your visitor."

Don Alessandro squirmed and rose from his chair. Sophia's wide skirts and ruffles blocked his escape.

"I only want to know," she continued, "are you so very disappointed that I am not married that you would even consider allowing that commoner to court me?"

Don Alessandro rolled his eyes. "Any man who marries you will have to watch his conversations and look behind every curtain and around every door to make sure he is in private with his fellows."

"Don't try to divert me, Father," Sophia cautioned. "I have asked, are you so very sad that I have never married?"

"No," came the sullen response as he sat once more, then, "Yes... Sophia, you have tried to take your mother's place in this house for too many years. Now, Cassandra is gone, your little sister Gemma is married and your brother away at school. It is time to start looking for a man from the right family who will be able to take care of you and the estate until your brother reaches maturity. I would like to bounce a grandchild or two upon my knee before I join our ancestors. Gemma married Roberto for love, which is her right. But, I have always hoped that with your sensibility, you would marry a man of influence and tradition, and be the power behind him… Instead you seem intent on everything other than a proper future. I have indulged you, hoping you would outgrow this foolishness, but no…" He caught her large dark eyes, mirrors of his own. "If anyone understands your reluctance to marry, it is I, Sophia. I, too, resisted in my youth. But as I grew older, I came to see the value and purpose and importance of family. It is time you did so, as well."

Don Alessandro paused to let his words sink in, then, "Carlo told me that when he took you to Milan to shop last week that you demanded he take you to La Scala," he accused with a touch of humor, as he resumed working on his small device. "He said you were inside the opera house for over an hour. Is it true?"

Sophia turned away in a swish of taffeta and lace.

"Is it?" her father insisted gently.

"Yes," Sophia admitted, looking down at her twisting fingers.

"And what were you doing there? I happen to know that auditions for the upcoming season were held last week, Sophia," Don Alessandro suggested. He laid down his screwdriver and turned to face her. "I know that you are restless – that is what marriage and babies are for – to keep you busy and focused on what's important: family! I urge you to consider it, daughter. You need a reliable man to take care of you and help perpetuate the D'Amici line."

"Like that... that lawyer?" Sophia was astonished at her father's implication. "Papa, who would make sure you do not smoke if I run away and get married?"

Don Alessandro rose and looked his daughter in the eye.

"Forget about Aldo. He's nobody you need to think about, he's not important. The point is that you are the oldest of the D'Amici children. That is an awesome responsibility. Eduardo is only twelve and an unruly child on his best behavior. I still have hopes that he will grow out of it... But until then, the family needs someone with a level head, a stout heart and a strong arm to preserve and protect the D'Amici legacy for future generations. I am old and tired. Our world has changed, Sophia. It is changing even now, and even we D'Amicis must change with it or perish under its relentless progress."

"If change means marriage to a common *lawyer*, then I'll have no part in change," she snapped, spun on her carved Spanish heels and stalked from the room before her father could reply, her bustle swaying behind her.

Don Alessandro raised his hands in silent appeal to the heavens.

Shaking his head ruefully, he picked up a small, enameled stylus-shaped implement and pushed a button on its side. An intense whirring buzzed forth, and a brilliant blue light emitted from the tip. With steady hands, the Don applied the cobalt beam to the disassembled device spread out upon his table.

# Chapter Four

**14 September, 1872   Milan, Italy   8:00 p.m.**

Haldane entered the exclusive restaurant in the glass-vaulted Galleria Vittorio Emanuele II, and told the tuxedoed maitre'd in fluent Italian that he was meeting a Signor Aldo. The rich scent of fine Italian cuisine wafted in the air, making Haldane's empty stomach growl in anticipation.

"Ah, yes, Signor," the man answered. "He awaits you in the Red Room. Please follow me."

*Wonderful,* Haldane thought with an inward groan.

Aldo greeted Haldane in the pretentious private dining room. The swarthy, balding Sicilian was dressed in the latest conservative fashion. Aldo's round head was punctuated by a black, closely trimmed goatee framing thick, sensuous lips, a pug nose and two darting black eyes peering from beneath a bushy brow. Haldane observed the strained buttons of Aldo's maroon cut velvet waistcoat, pulled taut over his protruding stomach, with disgust.

*What an unappealing fellow.*

Aldo wiped the accumulated perspiration off his upper lip, as his shiny head bobbed in a fawning bow. Haldane enjoyed looking down his long nose at the groveling lawyer, who seemed so intimidated by those of higher birth. In the beginning, that is.

Not everyone shared Haldane's revulsion of Signor Sergio Aldo. Some found his sycophantic manner quite gratifying; hence he had made such inroads into the dealings and bank accounts of so many unwitting gentles.

Aldo's service with Garibaldi in Sicily during the war for Italian Unification a little over a decade before made him a hero amongst the rising bourgeoisie and political class. Though sick of hearing Aldo's old, tired war stories again and again, Haldane admitted that, like himself, Aldo had the uncanny ability to adapt to any prevailing conditions… and like Haldane, was willing to go to any means to achieve his goals. But the shared protean traits did not endear Aldo to Haldane. He had seen too many times to what ends Aldo employed his talents. Although Haldane did not pride himself on his own ethics, it made Haldane too uncomfortable to consider other traits he might share in common with Aldo.

The two men shook hands and exchanged pleasantries over *ossobuco in bianco,* rich veal cutlets and braised vegetables, and *risotto alla milanese* with saffron and savory cheese. Haldane credited Aldo for knowing the best restaurants in Europe, even if his crude sense of humor assaulted Haldane's refined tastes.

After they had finished their meals, Aldo was ready to talk business over espresso and dessert. In between cramming the rich, cream-filled pastry into his mouth and gulps of over-sweet coffee, Aldo outlined Haldane's part in the scheme.

"You see, I am brokering a contract between two quarreling old northern Italian noble families whose adjoining properties contain valuable mineral deposits. The deposits are high in the mountains and somewhat difficult to reach. I propose that the families jointly mine the land and build railways connecting the new mine here, in Milano, the nearest industrial center. Together, the two families borrow the monies to pay for this major undertaking from me. All I would want for my selfless efforts is a small fee… and a modest percent of the mine's future profits in perpetuity. Gross, not net, of course. And I would only charge them a mere twenty percent interest on the loan per annum. Nowhere else could they find such a generous offer," Aldo said with a smirk, as he stirred more sugar into his coffee. "I've even got buyers lined up for the ore, once it's mined."

*I'll wager you have,* Haldane thought, but held his tongue.

"Now, the part I wish you to play is to help convince one of the old dons of the necessity of putting aside their argument in favor of this bold venture, and to lend your credibility to mine. In return for your negotiations, I am prepared to reimburse you two hundred and fifty thousand pounds sterling, deposited discretely in your Bank of London account," Aldo concluded with oily seduction, as he laid his spoon daintily on the painted porcelain saucer.

Haldane casually sipped his black Earl Grey tea, concealing his astonishment at the figure Aldo was willing to pay.

*He must expect to make a staggering profit,* Haldane thought. He made a mental note to research the estimated worth of the proposed new mines.

"Christopher, what do you say? You are the only man for the job. And as you can see, the rewards are generous for just a few weeks of your time. Your own fine estate will be secure for generations to come and no one need even know how... no, not even your brother," wheedled the lawyer.

Haldane bristled at Aldo's implied threat and audacious familiarity, as if they were equals on a first name basis.

*But what a sum!* Haldane mused. *He must be planning to rob these poor unsuspecting houses blind. I wonder if there is some way I might help these two estates and still get the money the damn swindler's offered to pay? Now that should be a challenge worth pursuing. And if Aldo might be ruined in the process, well... this could be fun.* A tiny twitch of a smile tugged at the corners of his mustache.

But he felt in his gut there was more, that Aldo was withholding something vital from him. He knew he must tread with caution.

Haldane drew the uncomfortable silence out as long as he could. He watched the perspiration gathering on Aldo's upper lip, and observed a gravy stain on Aldo's gray silk cravat with disdain.

"Very well. I'll do it, but only on two conditions. First, this completes and fulfills my obligation to you. I shall repay you the sum I owe from these proceeds, and this shall be the final contract I negotiate for you. My obligation to you shall be at an end once this deal is concluded. Agreed?" He paused until Aldo nodded his reluctant assent. "Good. Secondly, I want you to transfer the funds to my bank before I begin," Haldane bargained.

Aldo's quick black eyes narrowed beneath heavy brows.

"I won't have it all until after the contracts go through. I can offer you half now and half once you get the contracts drawn and signed."

*Ah... there it is,* Haldane thought triumphantly. *He needs me to get the contracts signed. That means they don't trust him... Good.*

"I won't begin for any less than two hundred thousand up front," Haldane insisted with focused intent. "You can pay the balance afterwards." Haldane's words hung in the air in silent reverberation.

A blank look flickered across Aldo's face and was gone. He spread his fingers in surrender. "I'm afraid you have me over the proverbial barrel, Christopher. I can't start without you. You win. I will have that amount transferred by wire to London tomorrow morning, and we can begin immediately."

*How dare this fat peasant use my Christian name? The brass of it!* Haldane fumed in spite of his victory, though he was much too well bred to give any outward sign of his indignation. It didn't matter to him that Christopher was not even his preferred name, as most of his intimates called him by his middle name, Jordan. It was the principle of the thing.

"I'm certain you won't mind if I wait to receive confirmation from my banker that the proper amount is credited to my account before beginning," Haldane said in his most charming tone. "It should only be a few days at most."

"Well, I can see that you have become quite the businessman, Christopher. Very well. We'll wait for confirmation. Would you care for a cigar? I have a friend in Bavaria who just started importing them."

"Actually, no," Haldane replied. "I really ought to go back to my hotel. I didn't get much rest last night, and the train ride today was somewhat fatiguing. I do hope you will forgive me."

"Well, I won't pretend I'm not disappointed, but I must have you at your sharpest when we go to meet with Don Stephano Calendri. Go and rest yourself, good Colonel. You know how to reach me once you have received your confirmations," Aldo said, with honest regret.

"I thank you for the wonderful meal, Signor Aldo," Haldane said as he rose to leave. "I shall be in contact with you in a few days. Now I bid you good night."

The two men shook hands and Haldane went out.

As Haldane left the private dining room, Aldo pushed his chair back from the table and motioned to his co-conspirator to come out of hiding.

"Well... what do you think?" Aldo asked the tall young man in black with a sleek blonde ponytail, who joined him from behind the thick blood red tapestry.

"I think Haldane is getting edgy," the handsome newcomer replied with Bavarian-accented Italian, as he placed his hands on Aldo's table and loomed over it. "He's not going to be controllable for much longer."

"Well, just as long as the moody bastard doesn't get out of line before we no longer need him. I must say, I don't care for giving up that much cash up front. I don't think I will be able to recoup that until later, but I need him if I'm going to pull off this one. We must have that ore. Besides, this money might prove useful to ensure our hold on him. I can always threaten to make his extracurricular activities public, should he become too obstreperous."

"Well, perhaps, but I don't want Haldane mucking up all our hard work. He's an uncontrollable variable. I don't see why we have to involve him at all. I could perform the negotiations you need," the blonde man argued, as he straightened, paced a few steps away.

"Not in a thousand years, Wittgenstein," Aldo rebutted irritably. "You had your chance with Calendri and failed, remember? Your skills might be formidable, but they are *nothing* compared to the Delivier gifts. Even wild and without any sort of training, Haldane has more persuasive powers than you and me and a host of demons combined. You just saw him in action, and he wasn't even trying. He just managed to talk me out of two hundred thousand pounds! *Me!* I couldn't even try to haggle. No, I won't proceed without him. I have sufficient leverage to keep him under control long enough to obtain the contracts I need. Then, after he's gone, we can move in, take over Villa D'Amici and you can peruse the Grail Archives at your leisure."

"I still think it's too dangerous," Wittgenstein muttered, his long thin fingers playing with a loose strand of his ponytail, as he padded back and forth. "My plan is the better one. If I could unravel the final secrets of D'Amici's mind-machine, I could use it on Calendri to get his signature. We needn't risk involving Haldane at all. I just need more time."

Aldo arose from his chair with growing menace.

"That's enough!" he bellowed, slamming his fist onto the table, jarring the dessert dishes and upsetting an empty wine glass. "We are going to do this my way! We need to move now if we are going to get production of the mine up by spring. Your way would take too long. We need guns and ships made from that ore now! It is my superior strategies that have gotten us this far, and it is my plans we will continue to follow! Capice?"

"All right. You needn't raise your voice," Wittgenstein sulked. "You'd just better make sure Haldane stays under control. And what about D'Amici? I know he's old and sick, but he's still as cunning as ever – this new mind device of his is proof enough of that. D'Amici has tangled with the Illuminati more than once in the past. My Master in Munich wouldn't like it if anything were to go amiss. It was only by extreme diligence that I managed to compromise his suppliers and discover what he was working on in time to figure out how to protect against it. But I still don't understand how the damn thing works or all its functions. We don't know what else he might have in store."

"You worry too much, Otto. I have plans for old D'Amici, never fear," Aldo soothed, retaking his seat and prying at his teeth with an ivory and silver toothpick. "The Ectoplasmic Shield performed magnificently! My compliments to your clever Bavarian technicians." A rough laugh rumbled up from Aldo's belly. "You should have seen the old man's face when he realized his mind control toy wasn't working… Oh! I won't be needing it anymore tonight. I should preserve the power supply."

Aldo slapped the toothpick down on the table and pulled a small black oblong box from his breast pocket, fidgeted with it a few moments, and then tossed it gently amidst the empty dessert plates and coffee cups.

"Damn thing makes my ears ring, but it worked like a charm…" he continued. "Ah, Otto! I can see it all… Soon all this will be behind us, and I will be in sole possession of the Villa D'Amici. With the power that will give me, nothing will be able to withstand my will. They said the unification of Italy was impossible, but we showed them. Soon, I shall unite all of Europe under my guiding hand! Using the copper and iron from this deal, I will supply our army with the latest weapons; build massive battleships that will conquer the seas! I will create a new golden age! Think of it! A new Renaissance! Once more, the world will look to Italy to lead!"

"I think you are perhaps a little premature in your assessments, Aldo… although my master tends to agree with you, for some reason. But what about the rest of the Grail Guardians? They aren't just going to stand by while you ride across the Continent," Wittgenstein prodded.

"Pah! A bunch of old men and cowardly philosophers! They have no real power any more. Their day is over and a bold new day has dawned." Aldo dismissed them with a wave of his hand. "With the knowledge contained in Villa D'Amici, and the ore contained in those mountains, I will be invincible. This time next year, Otto, I plan to be the most powerful man in the world, and you can bank on that, my friend. I shall have the goods on every ruler in Europe. And unlike the weak Grail Guardians, I am not afraid to use that knowledge to reshape the world to suit my vision. But, I must confess to a certain perverse delight in using Haldane to deliver the Guardians' arcane secrets to me."

"Well, just don't let Haldane near Sophia D'Amici, that is, if you've still got your heart set on her," Wittgenstein warned with dangerous undercurrents.

"Of course I will possess Sophia!" Aldo growled at his underling. "It will be my crowning achievement to sire the next dynasty of Carbonari Caesars upon the remnants of the obliterated Grail Guardians, bending their millennium of bloodlines to my purpose. Haldane is insignificant in the scope of my plans. Besides, I think I might just kill him after the turn of the year, once the Villa is mine. He's getting rather insufferable."

"Acht..." Wittgenstein sighed his relief, as he sank into the deep-tufted leather chair Haldane had vacated. "I wish you had told me that sooner."

"Never fear, my comrade. I have accounted for every contingency. We'll only have to endure Haldane's arrogance for a short while," Aldo said smugly. "Soon, he and the Guardians will be gone and the whole world will bow down to its rightful masters: us."

Haldane returned to his fine suite at the Grand Hotel et de Milan, anxious to record the last twenty-four hour's events in his journal. He had noted all major happenings in his life in the large, leather-bound book ever since his brother, Richard, gave it to him on his twelfth birthday. The tattered old tome had been rebound and enlarged several times by Haldane's own hand.

Religious in his faithfulness only to his Queen and his journal, he tried to go no longer than three consecutive days without an entry. The only times he failed to do so was when he was on extended and hazardous missions, which seemed to be most of the time, these days.

Using a code of his own devising, Haldane painstakingly wrote every detail he could remember about this evening's meeting, as well as everything of note from the delicious night before with Gretel. He went on to record some late thoughts about the most recent mission he had just completed days ago, observing reports of atrocities and war crimes in the Spanish Civil War.

As he recorded his afterthoughts on what he had observed in Spain, he reflected that the mission had impacted him more than he previously thought. Earlier that spring, a group of Traditionalists had rebelled against the new Spanish king, Amadeo I, crowned by a few years before at the conclusion of *La Gloriosa* revolution. The Traditionalists wished to replace the new king with a successor from the old line, Carlos the Seventh. These Carlists were accused of abusing civilians loyal to the new king. Haldane had been dispatched to observe the situation and report back to the British Home Office, to assess whether or not Britain should intercede at the request of the new king, Amadeo.

Although it should have been a routine mission, Haldane was still haunted by images of the tortured and mutilated women and children he had interviewed. Having seen battle many times in his sixteen-year military career, Haldane was well acquainted with the chaos and collateral damage of war, but never had he witnessed such intentional brutality. The image of one young girl, not much older than his daughter, who had been tortured and abused to death by the Carlists arose once more in his memory.

He shook his head to dismiss the image and rubbed his eyes wearily. *I'm so sick of suffering and death,* he thought. *Maybe I should put in for a desk job in London... Lizzy'd love that. Then I'd be available to take her round to do the whole season.* He grimaced at the thought of attending London's high society events, his wife grinning at his side. *On the other hand, perhaps not...*

In spite of the atrocities he had witnessed, he had recommended that the resources of his mighty island nation not be extended to help stabilize the new government. He knew that politically, there was little that Britain could gain and much to lose through getting involved in Spain's interior skirmishes. Yet regret tugged at the thought of refusing to aid those blameless victims of civil war. *But it could not be helped*, he justified. *The needs of the Empire must come first.*

Haldane considered retiring for the night, but determined that he was now too restless to sleep. He decided to make an impromptu inspection of Milan's finer bordellos.

# Chapter Five

**September 15, 1872   Villa D'Amici   9:30 p.m.**

"Sophia! I must speak to you!" Gemma called as she raced down the hall in a flurry of yellow ruffles and skirts after her older sister.

Sophia stopped, her hand on the door latch to her bedchamber, and turned.

"Gemma, what's got you so excited?" she asked as she guided her flustered sibling into her room.

"Shut the door, Sophie," Gemma urged, her dark eyes dancing, dark D'Amici curls bouncing. She fairly skipped across the wide room and took a seat on the canopied bed. "…And lock it, too. Then come over here by me." She patted the white chenille bedspread on top of thick down duvets.

"All right, all right," Sophia answered with a chuckle, as she complied, settling her bustle as she sat. "Now, what's this all about?"

"Oh Sophie! I don't know how to say it! I'm so happy!" the nineteen-year-old girl gushed. "I think I'm going to have Roberto's baby!"

"Oh. So soon?"

"Aren't you happy for me?" Gemma asked, not understanding.

"Oh, sweetie, of course I am," Sophia exclaimed and enfolded her little sister in a warm embrace. "I just didn't expect it to happen so quickly. Are you sure?"

"Well, no, not positive yet," the younger woman admitted. She looked up at Sophia with a hopeful smile. "But I have not had a cycle since before the wedding. And this morning, I felt quite wretched for a spell. It passed along quickly enough though."

"So I saw," Sophia agreed, recalling her sister and her bridegroom's spirited display earlier that day on the croquette court. "Gemma, this is welcome news. Have you told Papa yet? I know this will cheer him greatly."

"Sophia, I haven't told anyone but you," Gemma confided, as she fingered a ringlet of hair. "But I just couldn't keep it to myself any longer. You understand, don't you?"

"Of course, dear," Sophia soothed as she again hugged her sister's shoulders. "I am amazed you kept it secret for this long."

"Oh, I almost burst out with it at dinner tonight," Gemma said with a giggle, "but I wanted to talk to you first. I wish Mama could be here."

"Oh, so do I,' Sophia agreed, thinking how much better their departed mother would have been able to advise and guide young Gemma through her future discoveries of motherhood.

A moment of awkward silence fell between the two sisters as they both were forced to acknowledge the growing gulf between them, as Gemma's actual experience of life had overtaken and outstripped her older sibling and surrogate mother's paltry few adventures into the mysteries of womanhood.

"Well, have you heard anything from that lawyer fellow who fancies you?" Gemma asked eventually.

"Oh, yes," Sophia answered with some amusement. "He's sent me this and asked to call on me." She reached to her bed table and picked up a thick tome she passed to her sister. "It's a book of Greek dramatic theory from a peculiar German writer with a funny name: Nietzsche. Signor Aldo has certainly gone to some lengths to discover my interests. I suspect he must have consulted my bookseller. I don't know if I like that or not."

"So, what are you going to tell him when he calls?" Gemma asked with a conspiratorial grin.

"Oh, what I've told all the others, I suppose," Sophia answered with a sigh. "I shall return his book and show him the door... after I've finished reading it. My German is pretty rusty, so I may take a while."

"Sophie, why don't you spend some time with him, get to know him before you send him packing..." Gemma suggested, with a wry grin. "You know, you don't get that many gentlemen callers anymore. After all, you've turned down half of Europe. Maybe you should give this Aldo character a fair chance."

Sophia stood up in disgust and turned on her younger sister.

"Not you too!" she cried. "Just the other day, Papa was giving me the same lecture. I've told you all before, I don't care if I never marry." Sophia turned and went to sit at her vanity, her back to her sister. She began to pluck the ribbons and filigree pins from her hair. "Someone's got to hold this family together. Papa's making himself sick worrying about Eduardo and this stupid mining nonsense that Aldo is stuffing him full of. And now, if you're going to be having a baby... well, someone's got to maintain a level head and take care of the daily necessities of running this place, what with the end of the growing season here and all. Someone's got to see to this fall's pressings. Papa's too sick to go to the vineyards, and I don't have the time to sit in a parlor while some boring counselor woos me."

"Oh, come on, Sophia," Gemma objected. "You know they don't really need you in the winehouse. The foreman knows much more about making wine than you. You're just afraid. Admit it, you're afraid that if you marry, you won't be able to act like a man anymore – you'll have to restrict yourself to more womanly arts and leave the vineyards and all those books you read to the men."

"That's not true!" Sophia cried, as she spun and stood to face her sister's accusation head on. "Never have I acted like a man! What a man would wear lace and ruffles? What man would allow himself to be bound up so tight in a basque that he could scarcely breathe, just so he could have a tiny waist? Oh no, little sister. I am a very far cry from acting like a man."

"Oh, you know what I mean," Gemma stood her ground, rising from the canopied bed to meet her sister, "You do whatever you please, without a care what other people are thinking about you. You are too proud and stubborn. You just don't want to be obedient to a husband. You don't even mind Papa half the time."

"Well, you've got that one right," Sophia agreed ferociously. "I don't want to be some man's pampered plaything, with no brain. To bear and run after his squalling brats with runny noses until my mind turns to mush... I refuse to be subservient to some idiot man. If that means I act as a man, then so be it."

Gemma's eyes softened as she whispered, "But what about love? If you love him, it's not subservience, it's a delight."

"Gemma, I'm glad that you have found love and are happy," Sophia relented. "But, I don't think that it shall ever be my good fortune to find the kind of sentiments you and Roberto share. You are right. I am too stubborn. And too old to change my ways now."

"Oh, Sophie, I had hoped that someday, our children would play together," Gemma mourned. "I know that it must be hard for you to understand, but I feel so fulfilled, knowing I will soon be a mother. This is what I've wanted all my life. I don't see how you can turn your back on such joy without ever even tasting it." Gemma moved to the door and opened it. "I just pray that someday, you will come to know some of the happiness I feel with Roberto before you die. We have known so much tragedy, losing Mama, and then losing Cassie just last year. Someday, Papa will be gone, and Eduardo grown up and married. I'll have my children and my Roberto, but you'll be alone, living on Eduardo's generosity, and even your title will be gone, given to Eddie's wife once he marries. You'll have nothing of your own. Think on it, Sophia."

Gemma slipped out the door and closed it behind her. Sophia stared after her sister for several long moments before turning to regard her reflection in the mirror. She touched her cheek as Gemma's words wormed their way into her heart.

## 16 September, 1872   Milan, Italy   2:25 p.m.

Haldane strolled down the Via Corso di Vittoria, on his way to Aldo's business offices, whistling a merry tune. The busy street around him bustling with activity, Haldane ignored the people, the ancient stone buildings and the brilliant blue sky, alike.

In the preceding days, he had, by various means at his disposal, determined that the mineral deposits of copper and iron on the adjoining Calendri and D'Amici lands had been appraised to be among the richest in Western Europe, if deep and somewhat difficult to mine. Recent advancements in rail and mining technologies made the once inaccessible minerals now within reach, if given an ample initial investment.

He wondered if the aging dons were aware of the fortunes that they were sitting on – far more than what any back taxes or barrel makers' bills amounted to. He was willing to wager that Aldo had neglected to mention just how much the masters of those deposits would stand to make if they are able to put aside their age-old feud long enough to properly develop the project.

*Well,* Haldane thought, *I'll just have to make sure that the old boys find out, now won't I?*

He had learned from local gossip that these two ancient houses had been feuding over some minor slight for the last four hundred years, killing off most of their offspring in centuries long past, though in recent generations the violent hatred between the two houses had died down to silent loathing. It wasn't going to be easy to get these two to cooperate, even if it was to save both their estates.

Aldo had divided the negotiations between himself and Haldane. Aldo would work D'Amici and Haldane was to focus on Calendri. Local gossip also gave Haldane much needed information about the "Old Boys," as Haldane dubbed the two elderly lords. Don Stephano Calendri was fast approaching ninety, but was still sharp and straight as an arrow. Calendri had been a general during the Napoleonic wars, but had stayed out of the Unification of Italy. Haldane took that as being in his favor – he would be dealing with a fellow soldier. Calendri had the reputation for being a proud old bird, who would rather die than take charity – not an easy mark by any means.

The Villa Calendri was aged and decrepit, crumbling from over fifty years of miserly neglect. Old Calendri only kept a handful of servants now. Calendri's only son and heir, Vincente, was more interested in gambling and horses than anything else. Haldane could expect little help there. Vincente Calendri had never married and spent most of his time haunting the gentlemen's clubs and bordellos of Milan, so the great house was practically empty. Haldane was grateful that he wasn't going to have to stay there during the negotiations. At his own request for more neutral territory, he was being put up in Calendri's hunting lodge, in the mountains by the border between the two estates, about a two-hour ride from Milan.

Haldane also uncovered information about the other family, the D'Amici's. Don Alessandro D'Amici seemed an easier touch than Calendri. Though only in his seventies, D'Amici was plagued with bad health. He had married late in life, so his heir was still a child, away at school. D'Amici also had three grown daughters. The eldest was reported to have once been a beauty and shown promise in the opera, but had thrown away her youth on her doting father, music and exotic plants. He wasn't sure how much influence this faded spinster had over her father, but he was sure he could charm her if the situation should call for it. The other two daughters had married poor, though noble enough, men for love. The middle daughter had died in Paris during the recent uprisings the previous year, while on her honeymoon.

Local gossip said that old "Sandro" D'Amici still supported his great house in the old fashion, with many servants, thus running up a huge debt when his vineyards cut production by two-thirds because of a blight two years ago, and then had to sanitize or replace all the infected presses and bottling equipment. His troubles were worsened when the new kingdom government assessed a massive tax on D'Amici holdings. The old Don was desperate to hang on to his estate. Haldane agreed that Aldo could handle the likes of D'Amici without effort.

He shifted the valise he was carrying to his other hand, as he walked down the busy avenue, headed towards Aldo's dingy offices. He didn't know how long these talks would take, but he had pulled some strings to secure an extended leave of absence. He told his superiors in London that he needed to take care of "family business." Because of the extended and grisly nature of his recent mission in Spain, he was accorded special consideration. He wasn't expected back at the Horse Guards, as the Royal Army headquarters in London near Westminster Palace was called, until January fifth. He reckoned that gave him ample time to settle the negotiations, and still left plenty to spend with his family for the Christmas season.

Haldane looked forward to spending the holidays with his three children, whom he adored, when he remembered he had them. He hadn't seen them since before heading to the continent, some three months before. He especially anticipated time with his eldest, Victoria, his only daughter and child by his second wife. At ten years, Victoria already showed promise of becoming a beauty, like her departed mother had been.

He was looking less forward to the frantic social season his third and current wife, Elizabeth, expected him to attend smiling at her side. An arranged marriage, he and Elizabeth had agreed long ago that both their lives ran smoother when he wasn't in the rambling brownstone townhouse on Cherry Tree Lane in London's fashionable West End, a part of Elizabeth's generous dowry. As a result, Haldane spent much of his time abroad in the line of duty.

Haldane was genuinely fond of the ambitious social climber he had married, but although she had given him two fine sons, she had never excited his passion. The daughter of a wealthy rug and furniture importer, Elizabeth, in unspoken agreement, ignored Haldane's womanizing abroad. In return for her blind eye, she expected him to maintain the semblance of a happy marriage when in London, and to escort her to the many social functions with which she was so enamored. She had even agreed to convert and raise their children Catholic, though she herself had had a staunch Protestant upbringing.

Even with being a Catholic, Haldane was a great catch for a daughter of the merchant class, establishing Elizabeth in the best of society. A portion of her impressive dowry, judiciously invested, had eased some of the strains of running the large Malwick estate, for a while.

*I regret not having more time to spend with the children,* he reflected, as he walked the busy Milan street, miles and days away from home. *They grow up so fast, and with another coming in the spring. But it can't be helped. Duty calls. If fortune smiles upon this business with*

*Aldo, I might even have as much as a month to spend with my growing brood afterwards. With the funds from this deal, I shall be able to finally pay off my creditors and perhaps take the whole family to Paris for a week or two to make up for being gone so long... Assuming Lizzy hasn't racked up another slew of bills for me.*

Haldane watched a pretty, olive-skinned lady's maid on the walkway. As he opened the door to Aldo's dingy offices, he hoped he wouldn't find things intolerably dull at the Calendri estate. Something about the coquettish way the maid smiled and tossed her head as she passed reminded him... at once his elation crashed.

Aldo's sleek black brougham carriage took them on the two-hour ride to the Calendri holdings. On the way, Aldo worked on some account books with a small stub of a pencil, while Haldane stared out the coach's window, absentmindedly stroking his dark mustache. Aldo wondered what was so fascinating about the endless groves of olive trees and vineyards whizzing before far mountains. He watched Haldane out of the corner of his eye, but Haldane only stirred to brush an occasional unruly lock or two of hair from his eyes.

Haldane stared at the green blur flying by the carriage without sight, lost in dismal reverie. His thoughts dwelled on by-gone days of his early manhood. He was aware of Aldo's curious glances, but felt no inclination to talk to him. The less contact Haldane had with Aldo, the happier he was.

The sight of the pretty maid on the street had brought back searing memories of Haldane's second wife and mother of his little Victoria, the late Contessa Marguerite Du Monde. The mere thought of her was like rubbing salt in an open wound, even almost nine years after her death. Though their marriage ended in stinging rancor, Haldane still thought of Marguerite as the love of his life. Time had not healed this wound in his soul, even as he sought relief by relentless pursuit of his career and countless women.

As his thoughts flew back over the years, Haldane still could not understand what had gone wrong, how he had let the situation deteriorate so, how he had lost control.

*If only Marguerite hadn't found my journal,* he thought, wallowing in the bittersweet memories. *But enough of that, old boy,* he told himself, even as he allowed himself to sink into the well-worn grooves of what might have been.

If only the impoverished Contessa had not discovered how he maneuvered and manipulated her into marrying him, recounted in vivid detail in his journal, before he had developed his own secret code... If only she not discovered the acts of betrayal he committed while still married to her.

In his imagination, he constructed a world where he and Marguerite were still happy together, like when they were newlyweds. A private smiled played around his lips as Haldane dwelled on the fabricated details of the daily life with his deceased second wife. In wayward volition, his left thumb tugged at the simple gold band that he had given to Marguerite on the day he had finally convinced her to elope, now adorning his little finger.

Aldo glanced at Haldane again, wondering what the annoying Englishman found so entertaining.

# Chapter Six

Don Alessandro D'Amici sat in the large wood-paneled library in waistcoat and shirtsleeves, his chocolate brown frock coat flung casually over the back of his chair, putting the final touches on a small round clockwork device. He pushed a little button on the side of the device, and a tiny red light glowed on its ornate base.

"Ah! Perfecto!" he congratulated himself aloud. "Now all that is needed is a subject to test its effectiveness…"

Don Alessandro stood, retrieved his jacket and slipped it on. He then took the round metal device and dropped it into his pocket, preparing to seek out the needed test subjects for his newly overhauled Telepathon. He glanced around the library, mentally evaluating his family and staff as potential guinea pigs.

"Not Sophia," he muttered. "I shouldn't like to explain such a contraption to her, if it were to still have any problems operating… But she would make a fine test subject, for sure… once I am positive it's working. Hmmm…"

The door to the library opened, cutting off Don Alessandro's ruminations, as his youngest daughter, Gemma came through the entrance, in a swath of red and cream striped silk taffeta ruffles.

"Oh, Papa," she said, her cheeks suddenly turning a brilliant crimson that complemented her gown once she caught sight of Don Alessandro. "I didn't realize you were in here. I – I was just wanting to find something to read for tonight."

A sneaky smile crept upon Don Alessandro's face.

"Not at all, my dear! I am delighted to see you," he welcomed, motioning for her to come closer. "It's seems we've seen all too little of you since the wedding." He leaned in as Gemma came around his desk and kissed him on the cheek before taking the nearby leather armchair.

"I'm sorry, Papa," the girl said, "but now that I am Roberto's wife, my first responsibility is to him, you know."

"That is how it should be," he replied. "You're a good girl, Gemma." The young woman glowed with her father's approval. Deep within his pocket, his fingers pressed a hidden button, as he retook his seat. "Now tell me something my dear..."

"Yes, Papa... What do you wish to know?" she asked, gazing upon him serenely.

"What did you *really* come into the library to find?" he probed intently.

Gemma hesitated, her expression blank. Don Alessandro pushed another button on the device secreted in his pocket.

"I came to find a – "

"Yes...?" Don Alessandro encouraged. "To find a what?"

"I came to find a book on anatomy," she finally managed to get out.

"A book on anatomy? You've never showed an interest in the sciences before..." Don Alessandro quizzed. "What piqued your interest in anatomy now? And why are you so embarrassed to tell me?"

The young woman squirmed uncomfortably under the control of the mind mechanism, but was compelled to answer, nonetheless.

"I suspect I may be carrying Roberto's baby, but I am not sure. Sophia does not know how to find out for sure without waiting and going to the doctor, but I wanted to see if there was anything here in the library that might help me to ascertain the true state of affairs."

"Ah! My Gemma! My little jewel!" Don Alessandro cried rising from his chair to embrace his daughter, repressing a small cough. "Why didn't you tell us? Why all the subterfuge?"

Gemma smiled remotely at her father's enthusiastic hug, still under the influence of the Telepathon.

"I did not wish to disappoint Roberto should I be proven incorrect. I wanted to wait until I was sure before announcing it to the family. I did tell Sophia last night, but I made her swear she would not tell a soul until we knew for sure."

"Gemma, your secret shall be safe with me, as well," Don Alessandro pledged. "In fact, you shall not even remember that you told me..." He reached in his pocket, pressing more buttons.

Gemma blinked her eyes several times, as the machine removed the last few minutes from her memory. Then, she glanced around the room in confusion, as the machine released her from its grip.

"Well, my dear," Don Alessandro said as he stood and headed towards the library door, "I fear I am a bit fatigued now, and would like to lay down for a bit before supper." He stifled a small cough significantly.

"Oh of course, Papa," Gemma replied, springing up from her chair and accompanying him to the door. "I'll just find a nice novel or history book, something boring to help put me to sleep tonight, and then go check on Roberto."

Don Alessandro kissed her check, satisfied in the knowledge that not only was the Telepathon working perfectly, but also that the D'Amici line would continue into the future. As he walked away from the library, he gave a little jig in his step.

## 20 September, 1872  Calendri Estate, Northern Italy 5:00 p.m.

Aldo's hired coach arrived at the Calendri estate's gates in the long shadows of late afternoon. Villa Calendri was a strange conglomerate of geometric shapes. Primarily a cube, it had rectangular outbuildings and a giant glass pyramid peeking up from behind, where the household kitchen gardens were located. Located high on the side of Monte Calendri, Villa Calendri overlooked deep-forested canyons and swift, glacier-fed rivers. The Georgian style villa had been built in better times, over one hundred and twenty years before. Now, its once-fine façade was cracked and peeling.

Ushered inside by a frail-looking butler, the two visitors were introduced to the erect old lord of the manner. He looked just as Haldane expected he should. Tall and narrow, with thin wisps of white hair curling out from his head. His face was as narrow as the rest of him, brown and wrinkled, with a great hawk-like nose protruding out the center. He welcomed his guests without flourish.

"You must forgive me," Don Stephano Calendri told them. "We are not accustomed to many visitors here."

"Oh, no, my lord. You have nothing to apologize for," Aldo exclaimed. "I prefer to conduct my business without frivolity and the good colonel here is another Army man, such as you and I. I'm sure I can speak for us both when I say that we appreciate your straightforward ways."

*Toady,* Haldane silently sneered.

The ancient Don sniffed at Aldo, and turned to behold his other visitor. Don Stephano studied Haldane intently for several long moments, as an awkward tension mounted. Then with a curt nod, he turned on his heel and barked, "Follow me. We can talk in my study."

The old man led the other two men out of the cavernous great hall into a small, adjoining room. This room was slightly cozier than the yawning ballroom they had just left. It contained worn furniture that had gone out of style half a century before. All the valuable furnishings had been auctioned off long ago. A large, battered desk filled the far end of the room, with an equally battered leather chair behind it, into which the don slowly lowered himself.

"Please be seated."

It was more an order than a request. Haldane and Aldo seated themselves in the two mismatched worn armchairs that faced the desk.

Aldo cleared his throat nervously. "My lord... there is so much for us to discuss, but first may I offer you a cigar?"

"Signor, I told you at your last visit, I do not smoke or imbibe spirits. I'll thank you to not forget again," snapped the old man.

Haldane had a gnawing premonition that he was in for trouble.

At his own request for more neutral territory, Haldane was put up at Calendri's hunting lodge in the woods between the two estates. More a cabin than an actual lodge, containing only one large room, sparsely furnished, it suited Haldane just fine. It was far enough away from the Villa Calendri that he could relax, yet close enough to be convenient for his negotiations.

The negotiations proceeded at a snail's pace. If Calendri agreed to something, then D'Amici disagreed. When D'Amici was finally convinced, then Calendri changed his mind. Even the choice of maps set off days of negotiation. Mineral assays, projected expenses, the hiring of mining teams and the purchase of large equipment... Every detail of the contract became a separate pitched battle. Each night, Haldane always seemed to return to the hunting lodge between the two estates tired and cranky, his head bursting. He was grateful that at the end of each day's long wrangle with Calendri that he didn't have to be civil to anyone.

## October 27 1872   Monte Calendri, Italy   5:09 a.m.

Haldane lurched forward as the brown gelding beneath him came to a halt, jarring him from his light doze in the pre-dawn dark. As he roused himself back to wakefulness, he looked around for signs of danger, but found none in the shadows of the deserted wood-lined road. He tried to take his bearings, but realized he did not recognize his surroundings. The woods on both sides of the dirt road were denser than where his cabin was located, making him suspect that he was higher up the mountain, but he wasn't sure. The trees obscured his view of the sky, as steep mountains rose on either side of the road. The narrow strip of starlit sky above him gave no clue of orientation.

"Oh bloody hell," he murmured, as he realized he was lost. He chided himself for choosing to return to his cabin instead of accepting his lovely hostess' offer of a comfortable room in Milan. "Could have been cuddling in a warm bed, instead of lost in the middle of nowhere." Then he recalled why he had chosen to brave the mountain roads at night and relaxed his self-accusations.

He had gone to Milan to celebrate his thirty-third birthday at a musical salon after five weeks of hard negotiations at Villa Calendri. The hostess had taken a liking to Haldane, and it would have been unlikely he would have gotten much sleep that night, had he stayed. Although he found the widowed countess attractive, his usual appetite for new conquests deserted him tonight.

He kept seeing the image of that poor abused young Spanish girl from his last mission, instead of the glamorous society woman coquetting him. The girl was not much older than his daughter, stirring up ripples of regret. Although he knew it impractical, he still wished there had been something he could have done for her – for her people. *The needs of the Empire must take precedence over personal sentiments. I can't save every innocent from becoming a casualty.* He knew that contrary to popular belief, the greatest victims of war were helpless women and children, not male soldiers dying in battle. *That's the way it has always been – men make war and women pay the price. I may not like it, but I can't change the way the world works.* Yet he could not shake his disquiet.

It was this same odd mood that had kept him from the taverns as well, preferring the solitude of the cool night instead. So he had declined his hostess' gracious invitation, assessing himself alert enough to make the trip up the mountain to his lodgings. But his current predicament argued otherwise.

Shaking his head to clear the cobwebs, he shivered a bit in the pre-dawn air as he considered his next move. He knew that he had passed the tiny hamlet of Lecco before he fell asleep, but he was not sure how far up the road he had gone. Since he did not know if he had missed his turn off or not, he decided to proceed until he either recognized a landmark or came to a clearing where he could figure out his location. He shook the reins and prodded the horse he had borrowed from Calendri to an easy gait. They proceeded along for several minutes without any change in the thick, close landscape.

*Hell of a good place for an ambush*, Haldane thought as he came to a fork in the road, where his road along the valley joined with the path from above along the tree line. He looked about cautiously, but only the rhythm of his gelding's hoofbeats, the rustling of the leaves, insects and an occasional howl in the distance stirred the quiet night. A few hundred yards further and he recognized the path to his cabin to the right. He let fly a sigh of relief and started to turn the horse onto the path.

All of a sudden a bright flash in the dark sky caught his attention. He looked up to behold a brilliant falling star and smiled. The meteorite was falling fast, and he realized that its low trajectory would pass his position. The green-hued star flamed past, some one hundred feet over his head and kept going, leaving a streamer of smoke trailing behind. Impulsively, Haldane turned the horse from the path to the cabin, galloping up the road in pursuit of the falling star.

He rounded a curve at full speed, just in time to see the meteorite fall into the middle of a large dark lake, with a loud sizzling splash he could hear even from the shore. As Haldane approached the water's edge at full speed, pulling up only at the last moment before reaching the water's edge. Remembering the old tradition, he decided to make a wish. Since this was the closest he had ever been to a falling star, he reckoned his wish should be a big one.

"I simply want to be happy," he whispered softly to the breeze in his native tongue. "Even if it only lasts one day – one hour, even. I want to know what it is to be completely and totally satisfied. Wanting nothing, dreading nothing, fearing nothing…" He closed his eyes and focused on this wish, imagining what it would feel like to be released from the constant gnawing in his soul, the dark fears and sharp regrets.

With a slow smile, he opened his eyes and looked at the black, star-reflecting water and the mountains that ringed the lake, deeply breathing in the fresh fragrance of the piney trees and water. *Lago di Lario*, he thought, recalling the name of the lake, one of the most beautiful in the region.

Again, indulging in his peculiar mood, Haldane dismounted and wrapped the horse's reins around a nearby tree branch. He pulled a feedbag from his saddle and hooked it to the animal's harness. Immediately, the gelding began munching the oats inside. Haldane patted the faithful horse and made his way to sit on a boulder by the water's edge.

The half moon overhead bounced off the waves, under a crystalline indigo sky. Millions of stars blazed out from the heavens. Looking to the east, he could see the first flush of the coming dawn reflecting on a few low clouds over the eastern mountains. The rhythmic lapping of the waves against the rocks, the soft rush of the breeze and the faraway sound of birds heralding the coming dawn made a suitable accompaniment to the lovely landscape before him.

He looked up into the Milky Way, stretching overhead, losing himself in awe of the vastness of the night sky. Suddenly, he had the sensation of momentum, and he felt his petty life crumble into insignificance before this new awareness. Compared to the infinitude of space, his little life seemed but a momentary flash in the velvet eternity. His many problems and mistakes had no meaning, no hold upon his spirit. A sense of contentment filled him, his harsh thoughts subsided and he experienced himself at one with this place. For the first time in a very long time, he felt a respite from his relentless yearning, at peace within himself and the world. With a grateful heart, he recognized the promise of fulfillment of his simple wish.

He leaned down, gazing into the inky water, reflecting ripples of stars. Reaching out, he touched the cool water, then bent down to take a drink. The water was cold, sweet, invigorating as it trickled into his belly. Suddenly, he began unbuttoning his caped overcoat, stripped it off and tossed it gently on the rocks. Then he pulled off his boots and stood to remove his uniform tunic, shirt, breeches and undergarments, dropping them on the rock in a small pile. He yanked off his stockings as to cool night air bit into his tightening flesh, making every cell alive. His pale skin glowed in the half-light of the new moon and stars. He vigorously shook himself to remove the shivers of cold before scrambling down the rocks to the water's edge.

Stepping into the stinging water, he ignored the sharp protests of his flesh against the cold, savoring his mastery over his instincts and the exercise of his will. He waded in on the rocky sand until he felt it slope downwards to greater depths. Filling his lungs with the chilled night air, he dived into the cold water and swam underwater until the need to breathe forced him to surface. It felt good to use his muscles, to feel his heart and lungs pumping, the tingling cold buoyancy of the water. He looked up at the starlit sky above as he floated on his back, feeling as if he were floating in space amongst the stars. All of his cares seemed insignificant in the vastness of infinity. His body adjusted to the temperature of the water, as he lay upon the face of the water.

Floating weightlessly, staring up into the pre-dawn sky of cobalt blue to black, he relinquished the ties that bound him to a life grown too tight. As thoughts of his habitual worries and fears arose, he chose to ignore them, instead focusing on the reports of his senses – the stars, the interface where the cold water met colder air on his skin, the rhythm of his own strong heart. When his habitual regrets arose for his consideration, he chose instead to listen to the lapping of the water in his ears, to feel the buoyancy of the lake supporting him. Without fears or regrets, his mind stopped its restless questing to the future and past, and became rooted in the present moment. He closed his eyes and deeply inhaled the crisp, fragrant mountain air. His mind became utterly still.

He saw himself as if from above – his pale body adrift in the dark waters, and knew that he was not that fragile body below, so prone to weakness and death. Rather, he was that which looked out through the body's eyes. And he knew that which he was had never been born, nor could ever die.

As soon as this knowing registered in his consciousness, he was back in the cold lake, sputtering as his head bobbed beneath the water, his peaceful flotation sunk.

"What the bloody hell was that?" he sputtered.

He righted himself, returning to his floating position, trying to recapture the vision of the spontaneous vision, to bring it back, to seek answers to the hundreds of questions burgeoning up within him. But his mind would not go still, no matter how hard he tried to force his thoughts away, and his body refused to relax, forcing him to tread water to keep from sinking. Yet he continued to try to force his mind, body and spirit to obey and return to that moment of vision, grasping at the fading wisps of memory.

A cool dawn breeze came up, rushed across his wet skin, raising gooseflesh and shudders, finally convincing him that his body did have its limits of tolerance. Giving up, he turned back and swam to the shore. After drying himself off on a rough blanket from his saddlebag, he got dressed and retook his seat on the boulder by the shore. He remained there unmoving until the darkness faded and the wildlife about him stirred to wakefulness with the brilliant dawn. Haldane couldn't honestly say he was happy, as he knew his problems still awaited him, only a thought away. But those worries were connected to his body, not to that awareness of himself that he had just discovered. He realized that however those problems were concluded or not, no impact would ever change that awareness he had just experienced.

The weeks of negotiation dragged on longer than Haldane expected, with Calendri questioning every item, every expense, every clause of the proposed contract, requiring hours of careful research and explanation. Five times assaying teams were sent to take samples. Three different laboratories were used to analyze the samples. Although the exacting old don would never admit it verbally, Haldane knew that he deeply mistrusted Aldo. Yet, Calendri seemed committed to continuing the negotiations nonetheless. But the drawn out process began to take its toll on Haldane.

He attempted to soothe his jangled nerves reading some novels about the American Wild West and Civil War he had bought before he left London, but found scant relief. Even a copy of the latest controversial bestseller that he had picked up on one of his trips to Milan, *The Descent of Man,* written by that clever chap from back home named Darwin, could not do more than take the merest edge off.

The books and solitary rides to the lake were his only entertainments for the long weeks he spent as guest at the Calendri estate in the small cabin in the woods. He returned to the lake several times in hopes of recapturing the magic he had felt the night of the meteor, and while he did regain some modicum of ease each time he went, the fullness of his first experience escaped him, leaving more dissatisfied than before.

Occasionally, he would hazard the two-hour ride into Milan to seek amusements there, providing a break in the tedium. But even these, he found, soon lost their savor. He quit making the unsatisfying journeys, and resigned himself to a monk-like existence in the isolated cabin in the wooded mountains of Northern Italy, rage at his self-made incarceration simmering in his blood.

By the second week of November, he thought they finally had an agreement they could work with. That is, until Calendri brought in a team of lawyers from Rome to go over the contracts with a fine toothed comb. The battles began anew, and Haldane's wife's letters grew more and more insistent upon his hasty return.

# Chapter Seven

"What do you mean you *still* haven't got the Telepathon in working order, Sandro?" Calyx demanded incredulously, his voice echoing off the hard volcanic rock of the vaulted ceiling high above. "I was under the impression that everything was going fine... That's what I already have reported to the Matriarch. And now you tell me it has *never* worked on Aldo? What have you done? What were you thinking?"

Don Alessandro, in shirtsleeves, tried to shrug casually, as he turned back to his workbench and began puttering with buzzing gadgets. In the huge, black-domed underground room beneath the north tower of Villa D'Amici, Don Alessandro had turned an empty ancient lava chamber into a large workshop filled with technological wonders born of his unique genius. Inspired by the drawings of DaVinci and the ancient knowledge of the Grail Guardians, coupled with recent technological advances and his own discoveries, Don Alessandro's chill, damp workshop contained random prototypes and blueprints for everything from the gigantic Phlogiston-powered war machines to the latest version of the Vibralance tool, no larger than Don Alessandro's little finger, and devices of every conceivable size and purpose in between scattered on tables and under drop cloths throughout the large space.

"Well... You know that I have had my share of mechanical failures in the past, so I tend to take them in stride, and... well... Things have always worked out well enough in the end," he said.

"That's because I was always able to swoop in at the last minute to save your sorry arse," Calyx accused, as he took off his glasses and began wiping them on his monogramed handkerchief. "So what is your contingency plan?"

Don Alessandro coughed uncomfortably and moved further away from his friend.

"That you would swoop in at the last minute to save my sorry arse," he quipped with tentative humor, but quickly saw that Calyx was not amused.

"Truly, Giuseppe, I was positive that I could make it work. It has worked in all my experiments. It worked on my valet... It worked on my daughter Gemma. It even worked on Sophia, and you know how hardheaded she is. But for some reason I have been unable to ascertain, it hasn't worked on Aldo," Don Alessandro confided. He paused once more to cough before continuing. "I keep wondering if he has somehow found a way to counteract the Telepathon... But how? He shouldn't even know it exists."

"Counteract the Telepathon? Alessandro... This is serious. Without the Telepathon, you cannot gain control over Aldo. Our trap has no spring." Calyx rubbed his puckered forehead and paced past the device laden tables and sheet-covered mechanisms. "What are we going to do? This is *terrible*. You should have said something sooner. Oh dear God - I've lied to the Matriarch. I told her the Telepathon works. I can't believe you've done this to us!"

"I know, old friend," Don Alessandro said as he reached up to pat his tall friend's shoulder. Another bout of coughing overtook him for several seconds before he continued. "But I am sure the Telepathon *is* in good working order. The problem lies elsewhere. It's not my devices this time," he said with a half-smile. "Oh, I can hold Aldo off. Between Calendri and I, we have kept Aldo running in circles for weeks, and we can continue that for some time yet. At least we are keeping Aldo occupied while the Matriarch gets prepared to launch the main assault to bring the Illuminati down. But I think we have an even bigger problem, Peppe."

Alarmed, Calyx stared at his friend.

"What?" he breathed.

"If Aldo knows about the Telepathon, then we must have a traitor in our midst."

## 2 December, 1872   Villa D'Amici   2:12 p.m.

Sophia greeted the interloper in the cool verdant of the arbor, what she instinctively felt was her strongest ground, her maid acting as chaperone seated on a bench a discrete distance away. She was prepared for war, having donned her prettiest day dress and urged her maid to squeeze that extra inch out of her basque to give her figure an impossibly small waist, her curling dark masses of hair carefully pinned up to balance her delicate features and a single pink rose bud peeked out from its nest at her bosom.

Signor Sergio Aldo was equally turned out for battle, in a claret riding jacket and doeskin breeches, the cut of which disguised his paunch, while high black boots elongated his form. His goatee was neatly trimmed and a large cabochon ruby adorned his dove grey ascot. He approached with determination, his first volley ready at hand.

"Donna Sophia, let me express my thanks for agreeing to see me," he began solicitously. "I wasn't sure you would receive me when you took so long to respond. I had hoped to hear from you weeks ago. Did you enjoy the book?"

"Yes, thank you," Sophia replied, giving no hint of acknowledgement of his mild reprimand. "I see that you have put yourself out to obtain the unobtainable for me, Signor Aldo. The largest bookseller in Milan told me that this book you sent was not yet available in Italy. You must have gone to some trouble to procure it."

Aldo met her challenge with level eyes and a knowing smile.

"Such is always my habit when I meet a pearl of great price," he replied smoothly.

Sophia smiled her amusement.

"Am I a pearl of great price, Signor?" she asked.

"Indeed, the rarest, most beautiful pearl I have had the pleasure to behold, Donna," he said with a suave bow.

"And do you intend to purchase me, then?" she parried, icicles creeping into her voice.

"I would give all I have to make you mine," he answered, undeterred by her rebuff.

Sophia smiled and tapped his shoulder with her fan as she moved past him, forcing him to turn to continue to watch her as she spoke. "Would you really, now? Give all you have? For me? Indeed, I know your fortune is not insignificant. Signor, you flatter me."

"No, Donna. It is truth," he protested, grasping her hand and raising it to his lips for a soft kiss, while his black eyes held hers. "I fell in love with you the first moment I saw you."

Surprised at his audacity, Sophia resisted, yet found herself relenting as the warmth of his thick, sensuous lips touched her hand. After a long moment, Sophia retrieved her hand and withdrew a few paces to regroup her forces.

"So, Signor Aldo," she began, fanning herself to cover her discomfiture, "tell me about yourself. What manner of man are you?"

Aldo grinned broadly, as he recognized his victory in the first skirmish. He strode over to a nearby bench and set his boot upon the seat, striking a jaunty pose, his arm resting upon his knee before he deigned to answer.

"Well, Donna, what would you like to know?" putting her back on the defensive.

"I don't know," she replied, taking the charge into his territory. "Tell me about where you come from, about your family."

"Alas, dear lady, I have no family," he told her sadly. Sophia looked up sharply at his words. "You see, I am an orphan. I never knew my father and my mother died when I was but a small boy. I don't even know what my own birthday is, I was so young when she died."

"Oh," Sophia whispered, new compassion creeping into the place of recent disdain. "I, too, lost my mother young, but not so young as that."

"Indeed, Donna, and you have been graced with a great don as father. I much admire him, you know. I was very disturbed when he took to his bed after our meeting today," he declared, an emotion Sophia could not quite identify tinging his words. "Would that I had had a father like that. I pray he makes a hasty recovery."

"As do I, Signor. As do I... So, where did you grow up? With some relative or family friend?" Sophia empathized, sucked in by the tragedy of Aldo's past.

"Ahh, dear lady, if only it had been so, the story of my childhood would be a much happier tale," he lamented. "No, Donna, I grew up in an orphanage in the countryside outside Palermo for my first years, where I earned my keep as a shepherd. Around ten, I counted myself old enough to seek my fortunes, so I ran away to Palermo, where I learned to live by my wits. A few years later, a kindly, if eccentric, old lawyer hired me, and taught me to read and research for his clients. He showed me the ways of business and I worked for him for many years. When Garibaldi and his bright troops were sweeping across Italy, I worked my way to Syracuse, where I joined their gallant ranks. As reward for my brave service in the cause of unification, Garibaldi himself pinned a gold medal on my chest and paid for my education out of his own coffers. I found I possess a talent for business, and so was able to provide a comfortable life for myself. But I have no one to share that good fortune with, nor heirs to pass it on to. That is why I present myself at your feet, Donna," he said as he left the bench and approached her once more, taking her hand. "As you see, I am a self-made man, and while not of noble birth, I belief I have acquitted myself well, given the dreadful circumstance of my childhood. I have both the means and the desire to make you a happy wife."

"Well, sir, I hardly know you," Sophia objected. "You cannot expect a response to your proposal today."

"Indeed, dear lady," he whispered, as he took her hand once more and planted a delicate kiss on its back. "I hope that, in time, you will come to love me, even as I love you."

Sophia laughed sharply and extricated her hand from Aldo's grip.

"Sir, I have no use for love. It muddles the thoughts and leads to trouble. If you seek to woo me, thinking me some romantic fool, you will be sadly disappointed, Signor. Any man I should to choose to marry, it will be for practical, rational reasons. Not because my head is all full of hearts and moonbeams, like some silly goose."

"Indeed, Donna?" He straightened at her challenge. "Then allow me to present you with such rational justification why you must consider me." He stared straight into her eyes. "Your family estate is on the brink of economic calamity, Donna. Your father, while a wise and noble man, does not possess the business acumen - the knowledge, connections nor capital to pay off his bills or to develop what resources he does own... I do. He is deeply in debt and owes a great deal in back taxes. If you consent to marry me, I will save your family from certain ruin and would not expect repayment for the money I would invest in paying off the taxes on this fine villa or for undertaking the construction of the mine. Not only could I make you a happy wife and mother, but also I promise that you and your family shall have the financial security you sorely need. Now what do you say, Donna?"

"I need to think about it," Sophia managed to spurt out through the overwhelming information he just provided. She knew that her father had some debts, but on the verge of financial ruin? She had no idea things were so bad. Yet, it made sense, as she recalled her father laying off vineyard workers despite this being the busiest season of the year, and cutting back on the house staff a few weeks before, not to mention the heavy weight her father seemed to bear these days. "I will speak with you again later, Signor Aldo. Now, if you will excuse me..." She gestured towards the door, indicating the interview was at an end.

"Yes, Donna, do think on it," he replied with an oily grin. "I shall call on you again next week."

As the Sicilian departed, Sophia pondered his words.
*Is it true?*
Was her family so endangered? She didn't want to admit that her father had anything but absolute control of the family's fortunes. But there had been that failure of the vines a couple of years ago, and the new winepresses her father had bought last year had been a major

expenditure.

What would her Alcibiades, with all his worldly knowledge, counsel her to do? She bit her lip in consternation as she tried to see what path to take. But she could see no apparent solution that would satisfy propriety. If things were different, she could maybe support her family by singing in the opera or in music halls. But Sophia knew her father would never allow her to perform publically, much less earn wages. That left only an advantageous marriage as solution to her family's financial woes.

*I must talk to Papa about this, see what he thinks of this Aldo fellow*, she decided with a start.

She passed through the winding halls and climbed the curving staircases to reach his bedchamber, where her father had taken to bed earlier in the day.

Upon her soft knock, Don Alessandro bid her enter in a weak voice.

"Yes, child," he gasped in rough breaths. "Thank God you –" He broke off, overcome by a wet cough.

"Papa..."

Sophia was greatly taken aback at the change in her father's appearance from the last time she had seen him, just a few hours before. His face was gray, with dark circles under his eyes; his lips bluish and a harsh rattle accompanied each of his labored breaths.

"Papa, how are you feeling?" she asked, her own questions purged from her mind in her concern for her father.

"Very weak, Sophie..." he whispered. "I fear I have not much time left to me. I am so glad you are here. There is something I must tell –" his words were broken off by the fierce wet hacking that shook his form.

"Papa, please... Where is your medicine?" She cast her eyes about the room, seeking out some means to alleviate her father's suffering.

Don Alessandro grasped his daughter's arm, his fingers hot and dry.

"That's not important now," he gasped around his frequent coughs. Sophia returned her attention to him.

"What is it, Papa?" she asked, bending over him.

He lay back on his pillows and gazed up at his eldest and dearest daughter. Flecks of blood stained his lip. Sophia gently wiped his sweat-beaded face with a cloth. He raised a shaking hand and pointed to a nearby desk.

"There," he croaked. "In that desk..." The effort to speak brought the return of his cough.

"Over here," Sophia prompted, moving to the desk. "You want something from the desk?"

The don nodded weakly. Sophia opened the heavy roll top and peered inside at the assemblage of clockwork gears, tools and gadgets of her father's hobby.

"Key – Get the key from that little drawer," he directed.

Sophia found a miniature drawer near the top of the desk. Opening it, she found a small key.

"Good, good," Don Alessandro gasped. "Now... take that key downstairs to the library..." His words were once again cut off by a fit of cruel coughing. When he regained control, he resumed his instructions. "In the library, in my desk... That key will open the bottom left drawer. Inside, under the papers, you will find that the drawer has a false bottom." He paused to gasp a few moments before continuing. "Under the false bottom you will find a small silver box. Go fetch it and bring it to me."

"Papa, can't this wait?" she asked with concern darkening her bright eyes. "You're tired. You need your rest if you are going to get well. I'll bring this box to you in the morning."

"No!" her father cried. "Tomorrow may be too late! Too late for us all... I've failed... failed you, Sophia... failed us all!" The painful hacking returned. "Hurry - Go!" he gasped.

"Very well, Father," she relented. "I shall go get this box and bring it to you. But you must lie back and try to rest while I'm gone."

The old man nodded.

"Don't let anyone see – " he admonished, "don't let any see the box or know what you are doing..."

Sophia ducked into the library unseen. She quickly located the box her father had described. As she drew it forth, she was filled with concern for her only remaining parent. Never had she seen him look so bad, nor so agitated. His lungs had been weak ever since she could recall, but there was something *wrong* about the sound of his cough today. She slipped the small, cool box the size of a man's palm, emblazoned with the family crest of two crossed keys, into her full sleeve for safekeeping, then traversed the distance back to her father's bedside.

In the tawny afternoon light, his face looked a sickly green, the furrows on his face deep and sagging.

"Here, Papa. Is this it?" She proffered him the small box.

Don Alessandro let go a sigh of relief.

"Yes. This is it. Sophia... it is imperative that you keep this safe for your brother."

Another harsh bout of coughing interrupted him. He sat up, bending with the spasms.

"Careful, Papa..." Sophia whispered, as she placed a comforting hand on her father's shoulder.

"Never mind me," he gasped. "I sorely misjudged our enemies...

and my own abilities. I was warned, but I was so sure... My hubris has undone us!! You must safeguard this until your brother is old enough to claim his heritage. Seek out my old friend, Calyx, your godfather..." The coughing again detained his speech. When the bout finally stopped, the bedclothes beneath Don Alessandro's face were spattered with blood.

"Papa!" Sophia cried in alarm at the sight of it. "I'm going to send Carlo to fetch the doctor. I don't care if you want to see him or not!" She stood, as if to carry out her plan, but her father's harsh voice halted her steps.

"No! There's no time for that now!" he barked with the last of his strength. "All our work must not come to naught! This is urgently important!"

Sophia rushed back to his side and knelt by the bed, her stomach knotted, her ivory brow knit.

"What is it, Papa? What do you want me to do?" she pleaded.

"This box... it is the key to the D'Amici legacy..." he wheezed, with failing breath. "Now, it is for you... for you to protect with your life... until..."

A hideous rattling issued from Don Alessandro's throat and bright blood bubbled forth from his lips, dripping into his beard. Sophia clapped her hand to her mouth in horror. Tears welled up in Sophia's eyes as she witnessed her father's agonies, yet she could not tear herself away from his side long enough to summon help. He shuddered violently, as blood gushed forth with each ragged breath.

"Sophia..." he whispered, his voice barely audible above his breath. "Now it is in your hands... Protect...."

A final spasm of coughing ravaged the old man's body. Unable to endure any more, Don Alessandro released his tenuous hold on life and joined the ranks of his honored ancestors.

Sophia watched the life drain out of him with his last, shaking breath.

"Nooo!" she wailed, as she realized he would not draw breath again. "Papa! No! Don't go! Don't leave me here all alone!" she cried as panic grew in her breast. "You can't die yet! Not yet! What about Gemma's baby? You must live to bounce him on your knee, Papa!... Papa... I'm not ready yet..."

Her inconsolable sobs filled the still room.

# Chapter Eight

**13 December, 1872   Milan, Italy   10:45 p.m.**

"I came as soon as I received your telegram," Delacroix told Calyx, as he removed his dripping overcoat, draping it across a leather chair in Calyx's warm rented parlor. "I'm sorry to have kept you waiting, but the trains were backed up for leagues." The Frenchman removed his brown bowler hat and wiped the raindrops from his face and beard. "I am so sorry, Giuseppe."

"Travel at this season is always trying," Calyx agreed, embracing his comrade with a welcoming hug. "Especially when you know ill news is awaiting at your destination."

The two men stood behind the closed hotel doors, as fierce thunder and lightning racked the skies above. Cold rain pattered against the curtained window.

"I still can't believe it... Alessandro said his plan was foolproof, God rest his soul. How could Aldo have managed it?" Delacroix asked, quickly crossing himself.

Calyx also crossed himself. "Over thirty years we worked side by side. All our discoveries, all our adventures... I can't believe he's just gone like that," he said as he snapped his fingers. "I know he is in a better place with our honored ancestor, that this life is but a speck in the eternity of the soul. But it is still difficult..." He looked away, mastering himself before turning back with a stern countenance. "Sandro was never able to get his Telepathon to function properly on Aldo, but he was too proud to tell me until it was too late. I suspect he was poisoned, though my agents have not been able to ascertain how. There is not enough evidence to charge Aldo with murder, but all the signs point to him. I made sure Milano's top police sergeant was assigned the case. My secretary is assisting him. But the family doesn't know any of this, of course, in accord with the Code... Damned rotten time for Fra Diego to be on the frontlines in Spain."

"Murder? That bastard! But what of our plan? Without Alessandro and the Telepathon, we cannot hope to entrap Aldo," Delacroix despaired.

"I'm afraid it's worse than that," Calyx said quietly, as he removed his glasses. "My secretary sent me an update this morning... Aldo has also managed to seduce Sandro's eldest daughter, Sophia. Aldo procured a special dispensation from the Pope and they are to be married this week. Now, he will have legal possession of the Villa D'Amici until Alessandro's boy comes of age, in four years."

"My God! This is worse than I could have possibly imagined," Delacroix gasped as he eased himself into an armchair before a roaring fire. "We are lost... lost. I warned Alessandro about this. I had a bad feeling from the start. If only Alessandro hadn't insisted on facing Aldo alone. This isn't like the old days. He's no longer a young man. Now Sangraal hangs in the balance. How could we have let this happen? Have you heard from the Matriarch?"

"Yes," Calyx grunted. "You won't like it any better."

"Why? What does she say?"

"She says the scheme has become too costly, and orders us to abandon it. I can't even go visit my godchildren. It's become too dangerous, should Aldo decide to take me hostage," Calyx told him softly.

Delacroix looked up incredulously.

"But... but what of the Illuminati and Carbonari? We can't just let Aldo get away with this. If he can gain entry to the Archives or even Alessandro's workshop – especially Alessandro's workshop, there will be no stopping him! God help us! What have we done?!"

"I know, Anton... It is horrible to contemplate. But Mother Magda thinks that the safeguards should hold. Even though it's over four hundred years old, our most brilliant defensive architects designed that castle. It could take Aldo years to even discover the entrance to the Archives, much less gain access to the hidden chambers or Alessandro's workshop. Mother Magda thinks the Grail knowledge is secure for at least a while, until she is able to spare sufficient personnel to tackle the task," Calyx said without conviction.

"You're right, Peppe. I don't like this one bit," Delacroix

boomed as he stood to pace the comfortable hotel room. "Sandro was foolhardy. We never should have risked the Archives. You warned him... I warned him... the Matriarch warned him... but would he listen?"

"I know, I know. He was a stubborn, proud man," Calyx agreed. "But what can we do? We are ordered to abandon the mission."

"What, we are just supposed to abandon the Archives, too? We have lost so much and so many." Delacroix pulled back the curtain to gaze out the dark rain-streaked window with haunted eyes. "And what of Alessandro's girl? Are we just supposed to leave her to the wolves?"

Calyx nodded despondently.

"Mother Magda said that Alessandro knew the risks. We're not strong enough for a frontal assault, so we must try to weaken Aldo's base."

"So much is gone... so many children sacrificed...." Delacroix turned to face his comrade, his fine brow furled. "And for what? No, I cannot allow this. Sandro was my friend... For Christ's sake, Calyx, you were his partner for all these years, godfather to his children. We cannot allow his death to go unavenged, his children to fall into darkness."

"What can we do?" Calyx asked. "There's just the two of us. Aldo has the backing of two very powerful dark lodges. Alone, we can't possibly hope to win against odds like that. The Matriarch and the council are much better equipped to deal with the likes of Aldo than we. We should leave things up to their greater wisdom and just follow orders…"

Delacroix stood and paced across the room, then pivoted towards the door as sudden inspiration dawned, grabbing his still damp overcoat and hat en route.

"Where are you going, Delacroix? " Calyx called after him. "What the devil are you up to now?

"Something I should have done long ago, regardless of what the Matriarch orders," Delacroix answered in a dangerous voice. "I'm going to see about evening up those odds a bit."

## 14 December, 1872   Villa D'Amici   11:23 a.m.

Sophia sat at her vanity, gazing at the pale reflection before her. The dark gray skies and cold rain which beat upon her windowpane matched the unshed tears and chill in her heart.

Her sister's wedding gown, used but a few months before, was again pressed into service. Sophia had refused to spend a single lira on a new gown for a marriage of convenience. Even so, she could not help but respond to the image of loveliness she presented to the mirror in her borrowed lace and veil. Her small white-gloved hands trembled, as she firmly resisted the impulse to tear the veil from her hair and run from this fate that loomed before her.

Grief-stricken, less than two weeks since the demise of her father, Sophia could not afford to also mourn the loss of her own romantic hopes. Her father died unshriven, and she feared for the state of his soul, so much of her time was filled with fervent prayers. Don Alessandro's untimely death created a void she feared would always be empty. Her family and all their retainers now looked to her for guidance and leadership. While Sophia was quite well educated for a woman of her time, she knew she lacked the knowledge and experience required to faithfully regent her house until her brother, Eduardo, should reach maturity.

She had tried to contact her godfather in Milan, as her father had bidden her upon his deathbed, before she accepted Aldo's insistent proposal. But Judge Calyx's secretary informed that the magistrate was away on urgent business, and promised to send her message on. The family chaplain, Fra Diego, had taken his leave to Spain months ago to care for his ailing elderly mother. So Sophia was left to her own council - her own and her inner dream lover, Alcibiades, who urged her to undertake whatever heroic efforts were required in order to protect and safeguard her family's heritage.

Although she found the idea of marriage to Sergio Aldo repellant, she knew that she was acting in the best interests of her family's legacy. This and only this was to be her consolation. She agreed to marry Aldo once he finally yielded to her single condition that this was to be a marriage in name only, but the lawyer promised to win her love someday.

*Well, whatever else Sergio might be,* she thought as she examined at the huge ruby engagement ring he had given her just the week before, *he certainly has the resources to keep us afloat until Eduardo grows up enough to take over.*

*If only I was a man, I wouldn't have to depend on anyone. I would take care of the family...* She considered how she would respond had she been male – how her Alcibiades would handle this crisis with firmness and expertise.

A new strength flowed into her heart, as she drew comfort from just the thought of her Alcibiades. Even though the conditions of this arranged wedding guaranteed that she would never know the sweetness of romantic love, she knew she would always have her Alcibiades. He was that part of her which, freed from the restraints of nineteenth century womanhood, dared and achieved the impossible. Alcibiades would never shirk from a distasteful task, if it furthered his goals.

A sharp knock on the door broke into her thoughts.

"Sophia, aren't you ready yet?" her sister Gemma asked gaily as she came in, followed by three other women in bridal finery. "The Bishop is waiting for you."

Sophia sighed, and stared into the eyes of her reflection, finding there the resolve of Alcibiades.

"Yes, I'm ready."

Don Alessandro D'Amici's unexpected death threw a new kink into the mine negotiations. Without Don Alessandro's strong hand to guide them, the D'Amici clan floundered. Aldo spent precious days explaining the transactions to the bereaved family, and convincing them of its necessity and the need for haste. Haldane began to worry he would not be able to return home to England in time for Christmas.

*Why did the old boy have to choose such an inconvenient time to die? If only he could have hung on another week, I would be on my way home now,* Haldane thought when old Don Stephano gave him the news.

Haldane had helped negotiate treaties affecting the lives of hundreds of thousands of people with much less fuss than these two old families with their petty bickering. The frustration of the past several weeks was telling on him, as evidenced by the reappearance of the blinding headaches, which always came to plague him when he overextended for too long.

Then, in one of his brilliant flashes of business prowess, Aldo secured the power of attorney for the young heir by a hastily arranged marriage to D'Amici's elder daughter. The contracts would go through as planned. Personally, Haldane thought Aldo could have gained the power of attorney without the arranged marriage, but reckoned that Aldo must have his reasons.

Haldane did not attend Aldo's wedding. Instead he spent the day nursing a fierce headache, alone in the Calendri's hunting lodge. But now, with Aldo in firm control of the D'Amici holdings, Haldane began to look forward to going home soon. Maybe if he was lucky, maybe he could still make it home before Christmas Eve.

# Chapter Nine

**21 December, 1872   Villa D'Amici   7:15 p.m.**

The loud crash from the corridor outside the glass arbor shattered Sophia's solitude, jarring her already frayed nerves. She threw the book she was attempting to read onto the seat beside her and rose to investigate the noise, all the while hating the idea of change in her ancestral home.

Flying out of the french doors and into the corridor, she found two workmen digging a trench through the floor to lay the pipes that her husband of seven days had ordered. It nauseated her to see the fourteenth century Venetian tile laying in shards on the floor, broken beyond repair by the clumsy workers commissioned to install 'modern conveniences' into the ancient villa.

"You fools!" she cried, as she came upon the workmen. "This tile is irreplaceable!"

"Donna, be careful," one of the rough men called to her. "This place, she is dangerous with the holes in the floor. You wouldn't want to fall and hurt yourself. Then Piero and I would have to carry you to safety. That would be too bad, no? You might tear your pretty dress, Donna Bella." The man smacked his lips and leered.

*Papa would never have allowed such a rude worker into his house,* she thought with scorn. *But this is no longer Papa's house. It's not even my house anymore.*

"You are not to address me in such terms." Though her tone was cold, Sophia's dark eyes flared with a fire that took the workman back to his place.

Sophia was surprised at how quickly her new husband had somehow managed to get a special dispensation from the Pope to suspend the customary ban on weddings during the mourning period. Now, days later, after all her hopes were crushed by cruel practicality, Sophia came to realize the depth of her misjudgment.

*Oh Papa! Papa! What have I done? How could I have known?* Silent, unshed tears stung her, as she again looked at the ancient tile, broken beyond repair.

The anger and despair did not leave her as she walked through the corridor, her fists clenched tight. The sight of yet another tile lying shattered made her catch her breath. This one, colored and patterned with the ancient D'Amici crest, was the last fragmentation of the past she could tolerate. She bent and picked up a large spike of broken tile. Holding the shard like a dagger, she charged the workman.

"Get out!" she shrieked, unsure whether she was actually speaking to the men before her or to their absent master. "Get out of my villa! I don't want you here!"

"She's mad! Crazy, out of her mind, she is!" the shocked worker declared as Sophia descended upon him.

"Donna, a thousand pardons," pleaded the other worker. "We are only doing what we were hired to do."

With a strange, inarticulate cry, Sophia lunged for the first man, slicing her makeshift weapon deep into his arm. The man howled in pain and disbelief, attempted to back away from her. His feet went out from under him, as he slipped on the broken tile, sending a small shower of shards down into a nearby hole. A plume of steam erupted from the hole in the floor and crept along the corridor. The other man let out a small yelp and bolted through the nearest door.

Emboldened by the sight of the fleeing workers, and suddenly drunk on the exercise of her own power, Sophia resolved to drive all trespassers from her home. With a feral grin, she advanced on her cringing prey like an avenging angel, thoughts of anything but cleansing her home gone from her mind.

"Leave my villa at once!" she screeched at the growing crowd of astonished workers, who had come to investigate the commotion.

Anxious to obey her, the hapless workers scrambled and stumbled away from the small woman who was as dangerous as a wet cat.

"Sophia!"

The masculine voice cut through the thickening fog and tore into her skull. She jerked to a halt and turned. She caught her breath as she glimpsed the furious eyes of her dreaded husband through the rising steam escaping from the cracked pipeline beneath the floor. She forgot her mission to rid the house of all intruders. Now, only escape was paramount.

"Donna Sophia," Aldo addressed his bride with the same measured tones he used in boardrooms and business negotiations. "I am given to understand that you are not pleased with the workers. I realize you have some sentiment for this old place but... I will no longer countenance such childish behavior!"

"I-I...." she stuttered, unable to account for the wild violence which had overtaken her.

"What's going on here?" he demanded of the frightened workman, as he stepped out of the steam.

"The Donna, she's insane! I tell her to be careful, and she attacks me," the man whined. He held up his wounded arm. "She slices me open like a sausage, and all because I tell her to watch out for the holes."

Aldo glanced at Sophia, who avoided his gaze. Queasy with fear, she clasped her hands to stop their trembling.

"Go get that wound taken care of. I want to talk to you later," he told the workman. After the man had gone, he turned to the much-subdued Sophia, and spoke gently. "Donna Sophia, I know how upsetting this must all be to you, but I promise, it will be worth it. Please, just bear with me for the next few weeks. After I've found – I mean, after I've gotten all the new plumbing installed, you will see how wonderful everything will be. It will all be just as I have promised."

Summoning the tatters of her dignity, Sophia pulled herself up to full height. "When you said you wanted to put in modern water closets, you said nothing about tearing up the floors. I married you because you promised to help me protect this place for my little brother. But if modern plumbing means destroying the history of the villa, then we can do very well without those conveniences," she told him with cold fury.

"Sophia, my dear," Aldo cooed. "I understand your anger. I will tell those clumsy workmen they must be more careful, don't you worry your pretty little head. Why don't you go up to your chamber and I'll just give these fellows a good talking to."

"Tell them also to have more respect," Sophia added, with suspicion at his conciliation, as she turned and stepped through the rising mist spreading across the floor, yet grateful for his unexpected temperance.

Aldo surveyed the aftermath in her wake. It was true that the workmen were doing a lot of damage to the floors, but what did that matter, compared to what lay hidden beneath? He pondered the injury Sophia had caused to the worker, but workers were paid. If a job became more difficult, then more pay was given.

And this job had certainly become more expensive than he had expected. Almost a full week's worth of exploration by twenty workmen had failed to gain him access to the secret chambers known to exist somewhere on these premises. And Sophia's cool but firm rejection of him from her bed did not sweeten his mood.

The other workman returned from his refuge with cautious steps. Seeing him, Aldo addressed the trembling man.

"Piero, come look down here. Where's all this steam coming from?" A warm, moist cloud hovered about the level of his chest. "What the devil's causing it?"

"Signor, I can not work under these conditions," the man stated indignantly. "I have a wife and family to think about. I can't work around madwomen. I quit."

"Oh Piero, I'm sure she didn't mean anything by it," Aldo said in his most persuasive manner. "You know how women are. I'm sure it's just some phase of the moon."

"No, Signor. That one, she is crazy," the workman insisted.

"Very well then, what if I double your pay and promise to try to keep the Donna away from you?" he bargained.

"You promise, she would not come near us again?" Piero asked.

"I said I would try, but I need your help. Tell me, man, where is this steam coming from?"

The workman crossed and bent to peer through the thick steam that continued to rise from the hole in the floor.

"Broken pipe, Signor," replied the workman's voice from beneath the steam. "She brings steam up from the hot springs down below."

Realization dawned on Aldo as he observed the rising cloud.

"Can you tell where this pipe leads?" Aldo asked, already knowing the answer.

"To the greenhouse, Signor," the man told him.

"Are you sure?" Aldo demanded with a growing smirk.

"Yes, the old butler, he's very clear. He says we must be careful of this one. If the steam goes, then the flowers go, he says," the worker replied confidently. "You want I should stop the steam right away, no?"

"No... Let the steam run out," Aldo told him. "You wanted the Donna to leave you to your work. Well, my good man, you have provided the means. As you, yourself said, 'with the steam goes the flowers.' She'll be so busy trying to figure out what has happened to her precious flowers, she won't have time to bother you or your crew."

"Ah-h!" the man agreed with a conspiratorial wink. "I should look for this secret room again, then?"

"Yes. It is very important we find it as soon as possible. But try to be a little more careful with the old tile, will you? Seems she's mightily attached to it. In the mean time..." Aldo said as he spun around to head back into the villa. "I have a wayward wife to discipline."

Suddenly, a loud crack sounded as the floor went out from under Aldo. His foot fell into one of the many open holes the workmen had left behind, hidden by the thick steam. Aldo shrieked wails of sincere pain as heat seared his flesh from ankle to knee in the ruptured pipe. Instead of steam, however, this pipe carried hot water from the volcanic springs deep below the villa to the kitchens. Though the servants and workers heard his cries, none ventured through the blinding white clouds to rescue the new administrator of the villa.

"God's Balls! Can't anyone come to my aid?" He called out in pain, hauling himself from the torturous hole in the floor. "Annabella!" he roared for his serving maid. "Annabella, damn you wench! Come here and help me!"

## 20 December, 1872   D'Amici Villa   3:25 p.m.

Haldane rode the borrowed gelding down the drive leading to the Villa D'Amici. As he passed the vineyards that stretched out acre after acre on both sides of the road, filling in the gentle slopes of the mountain valley in graceful terraces, he admired the countryside.

*I say, what a picturesque place this D'Amici estate is. One could become quite attached to it if given half a chance,* he mused.

The D'Amici estate was a sharp contrast when compared to the Calendri lands, where all his negotiations had taken place. The D'Amici family had carefully tended their vineyards and gardens, while the Calendri's had turned their lands over to logging, grazing and cattle.

Haldane smiled at the sight of the impressive castle on its aery perch, as he rode through the wide iron gates. A graceful fountain sparkled and cast plumes of steam and rainbows in the cold air in the front courtyard of the grand old villa.

*No wonder Aldo wanted this for himself, the bastard.* Haldane's regret was compounded by his failure to find any weakness he could exploit to wreck his revenge on Aldo.

The afternoon sun painted the old castle gold and apricot, nestled atop its leveled mountain peak, but Haldane's practiced eye saw the fortifications and battlements underneath the tall gothic spires and buttresses. This charming fortress was a highly defensible holding, while appearing almost ethereal in the long shadows of winter.

A colorless serving wench admitted Haldane to the villa and immediately ushered him into the wood paneled library. Aldo sat grumbling, his left leg propped up on a stool, the desk before him strewn with papers and books. Tall, mahogany bookcases packed with books of every description dominated the elegant, yet comfortable room. The smell of wood smoke and old books prevailed.

Above the elaborate marble mantel hung a life-size painting of a dark-haired woman in the dramatic black and silvery gear that Haldane recognized as the Queen of the Night, from Mozart's *the Magic Flute*. The painting's impassive stare seemed to follow the Haldane's every movement with large dark eyes. Her ivory face was framed with masses of curling black hair, caught up in an elaborate coiffure and decorated with gems, stars radiating out from her. She had the slightest of Mona Lisa smiles on her sensitive, ruby lips. The face seemed hauntingly familiar to Haldane. His heart leapt as he wondered from where he could know this mysterious beauty.

"Ah, Christopher, come in. Please excuse me for not standing, but I hurt my leg the other night. What can I do for you?" Aldo asked in a pained voice.

"Good afternoon, Signor," he responded, wrenching his eyes from the fascinating painting. "I have welcome news for you. I have come to inform you that old Calendri has agreed to the final draft of the contract. My work is done. I leave straight away for Naples," Haldane told him.

"No, no, no. Not so fast my dear Colonel," Aldo snapped. "Our agreement was that you would stay until the contracts had been *signed*. I have invited Calendri to a celebration to sign the contracts on Christmas Eve. You can leave Christmas Day, after they are signed."

*You bloody bastard!* Haldane cursed silently, with a steely stare. "Signor, you know I promised my family that I would spend the holidays with them. Already, my wife is furious with me for having missed the start of the season in London. I beg you to release me from this final obligation. I have done everything else you demanded and more. Surely you can be satisfied with that."

"I'm sorry, Christopher, but an agreement is an agreement. You will stay until Calendri signs the papers on Christmas Eve. If you leave before that, he might become suspicious and refuse to sign, then our contract would be null and I would be forced to demand repayment of the two hundred thousand I so generously advanced to you. Is that what you desire?" Aldo asked in feigned alarm.

"No, of course not, damn you," Haldane snapped. "I should have known you wouldn't care. You've never had a family to return to for Christmas. You can't possible understand what a hardship this places on me."

"I'm sorry, Christopher. It can't be helped," Aldo said without sympathy. He was tired of Haldane's whining and he had to relieve his bladder, which meant the unpleasant experience of walking on his scalded leg.

"Well... couldn't we have Calendri sign the papers before then?" Haldane coaxed. "I could get him to sign the papers tonight and be on my way tomorrow."

"Out of the question!" Aldo bellowed. "The contracts will be signed on Christmas Eve as planned," he said with finality. "You see, I too have a wife now. I promised her a celebration, and a celebration she shall have. You will attend or I will cancel our agreement immediately."

Haldane looked down, clenching his jaw in anger.

*I'm not going to get to see the children at all, damn his buggering soul to hell.* He took a deep breath to regain his composure. "...Yes. I had forgotten... you married last week. Terribly sorry I was unable to attend the wedding. Did you receive my gift?" Haldane had sent an engraved silver punch bowl he had seen in a shop window in Milan.

"Yes, thank you. It was nice, my wife was very pleased," Aldo replied blandly.

"And where is your lovely wife? I would welcome the chance to meet her."

"No doubt you would," Aldo agreed acidly. "I have sent her off to shop for the party. She should return sometime."

Haldane practiced eye noticed the papers strewn across the desk. They were copies of the contract, one page with a scrawled note in the margin and an arrow indicating an insertion in the document. His curiosity piqued – there had been no addendum to the contract for several weeks, despite Calendri's petty balking. *I'd certainly like a closer look at that,* he thought as he stroked his mustache.

"Is there anything else you want, or may I go to the lavatory now," Aldo asked peevishly, and began to rise out of his chair. All of a sudden, Haldane was at his side, with a steadying hand under Aldo's elbow. In spite of himself, Aldo was grateful for Haldane's unexpected help.

"What happened to your leg?" Haldane inquired, compassion dripping from his words.

Aldo limped towards a door at the far end of the room, leaning heavily on Haldane's arm. "I'm putting some damned decent plumbing in this blasted place. Imagine a grand place like this having only old Romanesque water closets. I fell in a hole left by the clods doing the renovation."

"What a pity. It looks rather distressing," Haldane murmured. He assisted Aldo across the room and through the lavatory door. "I'll help you back to your chair when you're ready," he offered with gracious charm.

Aldo muttered an embarrassed "Thank you," and closed the door in Haldane's face.

Haldane rushed back over to the desk and caught up the page with avid interest.

*The damn greedy bastard!*

Aldo was planning to secretly change the contract, Haldane was sure of it. He looked through the other papers scattered on the table, realizing the full extent of Aldo's deceit. The rewritten contract would entitle Aldo to fifty, not twenty, percent of Calendri's profits in hidden fees and royalties.

*I can't allow Calendri to sign this,* he resolved. *It's unfortunate that it's already too late for the D'Amici family. There's nothing I can do for them now that the bastard has them in his grasp. But, perhaps I can still do something for old Calendri.*

Haldane sped back to the bathroom door only moments before Aldo emerged.

After taking care to be sure that Aldo was well settled back into his chair, Haldane told him, "If you have no further business with me, I'll be on my way back to my lodgings. Kindly express my regrets to your wife. I will see you on Christmas Eve," and swiftly took his leave.

On the ride back to the Calendri estate, Haldane plotted his revenge.

*Keep me from my family at Christmas, you bastard,* he thought with a wicked smirk. *Go ahead. You'll regret it for the rest of your miserable life,* he vowed.

As Haldane approached the main road, a fine carriage bearing the crossed keys of the D'Amici arms on the door passed him. *That must be Aldo's bride, returning from her shopping trip. I wonder what she looks like. I've been told that she was once thought a beauty, in her day. Maybe I'll do her just for good measure,* he thought, as he turned onto the road leading to the Calendri estate. *Things have been a bit dull of late.*

# Chapter Ten

**Christmas Eve, 1872   Villa D'Amici,   6:16 p.m.**

"It is done!"

The exultant voice of Signor Sergio Aldo rang out in joyous laughter, echoing off the gothic arches and dark wood bookcases of the D'Amici library. Aldo rubbed his thick hands together in glee and turned his newly acquired wheelchair to face his companion.

"The whole world lies before me, awaiting my next move. Everything is in position. Old D'Amici lies cold in his tomb, I possess his fabulous villa, and lovely Sophia is my bride. No one can stop me. After tonight, the final contracts will be signed and nothing will stand in my way. ...Ah, Otto, I wish you had one measure of my satisfaction. Maybe then, you wouldn't worry so much."

Aldo punctuated his point by downing half his snifter of pale Napoleon brandy.

"All that remains," he continued, as he wheeled toward the looking glass on the wall near the door, "is the signatures. Once old Calendri signs and Haldane witnesses it, this marvelous old place shall become my capital from which I shall rule Europe. Its rich metal deposits will finance the greatest army Europe has ever seen."

Aldo inspected his image in the gilded mirror with indulgence. Balding, his close-cropped black hair shot with quicksilver framed the sides of his shining cranium, while darkly sparkling eyes refuted his acquired social graces. The bespoken tuxedo fit was exquisite; the work

71

of fine Sicilian tailoring from back home, but the left leg had been savagely split to accommodate Aldo's thick bandage-wrapped calf.

"Your gloating is premature, Aldo," a cool voice chided from a shadowed corner of the luxurious renaissance library. "What wretched errors hath my heart committed when it thought itself so blessed never?" he quoted.

The tall, blond young man with a sleek ponytail emerged from a gothic archway, and stood before the swarthy Sicilian Aldo. A dazzling smile lit up his handsome face, but not his icy eyes. He held a small volume of poetry in his long, slender hand.

"Your tasks have just begun. It is true that you have disposed of the owner of this most strategic of Guardian strongholds, and married his daughter. You are indeed master of Villa D'Amici... but not without my help. It is only due to Illuminati intelligences and equipment that you escaped D'Amici's mind machine. I have delivered my part in our agreement. You have control of the castle. Now it is time for you to keep your part of the bargain."

Aldo flinched and looked away. Clammy hands fidgeted and trembled, in spite of the warmth of the roaring fire. The previously subservient Wittgenstein's attitude was becoming a problem.

"Yes, and you see how I have every intention of keeping my promise to you," Aldo began, gesturing broadly. "I have dug up almost half of the ground floor of the villa, looking for these damned catacombs you insist are here, and what has it gotten either of us? I've been scalded on the leg and can barely walk, while my new bride is so furious, she will have nothing to do with me. And you still do not have that which you seek. I do not think your secret records exist, Otto. My sources tell me that your precious Grail is in Southern France, not Italy. I cannot find it if it is not here! I beg you to release me from this task. Surely it is not that important. Your master already has possession of the Spear that pierced the side of Jesus... I shall happily honor the rest of our agreement, and utterly destroy the final remnants of the damned Grail Guardians, never fear. I shall make sure their bloody interference is stopped once and for all. The Guardians' days are numbered. Just allow me to focus on our true enemies, and not waste any more time seeking your damned old cup."

Baron Otto Wittgenstein put down his book and drew himself up to his full impressive height. As he towered over the seated Sicilian, Aldo could not tear his eyes away from Wittgenstein's crisp Aryan features.

"Sergio, I am most disappointed to hear you speak this way," he said, his deep voice resonating mild threat. "I strongly urge you to reconsider your words. We have worked together so beautifully up to now. I would hate for something to go wrong. It would be a horrible pity if the first joint venture of our venerable brotherhoods were to go astray. The combined might of the Bavarian Illuminati and the Carbonari is too potent to waste achieving mere fleeting political supremacy that is too easily lost in a few years' span. Our goal is nothing less than dominance of the next era of mankind, the coming Aquarian age. My master will not allow this opportunity to be misused."

Releasing Aldo from his stare, Wittgenstein moved to the fireplace, his back to Aldo as he spoke, his light tone giving lie to the heavy import of his words.

"The Secret Archives of the Grail Church *do* exist, Aldo. That which my master seeks *is* here. You haven't even begun looking under the towers yet. You have far to go to exhaust all possible entrances to the catacombs. You have until New Year's Day. If you have not gained entrance by then, I shall take the matter into hand myself. ...And, I assure you, my master would regard this matter as a breech of contract, with everything that implies, should you prove unable to access to the Archives. It is vital that we know the final resting-place of the Holy Grail."

"But what of my wife?" Aldo objected. "I am destroying her home to find your stupid books. Surely this relic is not so very important that you would risk alienating the affections of the future mother of the Emperors of Europe? What's the rush? We need Sophia's cooperation. Come, give me some time to woo her – to win her heart before you would have me wreck her castle. I suggest that we proceed with the rest of our plans, and perhaps I can even get Sophia herself to tell me where the entrance lies." Aldo observed no response from the baron's impassive back.

"Very well, Sergio. You have done us a great service in dispatching D'Amici. He has been a thorn in the Illuminati's side for many a year. I am inclined to be generous. You have until Twelfth Night to gain Sophia's trust… and her secrets," Wittgenstein answered after several long moments. Amusement lifted Wittgenstein's voice. "Should you fail to deliver your full obligation at that time, however, I shall be forced to do everything in my power to vouchsafe the plans of my brethren, my personal affection for your conniving, swindling soul aside."

"I promise, you shall not regret your patience."

"I should hope not," the baron said with a serpentine menace, as he turned to face Aldo.

"Tonight, the contracts will legally be signed and sealed," Aldo assured. "No one will be able to question our legal claim. Old Don Alessandro D'Amici is gone, and soon, nothing will remain of the Grail sect in Lombardi. The ore from the mine will be enough to outfit and supply an army of unprecedented size. No one will be left to stop our sweep across Europe."

"Excellent," Wittgenstein agreed, as he sat in a deep leather armchair. "I am gratified to see that in these other matters in spite of your injuries, you maintain your usual standards of professionalism."

"Otto, you sting me to the quick," Aldo disclaimed, in mock pain. "You know perfectly well how efficient I am. That is only one of many reasons why your master has so wisely chosen to back me. But I must have maneuvering room. You know I have sworn my life to our mutual cause, the same as you. I shall prevail. Mark my words. This injury is just a temporary minor impediment."

"Hmph!" Wittgenstein grunted, unimpressed, as he flicked a long golden strand of hair from his shoulder.

Aldo downed the last of his brandy. He pulled out a gold-chased pocket watch and glanced at the time in agitation.

"Where the devil is Haldane? He should be here by now. Let's go see if he has arrived."

Only moments after the men left, the two sisters crept into the deserted library, seeking a few moments to share their secrets, as they had since childhood. Gemma's dark eyes were dancing as she flounced down on a wide leather sofa.

"It seems like it's been such a long time since we've had a party. The old place looks quite marvelous. You've done a wonderful job fixing it up this week," Gemma enthused as her older sibling came and joined her on the couch. "I hope the rain doesn't keep the guests from coming."

"Yes, it has been a long time... over two years," Sophia agreed and sighed heavily. "I wish Cassie could have been here tonight." She smiled, recalling her long lost sister's irrepressible nature. "Wouldn't she be surprised to find you married to Roberto and expecting a baby, and me – married to anyone!"

"You know she would give you such a teasing! 'Solemn Sophie' – married to a bald, fat lawyer..." Gemma stopped as Sophia's wince told her that her words hit too close to home. "But you know, he's really not such a bad fellow, once you get to know him..."

"No, Sergio's not so bad," Sophia allowed. "He was genuinely grateful when I had Nana's old wheelchair brought down for him, so that he might get around with less effort tonight. And he has certainly been more than generous with his purse."

"Oh, yes," Gemma agreed. "Roberto and I would have never been able to afford such a fine house in Milano, if not for Sergio's help."

Sophia placed a protective arm about her little sister.

"Well, I couldn't let my very first niece or nephew come into the world without a proper home, now could I?" She squeezed Gemma's shoulders. "So, how is our little one progressing?"

"I saw the doctor yesterday," the young woman told her. "He says that it looks as though everything is as it should be... Good Lord willing, I should be a mother by next summer."

"I am so glad to hear it," Sophia said. "I just wish Papa could be here... and Mama and Cassie too – to share your joy."

Gemma lowered her head. She gazed at the black crepe sash of mourning tied to Sophia's arm, twin to the one on her own.

"Yes, I miss them, too." she admitted. "We have lost so may loved ones. That is why I am glad I conceived right away – to try to increase the numbers of our little family. I can never replace what has been lost, but maybe I can help to bring some new happiness into the world."

Sophia regarded her little sister with respect.

"Oh, Gemma, I'm so glad we've still got each other! You always remind me what is most important. Yes, we are part of a long line. Sometimes, I get so caught up in my petty problems that I forget that I am merely a small link in a vast chain of D'Amicis, which stretches back from the antiquity to far eternity. *Ire fortiter quo nemo ante iit.* I must remember that it is my duty to protect – to preserve that heritage for the future..." Sophia's words halted as she recalled her father's dying request.

"So, when are you going to start your family," Gemma probed, startling Sophia out of her reverie.

"W-well," Sophia sputtered, squirming on the deep-tufted leather couch. "I have no intention of having Sergio's children. You know that. I only agreed to marry him to help the family."

"Oh Sophia," Gemma wheedled. "Remember that Mama and Papa had an arranged marriage, and they truly fell in love. The man practically worships the ground you walk on, and you won't give him the time of day. How can you be so cold-hearted?"

"I am not cold-hearted," Sophia protested indignantly.

"Well, what do you call a woman who takes a man's money, name and his love, but refuses to return it?" Gemma challenged. "Besides, you don't know what you're missing.... You might just find that you like it."

"Gemma!" Sophia cried, scandalized at her sister's suggestion.

"My marriage is a simple business transaction. Nothing more. I don't care to continue discussing it with you..." Turning away from her sister, her eyes caught on her large portrait hanging over the mantel, reminding her of a more carefree time, when none of her choices seemed so freighted with duty and consequences.

"All right," Gemma conceded. "I won't mention it again. But you really should think about what you are refusing..."

"Gemma..." Sophia warned, annoyance flashing as she re-engaged her sister's eyes. "Didn't you say you had something else you needed to talk to me about?"

"Oh, yes," Gemma recalled. "When we picked up Eduardo from the academy today, the Headmaster requested to speak with us. He told us that since Eduardo returned from Papa's funeral, his marks have been dropping and he's been misbehaving in class. The Headmaster said they've had to punish him three times last week."

"Punish Eddie?" Alarm filled Sophia for her youngest sibling. "Why? Did the Headmaster say?"

Gemma continued her report, "He said that Eduardo is not paying attention to his studies. He has taken to disrupting the other boys with talking and silly antics. He even challenged this Latin master, calling him a fool!"

"Oh dear, this sounds serious," Sophia said, her brow furrowed in concern. "I shall have to have a talk with him..."

"But let's don't spoil Christmas," Gemma pleaded. "Let us at least have the holiday together before you get after him."

"Well, I shall see what I can do," Sophia replied. "But, I make no promises-"

She was cut short as the door to the library swung wide, revealing Signor Aldo, wheeled by his maid and Sophia's ancestral rival, the taciturn Don Stephano Calendri.

"Ah, my dear, here you are," Aldo began when he caught sight of the two women. "I am sorry to interrupt you ladies, but I'm afraid we need the library to conduct some business. The rest of the guests should be arriving shortly. Why don't you go see to the final preparations?"

The two women rose and moved towards the door.

"Of course," Sophia said graciously. "Thank you for coming out in this cold rain to honor us, Don Stephano. When you have concluded your business, I do hope you will join the rest of us in our modest holiday celebration," she said with a nod to her husband's guest and passed through the carved door, followed by her sister.

It did not seem right to be welcoming her family's long-standing enemy, to be joining into a business partnership with him. And yet, this was what her father had sacrificed his life to make happen. It did not seem just that her family's ancient nemesis should be the one helping her to save her beloved villa. She silenced her reluctance with duty, and proceeded towards the great hall to prepare for the other guests.

# Chapter Eleven

**24 December, 1872.   D'Amici Villa.   6:45 p.m.**

Haldane entered the dark paneled library where Aldo and Don Stephano Calendri were seated before the giant fireplace. The young Englishman's breath was still ragged from his cold and soggy march, taking in rough gulps of the musty-sweet book-scented air.

The midnight blue wool of his Royal Army Diplomatic Corps uniform was blackened on the shoulders where the falling sleet had soaked through his caped wool topcoat, and tiny crystals of ice still clung to his dark hair and military mustache. Dark storm-green eyes peered out from his pale handsome face.

"I know my tardiness is unforgivable, but I beg your indulgence, gentlemen," he began quickly, in fluent Italian. "Don Calendri, I'm afraid your brown gelding has thrown a shoe. I would be more than happy to pay for the blacksmith since I was riding him when it happened," Haldane offered the impoverished old mountain lord who sat rigid amid the opulence of Villa D'Amici.

"No, no, that won't be necessary," Aldo answered from his wicker-back wheelchair before the old man could reply. "I will have the blacksmith here take care of it. It will be no problem at all. But you look rather chilled, Colonel. Come, join us by the fire and have some brandy."

Aldo's huge carved wheeled chair sat beside a table laid out with the contracts to be signed.

"Thank you, but if it's not too much trouble, I would rather have hot tea," answered Haldane, as he took a tall-backed red leather chair between Don Calendri and Aldo.

Although he would have preferred brandy, Haldane knew he had to be in complete control if he was going to successfully execute his plan.

"Tea? No problem at all," Aldo said, as he moved to ring for a servant. The same washed out serving maid that had admitted Haldane appeared the instant Aldo's hand released the pull.

"Does Signor have need of me?" asked the woman.

"Some hot tea for the good Colonel here, Annabella. And quickly," Aldo told her. She bobbed her head and left. He turned back to Haldane. "Once again, Colonel, you have narrowly missed meeting my wife. The Don and I commandeered the library from her just now. You see what lengths I will go to ensure our success? I would even dispossess my own dearest bride," he said with a conspiratorial grin at Calendri, who stared into the fire with grim regard.

"Oh, what a shame," Haldane rejoined with abstract politeness. "You must be sure to introduce me to your wife once our business is concluded."

Haldane observed the emaciated Don's discomfiture with pity. *Poor old boy,* he thought. *Doesn't much like the idea of obligating himself and his kin to Aldo for the next thirty years. Can't say that I blame him. I've been in his shoes, and look at me now. I'm little better than Aldo's dollymop. All my achievements mean nothing as long as Aldo's got me by the balls.* Resolve hardened in his heart, as he glanced down towards the papers concealed beneath his uniform.

"Colonel Haldane is quite popular with the ladies, Don Stephano. That's the real reason all the negotiations took place on your property," Aldo explained with a wink. "Haldane doesn't know what he's missed, and I have planned it that way."

The serving maid reappeared with a tray containing a silver tea service, which she brought to a side table not far from Haldane's chair. She poured tea into a fine porcelain cup and handed it to him, while Aldo continued to attempt small talk with Calendri. The maid dipped a flustered curtsy and left after Haldane's half-smile and soft "Thank you."

Haldane sipped his tea as an uncomfortable silence settled about the three men. The heat of the fire and tea soon warmed Haldane's bones, yet did nothing to melt the hard lump of ice within his chest.

His departure for the villa had been delayed by a messenger's arrival as the cabin, bearing a cryptic note requesting an urgent meeting from some unknown fellow called Delacroix. The message unnerved Haldane, as to his knowledge, no one but Aldo and Calendri knew his whereabouts. He sensed impending trouble, especially as the strange request arrived just as he was to set out to deceive Aldo the deceiver. With no time for explanations, he had sent the messenger away without a reply.

His arrival was further delayed when the horse he had been riding threw his shoe almost two miles from the D'Amici villa. The tall Englishman had led the horse back as a light sleet began to fall. Now in the warm library, the humidity made his dark hair curl.

Despite these ill omens, he was still resolute to execute his planned revenge. What he needed now was a distraction. He ran his hand through his unruly locks while the other two men watched expectantly.

"Well, what are we waiting for? The sooner we get this signing done, the sooner we can join the party," proposed Aldo.

*Here we go! I've got to move now,* thought Haldane. "Just let me get some more of this warm tea first," he said, vying for time. Adrenaline quirked through his veins in anticipation. He willed his breath to slow and his muscles to release.

As he approached the table with the tea service, he unbuttoned the front of his uniform tunic and loosened the papers inside, his back to the other two men. He closed his eyes for a moment, steeling himself before picking up the fine metal teapot. Mid-pour, he suddenly released his grip on the silver teapot, letting it fall from his grasp. It clanked on the silver tray, spewing its contents across the table and fine rug. It bounced twice and came to rest on the hearthstones of the fireplace. Haldane jumped back in assumed horror.

"Oh, how unfortunate!" he moaned. "I'm so terribly clumsy. My hands must still be stiff from the cold. Please accept my sincerest apology, Signor Aldo. I don't know how it could have gotten away from me so fast." He knelt and retrieved the dented teapot. "I'm afraid I've destroyed your valuable pot. Of course I'll replace it. What rotten luck I'm having tonight – first the horse and now this," he exclaimed with calculated remorse.

Aldo wheeled forward to inspect the damage. "I hope you realize my wife will hang me for this, Haldane," he said with surprising good humor. "The table and rug, too. You do a thorough job, Colonel."

*I certainly hope so,* Haldane agreed silently. He turned to Calendri and said, "Sir, would you be so kind as to call for the maid?" He pulled out a handkerchief and knelt to dab at the growing stain on the thick Indian carpet.

The maid, Annabella answered the ring as before. She let out a small cry when she saw the aftermath and ran to fetch a cloth. By the time she returned, the three men were hovering around the scene of the disaster in helpless agitation. She bustled her way between the Don and

Haldane, who rose and stepped back to the table on which the contract was laid unobserved.

Turning his back to the others, who were actively engaged in the rescue mission, Haldane slid the pages out of his uniform tunic and traded them for the ones lying on the table. Hiding the unwanted contracts with his body, he crossed behind Aldo's chair and tossed the sheaths onto the crackling fire. He gulped a deep breath and released it, willing his heart to slow its racing.

*Fiat Accompli,* he thought with relish, as the pages flashed in the fire. The only witness to his deed had been the portrait of the ebony and cream woman hanging over the fireplace.

A shiver not caused by cold ran up his spine as he gazed up into the painting's luminous eyes. *She seems so familiar... who is she?* The sounds of the rescue recalled him and he forced himself to rejoin the others.

"Do you think anything can be salvaged?" a suitably chastened Haldane asked Aldo's maid. She shot Aldo a frightened glance before answering.

"I don't think the rug is ruined, though the teapot is badly dented, but I think it can be repaired," she answered in a quivering voice.

"Oh, thank heavens, what a relief," Haldane sighed. "Well, gentlemen, I apologize for the unfortunate interruption. Shall we resume our business?"

Annabella gathered up the damaged pot and tea-soaked rags and left the three men alone.

Haldane ushered Calendri back to his chair while Aldo maneuvered his wheelchair to face them. With visible reluctance, Don Stephano Calendri took the pen Aldo offered him and prepared to sign the binding legal document.

Both Aldo and Haldane held their breath while the old man signed the two copies of the contract, and both men sighed with relief when Calendri returned the pen. Aldo quickly wrote his signature in the place reserved for the executor for the D'Amici's with a flourish and handed the papers to Haldane to sign as witness.

Haldane bent to sign the papers, hiding his triumphant smile. *I have done it. There is no way Aldo can get his hands on any more of Calendri's profits now. It's a pity that he already has control of the D'Amici's.*

Haldane winced to think what a pig like Aldo would do to a graceful old place like this. He had noted the rough planks covering the holes Aldo had already torn into the floors in the name of progress. Haldane thought it dreadful to tear up such a historic castle so ruthlessly.

*Yet, this is the respect Aldo shows for heritage. Serves him right to be scalded for his efforts.*

After affixing his name, Haldane retrieved his teacup and took a sip. It was cold.

"Well, this assures a very happy Christmas for us all. I think we are all to be congratulated," grinned Aldo. "We have done what they said could never be done, and we shall all be rewarded our just deserts for it." The three men chuckled in forced appreciation. "Speaking of desserts, I brought in the best pastry chef in Milano to prepare tonight's delicacies. We have much to celebrate!"

Aldo reached for the cigar box on the nearby table, opened it and offered its contents to his guests. "I know you don't normally smoke Don Calendri, but surely you can make an exception on such a momentous occasion. We have become the proud parents of a newborn corporation! Let us revel in our accomplishment!"

"Actually, sir, I can't abide cigars, but don't let me stop the two of you," Don Stephano Calendri said with unaccustomed graciousness.

Aldo nodded reluctantly, and offered the box to Haldane.

"Colonel, I know you enjoy a fine cigar now and again. How about you? I had these specially imported from the Americas."

Haldane accepted Aldo's offered cigar, saying, "Thank you. If you don't mind, I'll keep it for later." He slipped the cigar in his inner breast pocket.

"Well, shall we go join the others?" Aldo invited, seeing that the other two men did not seem to share his glee. "I can't wait to taste what the maestro has cooked up for us!"

"Might I bother you for a spot more tea first? I promise I won't touch the teapot this time," asked Haldane with his most charming smile.

As the three men entered the grand hall containing the party guests, Haldane spoke.

"You know, Sergio," Haldane used Aldo's first name with calculated affection, "they have a name for men such as yourself in America. They call them 'carpetbaggers.'"

"Carpetbaggers? How queer. What does it mean?" Aldo inquired, surprised at the warmth in Haldane's voice.

"It's the word the dispossessed of the South used after the American Civil War to describe the selfless businessmen of the North, who threw a few belongings into bags made of carpet and rushed to the aid of the war-torn aristocrats of the South to help them rebuild their wrecked economy," Haldane replied, savoring Aldo's ignorance of the deep insult just intended him. "You now provide that same service to their European counterparts, dispossessed by the ravages of war and economics."

Aldo glowed with what he thought was Haldane's rare praise. "Well, anything I can do to help my fellow man," he muttered with some genuine embarrassment.

Haldane stood aloof, sipping his tea, anxious to leave as soon as it was polite – before Aldo could discover the switched contracts. But he was prevented from going until the blacksmith finished re-shoeing his horse. Although the scents and sights of the overflowing tables of food laid out for the meager party tantalized his rumbling stomach, he was in no mood to socialize with the few guests who hovered about the buffet, nibbling at panettone and salome Milano.

It was a far cry from the glittering diplomatic events he had become accustomed to in recent years. Because the family was still mourning the loss of its Don, there was no music or dancing, the mirrored walls of the ballroom were draped with black crepe. The few guests clumped together uncomfortably in small groups, sprinkled throughout the huge space.

Haldane felt strangely disconnected from the scene before him. Watching the grim celebration, he wondered what his growing family was doing now, on Christmas Eve back home in London. He was aware of some distant part of himself dispassionately watching him run through his familiar worries. It was like he was somehow aware of himself from two perspectives at the same time: one perspective was his normal daily awareness, with its accustomed feelings, but now this was joined by another perspective of himself as a part of a larger context, in which his longings and anxieties are viewed in all their manifestations and consequences, but somehow apart from him. This dual perspective quite disoriented him.

In his ordinary state of mind, he sadly imagined his family gathering without him. A few years ago, his long-suffering wife had taken up the new fashion started by Queen Victoria of bringing a live cut pine tree into the house for decoration. He envisioned his two young sons hanging gay strands of berries and popcorn, while his eldest and dearest child, Victoria, placed a tinsel angel on the top of the fragrant tree. *I've got to stop this melancholy. What a sentimental idiot I am.*

On the detached level of his dual perspective, Haldane observed as he reprimanded himself with accustomed self-discipline, noting the harshness in his self-judgment.

He scanned the others. *What a dreary gathering,* he thought. The party consisted of a strange combination of Aldo's shady business acquaintances, local minor nobility and rustics, for a total of not quite two dozen guests. Haldane had no wish to talk to any of them. He just wanted to go home. As it stood now, he might be able to make it back to London by New Year's Eve, if he was very lucky.

*Elizabeth will have my head if she misses Lord Northampton's New Year Eve Gala again because of me. I just hope I can get passage tomorrow.*

He worried anew that he would have little time to enjoy with his children before he had to return from extended leave to active duty. His thumb absently stroked the inner rim of the simple gold band on the little finger of his left hand.

From the other perspective he watched his ordinary self's stomach knot and throat tighten, noting all the minute reactions he had to his own thoughts. In this phantom state, he suddenly felt a familiar presence, magnetically pulling him towards reunion. Suddenly, his consciousness collapsed down to the single, ordinary perspective he was accustomed to. A small figure caught his attention. He made out the alluring image of a well-shaped young woman in a vibrant emerald velvet gown with masses of dark hair coiled up in a fetching coiffure, sailing from one group of guests to the next. He watched the woman across the ballroom, transfixed. She moved with accustomed grace and ease.

Haldane rubbed eyes with one hand, while balancing his teacup and saucer in the other. He shook his head, dispelling the lingering aftereffects of the strange double awareness that disappeared as mysteriously as it had appeared.

The woman moved closer. Haldane could now make out her features. A prick of mild recognition raised the hackles on the back of his neck and arms, yet he could not place where he had seen her before. *Who is this creature?* He forgot his misery in the mystery of the moment.

He appraised her appearance. Though not what could be called a classic beauty, she was certainly pretty enough. He reckoned that her head would barely clear the top of his breastbone, yet she was well proportioned. She reminded him of the fine porcelain doll he had bought for his daughter in Paris.

As she moved closer, he could make out the details of her face, surrounded by curling black hair. Her large, dark eyes inspired both worship and terror. Her ivory cheeks flushed a delicate rose with excitement, challenged only by the deeper blush of her lips.

*She looks so familiar. From where do I know her? Surely I have never met her before, I would remember that.* But the feeling of recognition would not subside, but rather compounded. He watched her approach and talk to old Calendri.

*I know her,* he thought, disturbed that no name came to mind. *Definitely getting tired,* he decided as he sipped at his tea. *I'm imagining things. I know I haven't met her before. There's no way I would ever forget her...*

Amidst the party gathering, Sophia found comfort and respite from her sorrows in greeting her guests and playing the well-practiced role of hostess. For the first time in weeks, she was actually enjoying herself. She approached old Don Stephano Calendri, her ancestral enemy, now her business partner, with a curtsey.

"Don Stephano, who would have ever thought we would see the day when Calendri and D'Amici would come together in peace and partnership? But as guardian of the D'Amici estate, I am glad that there is no longer enmity between our families. My father spent his last days to ensure it would be so, and I am determined to follow his will. I welcome you to Villa D'Amici."

"My dear, I grew up hating all D'Amicis," the old man began with creaking charm. "But, back then, none of the D'Amicis were so lovely. The times change, and we must change with them."

"Yes, so my father used to assure me..." Sophia muttered, as she scanned the small crowd of guests, then catching sight of a strange man in a dark uniform, across the room.

*Oh, hello again, my love,* she thought in automatic greeting to the stranger, then looked back again in shock. *How...how??? It's Alcibiades!*

She stared at the man and found herself moving towards him. She murmured some thoughtless word of excuse to Don Stephano and lurched towards the improbably familiar stranger, her thoughts slow and tangled. *What's he doing here? Who is he?*

Haldane looked up, surprised to see the object of his fascination approaching him with puzzlement written upon her face. She stopped momentarily to visibly compose herself before approaching him with regal poise.

"I am your hostess this evening. I am Donna Sophia." She extended a delicate white hand to him.

"I am most pleased to make your acquaintance, Donna Sophia," Haldane replied with a debonair bow, taking her hand brushing the back with his lips. "I am Colonel Christopher Jordan Haldane, of Her Majesty's Royal Army, at your service."

"Indeed you are," Sophia whispered under her breath to the top of his dark head as he kissed her hand.

"I beg your pardon," Haldane replied, confusion knitting his brow as he straightened.

"Indeed, you are at my service," she said, turning her tone and inflection impersonal, but still he did not grasp her meaning. "You have been in service to my family for a good many month, Signor Colonel. My husband, Signor Sergio Aldo, I believe commissioned your services during the recent business negotiations between my family, the D'Amici's, and the Calendri's."

*This is Aldo's wife! The bloody rat! No wonder old Sergio wanted to keep her from me. Why, she's absolutely enchanting. By Jove, I ought to cuckold him straight away, just for hiding her from me. But, she seems... so familiar, somehow. How should I know her? Where have I seen her before? She did seem to recognize me, though... or did she?*

"Ah, yes," he managed. "Forgive my stupidity, my dear lady. I was somewhat dazzled by your beauty. When you introduced yourself as La Donna Sophia, I should have realized that you were Signor Aldo's new bride. He is indeed a very fortunate man to have such a charming wife."

Uncertainty filled Sophia. She wasn't sure if she liked this stranger's flattery. Yet, he wasn't exactly a stranger... or was he? She bored deeply into his eyes.

*No, it can't be him. Alcibiades' eyes are brown. This man's are a funny hazel green. And Alcibiades never had that mustache... My Alcibiades is an American, not British.... Besides, it's all just a fantasy. I don't know who this man is... he just happens to resemble some man I made up. So what? It's just a coincidence. My Alcibiades is just a creature of my fancy, not a real person at all. This isn't him. It doesn't mean anything,* she assured herself and made move to extricate herself from his disturbing presence.

"Well, I must go greet my other guests, with your permission, Signor," she said awkwardly, turning away.

"I meant no offense, please don't go yet," Haldane pleaded to her back. "I only meant to say that I offer you my best wishes for a long and happy life, Donna Aldo."

The cold, dead sound of her married name spoken transfixed Sophia as if she heard it for the first time. She turned and spoke with the same frigidity she just experienced.

"My good Colonel," she began, "I realize that you have yielded great service to my family in... whatever it is that you do. I thank you for your felicitations and your conversation. I do hope you will enjoy our celebration. Good evening." Her sharp tone betrayed her polite words. She turned to leave once more.

Undaunted by her rebuff, Haldane rose to the challenge she presented. "I believe I would enjoy myself more if I were allowed to see the famous glass arbor in your trust which I have heard so much about," he said, content once again to address her back. Forgotten were all thoughts of his family or his own plight.

She turned slowly and glared at him.

"I am rather fond of botany, you see," Haldane continued pleasantly. "It is one of my many interests. Your palmhouse is the talk of all Lombard, I hear. Am I correct?" He placed his teacup on a passing servant's tray. "I am given to understand that there are exotic specimens from as far away as South America in your collection. I would be deeply honored if you would conduct me on a tour of your legendary glass garden." He flashed her his most intent smile and extended his arm with all confidence that she would take it.

Sophia hesitated for several moments at his audacious request, considering her options. She gave serious thought to the idea of stranding this presumptuous Englishman. At the same time, almost against her will, she evaluated this Colonel Haldane. He was handsome with mischief dancing in his eyes, and a boyish grin curling his dark mustache.

*But his nose is too long and he's much too tall,* she thought. *He is not Alcibiades.*

Yet, despite these few minor discrepancies, he definitely reminded her of the roguish American officer her parents had befriended in her girlhood – the one who had inspired her life-long forbidden fantasies.

But, what harm could come of spending a few minutes showing this tantalizing, yet disturbing man her most prized D'Amici legacy? *We won't be there long enough for anything to happen. I will make sure of that,* she decided.

"Very well, Colonel Haldane," she said as she took his arm. "I will be delighted to show you the eighth wonder of the world."

Sophia's palm tingled as it rested on the dark wool and gold braid of his uniform. She knew that accepting the colonel's invitation could damage her reputation and embarrass her new husband.

*My heavens!* she thought. *What is wrong with me? I should not be leaving the others without proper escort. Can I rely upon his honor? I've got to remember, he's not my Alcibiades. I don't know this man. And even if he is... Especially then, I should not be alone with him. What am I thinking?*

Yet at the same time, the possibility of Colonel Haldane taking advantage of her vulnerability sent delicious shivers down her spine. She marshaled her wayward feelings.

*Of course, he comes from a very good family, and he's an officer, Sergio said. A gentleman such as he can be trusted. After all, Sergio seems to trust him implicitly. He's not exactly a stranger, now is he? Why should I not follow my husband's example,* she reasoned, twisting logic to suit her heart's preference.

Together, they strolled out of the gathering, making small talk about the unfortunate change in the weather.

As they drew closer to the double glass doors of the green house, something seemed wrong to Sophia, pricking her to full attention. She observed no signs of the usual condensation that collected on the inside of the glass doors of the arbor. She hurried Colonel Haldane toward the entry with fixed determination, her panic growing the closer she came to the glass encased room.

With a small cry, Sophia released Haldane's arm and ran the few remaining steps to the doorway, all her previous thoughts lost in the moment.

Upon flinging open the doors, her worst fears were confirmed. The once glorious garden was freezing cold and dry. Rows of tropical flowers were wilted and limp in raised beds. Several plants were in such a deep state of shock that they would never recover. It was obvious that the plants' sensitive environment had been disrupted for some time.

Tears welled up in Sophia's eyes as she ran from one end of the garden to the other in survey of the damage. "What could have happened? I was only gone for a couple of days," she cried. "Everything is dying!"

Haldane stood in sympathetic silence, observing and sharing her shock and sadness. Things were not going the way he had expected either.

Sophia came and stood before him, unabashed tears streaming down her face.

"My mother's garden," she whispered. "It's ruined... Dead... What could have happened? It was fine two days ago... The heat and humidity systems must have broken... And I was too concerned with planning a stupid party to even notice! How could I have been so selfish?"

"I'm so sorry, Donna," Haldane offered, inadequately. "I'm sure you had nothing to do with this catastrophe."

"I should have been here," she moaned as she touched the brown crisp leaves of a dead fern. "Many of these species cannot be replaced. I let the gardener cut back to monthly visits after Father died. I was so sure I could take care of the garden. It was entrusted to me to keep, and I've failed!" Guilt propelled her around the glass arbor to survey her failure in detail.

The garden showed but little resemblance to its reputed glory. Looking around at the debris, Haldane thought there might yet be a chance. He recalled something he had heard once from an American Lieutenant he had met at a cabaret in Paris. It would take some doing here, and the proper equipment might not be at hand, but it was the only solution he could think of in the moment.

Sophia took in the extent of the loss of the garden, and the strain of the last few weeks descended upon her all at once. She wrung her hands and her whole form shook. Embarrassed by her blatant emotionalism, yet unable to stop herself from openly weeping, Sophia was all the more overwhelmed.

"Donna Sophia," Haldane said as he caught up to her, using the voice he reserved for soothing his daughter's tears after a bad nightmare. "Listen to me, I believe there is a way to save some of your garden. Now calm yourself, I will need your help. Here, have a handkerchief," he said as he pulled the cloth from his pocket. "Do you have any fire pots, small stoves, lamps, any sort of heat source that we can use in here without burning down the place?"

"I don't know," she said through her tears. She took the proffered handkerchief and turned away from his gaze as she wiped her eyes.

"Donna Sophia, please," he said, turning her to face him and taking her trembling hands in his steady grip. "I believe I know a way to help you. If you don't know what supplies are at hand, who would know? Sophia, which of your servants would know?"

"Carlo," she said in an unsteady voice.

"Summon him, do it now," he said, and hurried her on the way.

He remained behind to scrutinize the blighted garden. *What a shame,* he thought. He could not remove the image of Sophia's plight from his mind. Something stirred deep within his neglected soul. At that moment, Haldane would have done anything to help her without thought of the cost, effort or consequences, and he knew it.

It scared the hell out of him, and lured him on like no other bait.

# Chapter Twelve

**25 December, 1872.   D'Amici Villa.   8:20 a.m.**

As the morning light filtered into the stricken glass arbor, Haldane stood in suspenders and shirtsleeves, looking at the white linen sheets carefully draped around the maze-work of plants, smudge pots, lanterns and coals with measured satisfaction. Throughout the night, every resource available to the villa had been enlisted in the desperate mission of mercy, even the fine linen sheets that Signor Aldo had presented to his bride.

The glass arbor had taken on the look of some surreal dreamscape. The white sheets glowed in places where lanterns or smudge pots burned, adding fantastic reddish shadows and golden highlights to the panorama. Though outlandish in appearance, the apparatus was based on sound principles. Keeping the air and ground around the plants moist and warm was the goal of their contrivances.

Sophia sat on the earth of the garden, her legs dangling over the side of a growing bed, feeling the soil near a particularly bruised shrub now draped in fabric. Her elegant green velvet gown of the night before was crushed and soiled with mud. Her creamy cheek was smudged with soot, dark circles under her eyes.

Sophia watched Haldane walk to the bench near the entry where he had deposited his tunic jacket during the frantic rescue attempt, and remove a cigar from a pocket. His tall figure was well muscled and cleanly lined. He was athletic and poetic in his movements, even now in the grips of exhaustion. As he continued to move, Sophia saw his intention to exit to the courtyard outside in order to smoke away from the healing vegetation.

"Please," Sophia called to him. "Colonel Haldane, please stay with me. You may smoke in here, it can do no more harm than these beastly smudges." Without realizing it, she wiped more soot on her cheek with the back of her hand than she removed in her effort to provide a more presentable face.

Haldane returned, stifling a smile at her vain effort at grooming and her invitation. He drew a small silver box of matches from his trousers and struck one into flame. As he brought the match to the cigar, the light around his face revealed weary lines about his eyes.

"I believe that is all we can do for now," Haldane said, as he put one foot up on the wall of the growing bed a couple of yards away from Sophia and stretched politely. "Take some time to sleep now. Tomorrow I will wire a craftsman I know who lives in Venice, Master Giovandi Zagriello. I assure you, he is brilliant in all works of this type. If there is any artisan living who can repair and re-pressurize the old lines that heat this palmhouse, it is he."

He took a self-assured draw from the cigar and let fly small circular rings of smoke. Though tired, he was pleased with what he had wrought. He was sure at least some of the garden had been saved.

During this Christmas Eve's efforts at vegetative salvation, Haldane and Sophia discovered many interests and incidents in common. Both had lost their mothers at early ages, and they shared the same Catholic faith (though Sophia was still devout in her family's faith, Haldane admitted he had become somewhat lax in his spiritual duty). Both came from families steeped in historic pasts and noble titles. Sophia had been delighted to learn that history, opera, and fine works of art and literature were favorite past times for Haldane, too.

He appeared to Sophia to be a man who was self-assured, committed and driven to perfection in any undertaking. He had directed Carlo and the other servants to gather what was necessary for the construction and heating of the garden enclosure. So sure of his vision, he had placed every support with his own hands, wrapped every plant in the maze-work monstrosity that now occupied the glass arbor. Sophia was amazed at how quickly Colonel Haldane had organized a small army of house servants into gardeners, ordering what needed to be done and creating a sense of adventure that they all shared.

So exactly like what her Alcibiades would have done in such an emergency. *Could it be...?* She didn't dare to hope.

"How do you know so much about so great many people and things?" she drawled.

"Because I have been a great many places and done a great many things," he said, with an easy smile.

She looked again at his handsome face, marveling at the unaccustomed sensations he elicited. Throughout the night, she had found every innocent excuse she could to be physically close to him: to ask him questions, to solicit the aid of his strong hands, to offer help... She knew she was playing with fire, but depended on the presence of the servants to preserve her honor. Reason cautioned her to be careful, but her heart had already far outstripped rationality.

"Was this one of the many things you have done?" Sophia asked with an air of awe.

He heard the tone and responded with a lightness calculated to diminish the exaggerated esteem.

"It is now," he said with a little chuckle around the cigar he held in clenched teeth. In other circumstances, he would have encouraged hero-worship from a lady, but in Sophia's case...it was just different. Haldane avoided probing farther, lest these delicate sensations evaporate away, leaving him empty once more. At the moment he was content to just be of service to her.

He extended his hand towards Sophia, as she struggled to rise, and helped her to stand. He towered over her, and in the flashing lights of the myriad lamps, his stature seemed one moment menacing, then protective in the next. Haldane withdrew the cigar from his mouth and kissed her pearl-white hand. As his lips touched her skin, Haldane was suddenly lightheaded, and an unknown sensation moved through his chest.

Once more for only a brief moment, he perceived himself from that strange dual perception, observing himself responding to the stimulus of Sophia. *What the...? How bizarre*, he thought, as the new feelings reverberated through his being, reminding him of his experience the night of the meteor.

"Thank you, Colonel Haldane," she said, her hand tingling with his gentle touch. "I do not know what I should have done without your knowledge and good will."

"I do wish you would continue to call me Jordan, as before," he said, as he stroked the back of her delicate hand with his thumb, and took a half step closer to her. During the panic of the evening, he had invited her to call him by his familiar name, Jordan, rather than his first name, Christopher. Then, it had been a convenience of speed in communication. He sought it now as one might pursue kisses from a lover.

"Well, you have more than earned my eternal gratitude," she

murmured, resisting this added intimacy. Yet, she did not withdraw her hand from his.

An ineffable sensation flooded over Haldane, something known yet unknowable. He wanted to tell her how much he had enjoyed her company throughout the night, that he wished to make it last forever, but instead he found himself saying only, "It was my pleasure to assist my charming hostess for this wonderful Christmas Eve's celebration."

"Oh, my dear Colonel," Sophia said, as she extricated her hand from his at last and moved a few step away. She blinked at the morning's light, seeking more to turn away from his suddenly hurt glance than to evaluate the time of day. "It looks as if it might be as late as nine, by the patterns of the shadows." She continued to avoid his eyes as she looked out into the courtyard beyond the glass arbor.

"Yes, well then," he said, changing his tactic. "I believe we have quite effectively missed Christ's Mass." He took another puff off the cigar, careful to blow the smoke away from Sophia.

"Oh dear," Sophia gasped, as she turned back to him.

He was smiling, and she blushed to think that he had succeeded in maneuvering her into eye contact again.

"I should make amends to you, Colonel Haldane. I must ask you to join the company of my family for the holiday. Please allow me to extend the comforts of my household. It is the very least I can do for you after you have done so much to help me save my beautiful garden."

"I am most honored, Donna Sophia, " he replied. "In fact, I should be happy to enjoy the comforts of your household."

"Wonderful," she said. "We will have a beautiful meal, and some small presents, and you will tell us all about your travels and... Oh, it shall be very delightful." Her face glowed with an enthusiasm to match the sunlight.

"Wait," he broke in on her plans, suddenly very intent. "I meant to say, that I would cherish more time with you because... because you are very like someone I believe I must love very much."

*Bloody hell, why did I say that?*

Haldane had been unable to stop himself from speaking his true feelings of the moment. He hadn't even realized his feeling until the words were already past his lips. He stood in shock as he watched Donna Sophia's expression. Her confused, yet hopeful eyes told him that a reaffirmation of her invitation was mandatory for the decorum of the moment, yet he hesitated. An explanation for his behavior was simply not at hand... or was it?

The smoke of the cigar had an unusual bluish tint to it in the golden light of the morning. He pulled the crushed cigar band from his pocket and noted that it was not one of his own. It was the cigar that Aldo had given him the night before. Haldane's spine went cold as beads of icy sweat banded his forehead.

*Damn Aldo*, he thought. *I should have known that he would stack the deck in any way he saw fit. I've been drugged!*

Making a supreme effort to control himself, Haldane smiled at the ruse. He knew he had been dosed, but with what? The strange distortion of normal perception, his abrupt acceptance of Donna Sophia's invitation to spend Christmas in the villa, let alone his unbuffered honesty, proved even to his inebriated senses that he had been given a substance that made the will a pliable and honest agent to the suggestions of others. In light of this discovery, his next choices had to be carefully weighed. Donna Sophia awaited his explanation, her brows knit.

"Donna Sophia," he started slowly. "You will please forgive me. I'm so tired I don't know what I am saying... As much as I should wish to stay for Christmas, I fear I would be pale company in my present state."

*Good*, he had managed to speak without spilling his guts to her. Maybe, if luck was with him, he could get away and recover his wits before he revealed too much. He extinguished the cigar and returned it to his coat pocket for a more thorough inspection at a later time.

"Certainly," she broke in, "Of course, dear Colonel. You must rest and have some time to refresh yourself. I would not think of your leaving my care until you are fit to travel. All the more reason you must stay for Christmas supper."

He watched her dark eyes searching his in hopes of catching more of the previous moment's honesty. How tender she seemed to him, so aware and intelligent in her observations. He wanted to be fully honest with her, to tell her everything he knew about the dealings that Aldo had hired him to negotiate. He wished to expose all the corrupt contracts and backhanded deals Aldo had cut. He felt he owed her an explanation as to how she had been misled into this marriage, and how her new husband had stolen from her family in the guise of being their savior. And he especially wanted to tell her of his own efforts to foil Aldo. But he knew he couldn't trust himself to communicate clearly under the effects of the strange drug. Nor could he yet trust her with the knowledge that could endanger her life. Best to be away from the temptation until he had a better understanding of the perils of the situation.

Haldane started to protest that he must be leaving immediately, but instead he heard himself saying "Yes," he said, "Of course I will stay, Donna Sophia."

After a servant had directed Colonel Haldane to a guest chamber in the main house of the villa, Sophia returned to her own bedchamber. She shut out the light of the Savior's birthday with thick, burgundy velvet curtains. With her maid's help, she then struggled wearily from the bustled evening gown, and sighed with remorse as she examined its ruined condition.

"First the garden, and now this," she heaved a defeated sigh as she let the once rich garment crumple in a heap on her floor.

Clad only in her chemise and pantaloons, she fairly collapsed on the duvet and rolled herself into the cocooning comfort of its soft warmth. Exhaustion overtook her. She quickly slept, and deeply dreamed.

## 25 December, 1872   4:30 P.M.   Villa D'Amici

When Haldane awoke, he was still tired, yet refreshed enough to carry on. He lay abed and attempted once more to understand his unaccustomed response to Sophia. The strange double perception confused him. It seemed to have a whiff of the strange occurrence at the lake the night of the meteor, like a feeling from his childhood, when he had actively pursued an understanding of his being and reality. Although he was aware of all of his physical senses taking in his surroundings, if he calmed his mind and focused, he could almost reach that other, double existence of wholeness and perfection. But it seemed that as soon as he realized he had touched it, his mind became perturbed and he slipped away.

Cynicism and disappointment had buried his naïve longing for meaning for so long, he had forgotten any other way of being. But his yearning for purpose and connection now resurfaced, faint but distinctly unforgettable… and just beyond his grasp. He tried to understand his peculiar connection between Sophia and his strange visions. As much as he tried, the only concrete thing he could grasp onto was that Sophia somehow felt like *home* – that she held the key to unlocking a part of him that he never even knew existed. He did not know what this meant or how it should be, or even what he should do about it. All he knew were his raw feelings. Slowly, he realized the futility of seeking to understand the extraordinary with only mundane comprehension. Yet he still looked forward to seeing Sophia again soon.

He rose and set about determining the tangible: what drug had Aldo used on him? He couldn't know without getting it analyzed, but he suspected it was something such as he had seen used in high stakes military interrogations. Luckily, Haldane ingested only a small amount in the few puffs of the cigar he had smoked, and it wore off while he slept, but his suspicions were now fully aroused. Haldane did not put it past Aldo's ability or ambition to attempt to murder him or anyone else Aldo thought stood in his way, including Don Alessandro. But what truly alarmed Haldane was Aldo's power over Sophia, with its potential for abuse. Thus forearmed, Haldane readied himself for the evening to come.

Upon waking, the realization of the night caught up with Sophia She surrendered to the waves of grief she had repressed for so long. The life she had known was gone forever, just as the Arbor was in danger of going, just as the broken tiles had gone, just as her father and sister and mother were all gone...

And now, with the sudden introduction of Haldane into the situation, so looking and acting like her own dream come true, saving her garden in a moment of dire need – but, tragically, arriving too late to save her from a loveless marriage - Sophia felt her self-control slipping away. Deep sobs racked her body for several minutes before the storm finally waned and resolution returned.

"I am a D'Amici. Fortune cannot defeat me," she told herself sternly, and rose up out of bed. "*Ire fortiter quo nemo ante iit.*"

Her first order of business after dressing was to fly down the great staircase and rush to the garden in hopes of proving the memory of its ruin to be only a dream. Here, she found Haldane inspecting the cords that held up a particularly damaged specimen. He straightened at her approach, and turned towards her with a sad but hopeful smile.

The now-familiar tingling-twisting sensation embraced her body as she approached him. This time she gave no resistance to its presence. Suddenly, Sophia became self-conscious and wondered if he would be able to tell that she had been crying. She wished she had taken more time to examine her face in the mirror in the hall before her hasty entrance into the arbor.

"I believe our best efforts were not soon enough for this poor thing," Haldane said as he indicated the shrub he had been examining. "Tomorrow, I shall go to Milan and wire the craftsman I spoke of. I assure you once again, Donna Sophia, he will be able to do something to restore this prize," *if anyone can*, he finished silently.

"Colonel Haldane..." she began.

"Please, Donna," he interrupted, smiling as he stepped towards her. "I do wish you would call me Jordan again. I feel I must address you with formality when you call me by my rank."

"Yes, Sophia," came the rough nasal voice of Sergio Aldo from the entryway of the arbor. "This gentleman is more than our guest, he is our trusted and dear friend. I have addressed the good Colonel as Christopher for some time now in our dealings. It seems he offers you a special distinction in his request to address him as Jordan." Aldo's final word had a chill that easily competed with the cold mountain atmosphere outside the enclosed garden.

"What a waste," Aldo said. He motioned to indicate the whole garden.

"Yes," Haldane said, "I believe the shock may prove too severe to many of the more delicate plants."

"I was speaking of the linen," Aldo retorted.

"Surely, Signor Aldo," started Haldane as he clenched his jaw. "Surely, even you must see the tragic loss of living beauty evident in this place. If not amongst the flowers, you have but to observe the anguish in Donna Sophia's eyes. Sheets can be replaced, the memories which this place holds for your wife cannot."

"And what would you know of her memories?" Aldo growled back at the impertinent Englishman.

"Only what she herself has told me, Signor." Haldane left the statement heavy with unspoken accusations.

"Gentlemen," Sophia broke in, sensing their rising hostility. "Let us not forget what day this is." She moved towards Aldo's chair and slid behind him, her eyes fixed on Haldane's all the while.

"Indeed," replied Haldane. "Please forgive my shortness, Signor. It seems I am not as fully rested as I should be to provide civil company. With your leave, I shall be on my way. Happy Christmas, Signor… Donna…"

There was nothing to gain by an open confrontation with Aldo at this time. He still needed evidence if he was to prove Aldo guilty of any crimes. Haldane started to make his way to the exit now blocked by Aldo's chair. Self-righteous pleasure was written on Aldo's face and stark disappointment registered on Sophia's, before she could school her features to a more neutral expression. It was the look in Sophia's eyes that stopped his tactical retreat.

"Sergio," Sophia began. "I have invited the Colonel to spend Christmas with us. Colonel Haldane was very kind to spend last evening in an effort to save my garden. We owe him the Christian kindness of this holiday a thousand times over for his selfless deeds."

"Of course, my dear," replied Aldo. "Whatever you wish. I cannot refuse you on the day of the Lord's nativity, now, can I?" He switched his beady gaze to the discomfited Haldane. His tone took on a caustic edge. "*Jordan*, is it, then? Then, Jordan it is. Well, *Jordan*, how splendid you'll be joining us for Christmas supper. Sophia, conduct our guest, *Jordan*, into the villa so we do not have him catching a chill. I would never be able to forgive myself if my dear friend and associate, *Jordan*, were to be stricken ill in my own home on Christmas day."

Any remaining hopes Haldane had harbored of a pleasant afternoon with Sophia shattered. Haldane realized with a sinking feeling that his fate was now sealed. There was no escape in sight. He would be forced to also spend Christmas with the bilious Aldo.

Haldane and Sophia made their way to the sitting room, as Aldo's maidservant wheeled Aldo's chair behind them.

As she led Haldane down the winding corridors, Sophia pointed out the stalwart defenses cleverly built into the villa by her noble ancestors.

"During a siege, the D'Amici family could remain safe for weeks, perhaps indefinitely with the proper strategies," Sophia informed him. "The villa is not only protected by thick walls and heavy wooden doors, the twisting and turning hallways and staircases offers myriad opportunities for defensive positions, if the outer walls were ever overcome. Although the Villa has been sieged many times in its long history, never has it been breached," Sophia told him with pride as they entered a smaller family dining room filled with sunlight streaming through high clerestory leaded panes and a ten foot long table, laden with holiday treats. "We even have our own water supply, as there are natural springs, as well as hot springs on the grounds. This keep has proven impenetrable for over six centuries."

As he watched the members of the D'Amici family gathering in a private dining room for Christmas supper, Haldane could not help but ponder that for all its strength and security, the battlements and stronghold chambers of La Villa D'Amici offered small protection against the current invading hoards.

Sophia escorted Haldane into the drawing room and then left him to go back and help conduct Aldo's wheelchair through the halls of uneven tiles.

"God's Balls, woman! What are you trying to do to me, take my leg off, you stupid cow?" Aldo howled in pain as his injured leg grazed the wall.

Sophia gasped and recoiled as Aldo bellowed some curse quite unbefitting the nature of the season. She had never seen this new side of her husband.

"I'm so sorry, Sergio," she murmured numbly. "I-I'll be more careful next time."

Haldane's spine stiffened as he heard Aldo's harsh words

through the open door, but he remained silent.

*Temper, temper, old boy, stiff upper lip. You'll get your turn, don't spoil your case with haste,* he coaxed internally, clenching his jaw.

"Sophia, the servants can manage," Gemma quietly called to her sister. "Come here and sit by us."

Sophia moved towards Roberto and Gemma, who were already seated at the intimate dining table in front of the fire.

Gemma reached out and clasped her sister's hand in the knowing embrace of encouragement shared by all long-suffering wives. Sophia returned the pressure of Gemma's grip in silent acknowledgment.

A gangly boy in a blue tunic and pants snapped to attention at the sight of the gold braid and ribbons on Haldane's uniform, young Eduardo Alphonso D'Amici. The last male heir of the D'Amici family was outfitted, as he had demanded as condition of his attendance, in his full dress uniform of the military academy he attended in Padua.

"At ease, soldier" Haldane said to the youth, after their introduction. "We are on holiday, my good fellow. No need for military formalities on this occasion."

"Sir, yes sir," replied Eduardo, taking a formal at-ease stance. At twelve, Eduardo was already three inches taller than the diminutive Sophia. His dark, curly hair was clipped short, befitting a military school's regimentation. There was no mistaking the youth's proud ancestral blood in his manner or his physical similarity to his sisters.

Haldane regarded the youth's rigidity with a sigh. As he studied the young warrior, he thought back to his own youthful experiences with military schools. Haldane knew first-hand how it felt to be packed off to boarding school by a family who couldn't be bothered to take the time to raise or to understand him.

"I'll tell you what," said Haldane. "For this evening, it would be best if you and I held the same rank, so we can associate as fellow officers."

As Haldane spoke, he removed one of the golden emblems of his own commission from his left epaulet. As he pinned the insignia on Eduardo's vacant epaulet, Haldane's voice took on a sharp, official air.

"I, Lieutenant Colonel Christopher J. Haldane, in the name of Her Majesty, Queen Victoria, do hereby field commission Lord Eduardo D'Amici to loyally serve his own Kingdom of Italy as Lieutenant Colonel for this Christmas Day."

Haldane then gave his new fellow officer a jaunty, British salute, ignoring Aldo's snort of derision.

"Colonel D'Amici, do you accept your commission?"

"I do, Colonel Haldane," replied Eduardo in an awe-filled voice, returning the salute. Eduardo then rushed to Gemma's side to show her the shining emblem on his uniform. "Look, Gemma," said the excited youth, "I'm an officer!"

"That is lovely, Eduardo," said Gemma, her eyes sparkling with admiration as they met Haldane's own.

Sophia flashed Haldane a relieved smile, grateful that Haldane so easily deflected the boy's tantrum.

"Colonel Haldane, you recall my sister, Gemma and her husband, Roberto. They were at the arbor last night for a short time," Sophia said, as the young couple stood. "They have come up from Milano to join us for the holiday."

Haldane lightly kissed Gemma's proffered hand, and heartily shook Roberto's hand.

"Signor Manzini, Madame – it is indeed a pleasure to see you once again," Haldane said, recalling that the young couple had visited the heroic efforts, and that Roberto even had volunteered his efforts for a few hours hauling kerosene and charcoal to fuel the smudge pots and lamps.

"Don't mind Roberto," Gemma said with a merry smile. "He doesn't say much… But he's very handy to have around."

Haldane bobbed his head in salute at the silent young man.

"So I discovered last night," Haldane replied. "He worked tirelessly on your mother's palmhouse. I wasn't able to say anything last night, but I wish to take this time to express my gratitude for your assistance." He turned to Gemma with a charming smile. "Your husband here set quite an example for the rest of us. You should be very proud of him, ma'am."

Gemma beamed at her husband, who blushed at the fuss being made over him.

"At last," grunted Aldo as his chair cleared the final obstacle and wheeling into the room. "And, in time for dinner, I should hope." The rest of the table smiled and made polite sounds as he rolled his chair into their company.

"Come, everyone," Sophia urged. "Let us take our seats." Haldane found himself placed between Eduardo and Aldo, whose place at the head of the table was set without a chair to accommodate his wheelchair. Sophia was far away at the foot of the table.

"Well," Aldo continued as he reached his chairless place setting, "Jordan, what say you give grace. It seems I am in no temper to do so myself. Is that not so, my dear?" He turned to Sophia, as the smile slid from her face.

"If you say so, Sergio," Sophia said hollowly. Her fathomless, somber eyes gave no hint of emotion as she focused blindly on thin air.

"Have you ever seen her like, Haldane?" Aldo retorted in laughter at Sophia's measured response.

"No, Signor," Haldane replied with genuine admiration. "La Donna Sophia is unique, quite unlike any lady I have ever had the pleasure to meet."

He tilted his head in a slight bow of acknowledgment toward Sophia and lowered his eyes again.

The family silently joined Haldane, as he delivered a simple prayer of hope and happiness for this season and the coming year. All but Aldo made the sign of the Cross at the prayer's conclusion.

When dinner was finished, gifts were exchanged. Gemma received a beautiful yellow silken gown from her husband Roberto. Roberto looked dashing in the new top hat his wife gave him. Aldo was given a stylish ink pen by Sophia, one with the brand new mechanisms that carried its own supply of fluid in a refillable bladder. Aldo made a great show of giving Sophia two tickets for passage on an elegant steam ship, announcing that they would be taking a cruise around the world as soon as his scalded leg had healed.

Aldo gave Haldane a box of his special Cuban cigars, which Haldane graciously accepted. Haldane declined to smoke, however, stating that he did not like to imbibe in the company of ladies, whose delicate constitutions might be disturbed by the smoke.

Sophia gave Haldane the last remaining bloom of her garden, a pastel pink rosebud. She pinned the rose to the breast of his midnight-blue uniform with trembling hands, as Aldo glared from across the room.

When young Eduardo opened his gift from Sophia, he looked puzzled. Sophia had given her brother a large book.

"What is this thing," he asked, thumbing through the blank pages.

"It is a scrapbook, Eduardo," replied Sophia.

"What do you do with it?" wondered the youth, looking at his oldest sister with an expression as empty as the leaves in the book.

"Well, you can paste mementos into it, as I have in my own book. Then, when you are older, you can look back over what all you have seen and done, and remember."

"It's a baby's book," said Eduardo, slamming the volume shut, "for foolish girls, like you. What would I want with a book full of stupid newspaper clippings and opera programs?" Eduardo took the gift to the fireplace, with the obvious intention of consigning it to the flames.

The D'Amici clan watched in stunned silence as Eduardo

prepared to toss Sophia's gift into the fire. The sight of Sophia's dismay moved Haldane to action.

"Lieutenant Colonel D'Amici," Haldane barked, his voice filled with a crisp authority that brought the boy up short. "Your behavior hardly befits a gentleman of your privileged rank. Does this mean you are ready to resign your commission, sir?"

Haldane looked hard at the rebellious youth, knowing that his own actions might be considered as out of place as Eduardo's. But Haldane could not bear to see Sophia's heart broken, especially now. Besides, Haldane felt he understood the source of the boy's angst better than any one else present.

"Sir, no sir," said Eduardo, his dark eyes growing large as he tucked the volume under his arm, removing it from the harm he had intended.

"Very well," said Haldane, his tone measured and cool. "You should know, sir, that my own brother gave me such a volume as your sister has so thoughtfully given into your care, when I was just about your age.... Though I never pasted opera programs in it."

Haldane paused, wondering why he was allowing the members of the D'Amici family to share so much of his inner life. "Well," Haldane continued, "let's just say that I found another use for the book, as I am sure you will be able to do if you give it some thought."

The expression on Eduardo's face told Haldane that he was making some progress with the lad. Eduardo looked at the book, his eyes shining with new possibilities.

"I can write in it," said Eduardo, "can I not, Colonel Haldane?"

"Indeed you may, Colonel D'Amici," said Haldane with a fond smile on his lips. "Indeed, you may," *my boy,* Haldane finished silently.

"Thank your sister for your gift, boy," growled Aldo, annoyed with the attention the youth was receiving.

"I am an officer, and you must address me as such," replied the stalwart, young colonel.

"I'll address you with the back of my hand, if you do not immediately tell you sister that you are grateful to receive her gift," stormed Aldo.

"Thank you, sister," growled Eduardo, matching Aldo's own tone of malice.

*Damn you, Aldo,* thought Haldane, *I was so close to reaching the lad.* Haldane's jaw tensed, but he remained quiet.

"An officer," said Aldo, mocking the now sullen child. "You don't know what it means to be an officer. I, myself, gallantly led the great General Giuseppe Garibaldi, and his beautiful wife Anita, through the swamps of Comacchio during their escape from the Austrian forces sent to suppress our glorious revolution in '49, and I wasn't much older than you. That's what it means to be an officer, boy. Selfless service."

"Then you must understand," said Haldane to Aldo, leaping at the opportunity to deflect Aldo, "the humility needed for command. A humility that Colonel D'Amici was already feeling." Haldane fixed the perspiring Sicilian with a deadly gaze.

*Bloody hell,* thought Haldane, *if only he was not in that chair, why I'd take the damn bugger out into the courtyard and give him a lesson or two in humility right now.*

"Sophia," Gemma said suddenly, seeking to divert the mounting tension, "would you please sing for us? I have not heard you sing since Cassandra... I mean... well, it is Christmas, and I am sure that Colonel Haldane would love to hear your beautiful voice."

"Well," laughed Aldo, continuing his mocking tone, "if you plan to warble and screech like that Adelina Patti at La Scala, I'd just as soon hear a cat-fight. It is bad enough to suffer through such caterwauling in a respectable opera house. At least there, one can conduct business. But I simply will not abide it in my own home." Aldo lit a cigar and blew the smoke towards Sophia, who coughed as the cloud of smoke reached her.

"It seems your injuries have placed you in an ill humor, Signor Aldo," Haldane interjected, as if in answer to Sophia's unspoken plea. "I suggest that you take your leave and get some rest." Haldane spoke quietly, but intently. Aldo's face flickered blank for a half-second, and then resumed its accustomed scowl.

"Well," said Aldo, "I certainly never meant to cast aspersions on your lovely voice, my dear. Having never actually heard it myself, I stand corrected. That is, if I could stand." His attempt at humor went unappreciated by the company in the room. "I suppose I shall take my leave, as the good colonel suggests, and allow you to enjoy the evening without me."

Sophia's head jerked up at her husband's unexpected words, she then looked at Haldane, catching his eye for a fraction of a moment before he pointedly looked away.

Aldo turned his chair and wheeled himself towards the door of the grand drawing room, all silently driving daggers of ice into his spine through the back of his wheelchair.

"Oh, Jordan," he called out at the door, swiveling his chair to face them. "Don't suppose you'd have an interest in accompanying me into Milano tomorrow? I've some business to conduct there, and I should allow the doctor to examine this beastly leg again to see if it is healing properly. He said he would come around in a day or two after Christmas to check on my progress, but I thought I'd save him the bother of coming out of his nice comfy home since I need to go to town." He looked down at the bandages on his left leg and then surveyed the company in the room for sympathy.

"Yes," Haldane said. "I should be happy to accompany you." Refusal of Aldo's invitation could prove costly to his plans, even if the ride promised to be unbearable. He then turned to Sophia and took her tiny hand in his. "I also have an important mission to perform for Donna Sophia in Milan as well." He politely brushed the back of her hand with his lips. "And now," he continued as he released her hand, "I bid you good night, Signor Aldo."

As Aldo left the room, grumbling under his breath, Sophia looked towards Haldane.

"Thank you, Colonel Haldane. I must apologize for Sergio, he is in terrible pain," Sophia said, the excuse being more for herself than for her husband. "I'm sure he doesn't mean to be so rude."

Haldane knew that if he did not change the subject, distract himself and everyone else, he might not be able to control his future actions. The thought that he couldn't even depend on his well-honed self-control shocked him. He could not predict his own responses anymore, as if he no longer recognized himself. Though alarmed at this unexpected turn of events, exhilaration also filled him. He felt more alive than he had in recent memory. Automatically, the part of him that adapted Haldane to any situation demanded that he cover the awkwardness of the moment.

"Indeed," said Haldane. "How about that song? I see you have a pianoforte." Haldane strolled to the instrument, opened the keyboard and struck several chords upon the keys. "What shall I play for you to sing? I must warn you, however, my accompaniment may be somewhat wanting."

"Really, I would prefer not to sing this evening, if you will kindly forgive me," Sophia said quietly.

She listened as Haldane continued to play softly rolling chords. *How skillful his hands are,* thought Sophia, *Is there anything he isn't accomplished at,* she wondered.

"I am the one to be forgiven, not you," said Haldane, as he stopped abruptly and closed the cover on the keyboard, rising to face his hostess. "I have insulted your husband, and spoken out of turn regarding the behavior of your brother, and then demanded you entertain against your wishes. I have been unbearably boorish. I am still tired from last night. With your leave, I, too, should retire."

"Nonsense, Colonel Haldane," said Sophia with honest gratitude. "What you have done for Eduardo, and myself, will be long appreciated.

I have never seen my brother so taken with anyone. And nothing from the arbor would be saved at all if not for you. Surely Providence has sent you to us, and I am truly grateful." She smiled, softly bowing her head. "I promise to sing for you another time, when we are not so weary."

"I look forward to it," Haldane murmured.

"We, too, should take our leave," said Gemma, as she lightly tapped Eduardo on the shoulder. He had taken Aldo's new pen, and was actively engaged in writing his first entry in his new journal. As Eduardo responded to his sister's touch, he closed his now-cherished volume of self-exploration and marched ceremoniously towards Colonel Haldane.

"I guess it is time to resign my commission, Colonel," said the youth sadly. As he started to remove the loaned insignia from his uniform, Haldane's hand fell on Eduardo's shoulder.

"Keep it, Colonel D'Amici," said Haldane, smiling at the soldier-boy. "Only, remember to take it off when you return to the academy. You can't very well go about out-ranking your instructors." The two warriors exchanged another jaunty salute, the boy beaming. Eduardo then turned to his sister Sophia.

"Sophia," Eduardo spoke, unsure of how to express his feelings. "I love the present you gave me." He threw his arms around Sophia's neck and kissed her on the cheek. As he hugged his oldest sister to his breast, he whispered for her ears alone, "I love you, too, Sophie." With that, he fled the room, lest they see an officer cry.

Haldane returned to his sumptuous chamber in la Villa D'Amici, regretting having left his own journal at Calendri's hunting lodge. He wanted very much to record his suspicions about the cigars that Aldo had given him. He knew Aldo had offered the tainted cigars to Calendri, and now wondered if Aldo had given any to Don Alessandro D'Amici, as well. But mostly he wished to record the strange new feelings surging through him, in hope of gaining some semblance of control by locking his peculiar feelings into a cage of words.

As Haldane disrobed for the night, he alternately worried about Sophia's safety and wondered what she was doing now – was she thinking of him, as she prepared to retire, or was he just making all this up?

"You've got it bad this time, old boy," Haldane said aloud to himself in his native English, as the pulled off his uniform trousers, tossing them onto a nearby chair and stretching his cramped muscles.

Infatuation was a fairly regular event for Haldane, but he not had feelings of such intensity since the death of his second wife, Marguerite. Part of him wanted to dismiss all he felt as merely the strange combination of sexual attraction, pity, Aldo's drugs and his own desire for revenge. Yet, another secret part whispered that his feelings towards Sophia portended much more. It was the latter part that Haldane feared the most, for if that were true, then, life as he knew it would have to change. Resolutely, he purged these thoughts from his mind as he pulled down the coverings on the large bed and climbed in.

Instead of dwelling on such delectable mysteries, he forced himself to go over his plans for the morrow. He would ride into Milan with Aldo. *What a joy that promises to be,* he thought grimly. Then he intended to visit a chemist to determine what specific drug Aldo was employing on the cigars. He mentally reviewed the other various errands he needed to run in Milan.

*I must wire that plumber to come up as quickly as possible...Oh, yes,* he thought with reluctance. *I must wire Lizzy and let her know that I didn't embark today as I had intended.* Haldane was very glad that he didn't have to tell her face-to-face. *God, when will I be going back?* he wondered. Last night, he had been looking forward to leaving, but now he was more inclined to stay and see how things turned out with the D'Amici arbor... And Sophia.

He knew there would be hell to pay when he got home. He hoped it would be worth it.

## 26 December, 1872    Milan, Italy    3:34 p.m.

"Sir, where did you say you got these cigars?" the white-coated chemist asked Haldane in a concerned tone. The two men were in a laboratory of inorganic chemistry Professor Tommaso Renotti at the Polytecnico di Milano, recommended to Haldane by the Intelligence Officer at the Milan British Embassy.

"They were a gift from a business acquaintance," Haldane replied.

"Well, I would say your business acquaintance is not your friend," the chemist grimly said. "These cigars are loaded with what looks to be some kind of opiate... Not only is this debilitating; in sufficient doses, it is also deadly."

Haldane's eyes narrowed.

"Keep testing them. I want to know exactly what I am dealing with here."

"All right, sir. I will do. Don't accept any more cigars from this fellow," Renotti cautioned. "You can tell if a cigar has been dosed by the smoke. Look..." He picked up one of the cigars and held its tip to the open flame of a nearby burner. The wisp of smoke that curled up had a discernible blue tint. "See...?" Haldane leaned in to get a better look before the chemist snuffed the burning tip out and waved his arms to dissipate the noxious fumes.

Haldane nodded.

"I had noticed the strange smoke earlier. Thank you, Renotti. I will definitely stay away from strange cigars."

## 26 December, 1872   Calendri Hunting Lodge   10:20 p.m.

Back at his small cabin retreat, Haldane placed the carefully wrapped box of cigars that Aldo had given him, along with its accompanying card, in the bottom of his valise for safekeeping. They would serve well as evidence against Aldo, when the time came.

Haldane then turned his attention to the unopened envelope that he had picked up at the British Embassy in his travels. It was yet another telegram from his wife, Elizabeth. Haldane had avoided opening it all day, even as he carried it with him.

*Rather like my own personal cross,* he thought ruefully.

With a tired sigh, Haldane flopped down on the spartan cabin's davenport and tore open the envelope to scan its contents. Elizabeth was, once again, demanding that he return home at once. The terse telegram held none of the sympathetic conciliations of her previous messages.

Wearily, Haldane closed his eyes, released another heavy sigh and tossed the telegraph from him. In the light of day, miles away from Villa D'Amici, he pondered the wisdom of extending his stay in Italy, yet he had no choice now. He had been unable to obtain passage home, the trains and ships were booked solid for days.

He had wired Giovandi Zagriello, a master builder and plumber from Venice, with whom Haldane had had past connections. Haldane knew that if the pipes could be repaired, Zagriello was the man to do it. Haldane even arranged to pay for the repairs himself, laying out an exorbitant sum to lure the craftsman to the villa during the holiday season. He knew that Aldo would most likely refuse payment, and that Sophia did not have any monies of her own to spend.

*Surely that is enough,* Haldane thought. *I'll send Sophia word tomorrow to expect Zagriello, and I'll see if I can catch a coach back. It's probably best I don't see her again – too distracting. It could disrupt my plans with my dear Signor Aldo.*

Haldane faithfully recorded his new information and his observations into his journal before retiring for the night.

As he put his journal away for the night, a white envelope fell from the book. Retrieving the fallen envelope, Haldane found the forgotten message he had received two days before, as he had prepared to leave for Villa D'Amici. It now seemed like a lifetime ago that the note from the unknown Delacroix had arrived, requesting an urgent meeting.

*Well, I should look this old fellow up and see what the devil he wants.* He examined the message for the return address. There was none. *Bloody cryptic. How does this Delacroix expect me to meet with him if I don't even know who or where he is? I suppose I shall just have to wait for him to contact me again.*

Haldane flung himself into bed, exhausted, but sleep eluded him. Each time he closed his eyes, Sophia's sensual form swam before him. No matter how he tried to discipline his mind away from her image, it stubbornly returned. As he tossed and turned his body responded to the mental images that refused to stay banished, and he soon found he had an aching erection.

Haldane groaned and rolled onto his back, pulled up his nightshirt and grasped his hardened penis in one hand.

"Why can't you just leave me alone and let me sleep?" he asked his wayward anatomy.

He began to stroke himself, focusing his thoughts on Sophia. But the more details of her that he brought to awareness, the more uncomfortable he became. Shame and guilt crept into his awareness as his fingers slid over his stiff shaft, overcoming the physical pleasure. Disgusted at himself, Haldane left off his efforts and sat up in bed.

*What is wrong with me?* he wondered as he stared into the red embers of the nearby cast-iron stove that served to heat the small, dark cabin. He realized that despite his body's arousal, he had no desire to masturbate, to defile Sophia's memory with his lust. Disconcerted with this unaccustomed feeling, Haldane did not know what to make of this new discovery. *What is going on here? Ever since I came here, things have gone strange... I have gone strange.*

He decided to record this unusual occurrence in his journal, so he rose from the bed and lit two oil lamps with a twig. He pulled out his large journal, pen and bottle of ink, and set up to write in bed. Siting cross-legged on the mattress with the large book in his lap, he thumbed through the pages until he came to the end of the entries. Moistening his pen in the ink, he paused, unsure of where to even begin exploring the strange sensations and emotions.

Suddenly, he was *elsewhere.*

His consciousness was removed to that other perspective that he had experienced before, but this time, he was no longer connected to his ordinary perspective at all. He was wholly in that other state. His body was below him, in another plane of being. He was connected to his body through a shimmering silver cord, yet he was also apart from his corporeal existence. From this unaccustomed vantage point, his whole life, from birth to grave, was laid out before him. He was outside his life and viewing it as some strange piece of art, separate from his essential consciousness. It was similar to like what had happened the night of the meteor, but a thousand times more real, more intense.

Although from this distance, he could not make out the specific details of his daily existence, he saw definite patterns to the circumstances and choices. He saw how each choice led to the next and the next. He saw that the entirety of his life was of one complete whole, and that if any single detail were to be change, then the perfection of that whole would also be changed. His life appeared to him as a massively intricate work of art, all whole and of one piece, perfect in its dramas and challenges, just as a work of Shakespeare is perfect. Even the parts he had found difficult and miserable were now shown as integral to the storyline of his mortal existence. For once, the longing in his soul of answered in the overwhelming perfection of eternity.

His awareness expanded, and he now saw how all the choices and incidents of his life interacted with the lives of his family, friends and associates. Each of their lives was connected to his, and was part of the same strange expression of creativity. And from the lives of those touching his, the art radiated out, touching the lives of hundreds and thousands, encircling the globe, including all those peoples who's lives had been affected by him, the negotiations he had participated in, the Imperial policies he had carried out, the battles he had fought in, the seductions he had staged. Yet his consciousness was separate from the panorama of his life, observing from high above.

He sensed a familiar presence, and turned his attention from the squirming design of his corporeal existence below to behold a radiant being that seemed above yet permeating his consciousness. The presence encompassed both him and the planet below, with a definite impression of feminine nurturing. The being radiated infinite love and acceptance of him. But what shocked him the most was the identity of this entity. He recognized this entity as himself somehow, but larger, wiser, far more potent.

All superlatives faded in the presence of this vast being, who gazed upon him with such compassion, such infinite love. He recognized the entity as the same stuff, the same consciousness as not only he, but also Sophia, as well. He did not know who or what this vast presence was, but he did know with a knowing rooted in his own being, that it contained and animated both the woman he felt inexplicably drawn to, and his own soul – the ultimate source of both of their existences. The only difference between he and Sophia and this being was one of scale. Everything above and below was inextricably interconnected and complete.

Haldane knew he must speak, must somehow communicate with this entity that was himself. Never had he encountered anything remotely like this, and for all he know, he never would again. His whole being longed to reached out and unite with the vast consciousness before him more than he had ever wanted anything. Overcome with extreme astonishment, the only thing he could muster was: *Why do you go away sometimes?*

The presence gave a beatific smile of infinite compassion, as she replied: *I'm not the one who goes away. I am always here.*

Suddenly, Haldane was back in his accustomed corporeal form, back in the lamp-lit cabin in the woods, pen in hand, mouth agape. His heart pounding and gasping for breath, Haldane looked about the small room and its humble furnishings. Although the room had its normal sense of reality, it paled next to what he had just experienced. Never before had anything seemed so vivid, so true, so interconnected. Trembling, he put down the pen.

*What the bloody hell was that?!* he thought, as he glanced anxiously about the cabin. *Was that God? But she was female... I'm not sure I even believe in God. Surely it was merely some hallucination...*

Even as he tried to talk himself into dismissing the vision, he knew the experience was even more real than the present moment. For he could now see this moment as a specific point in that exquisite moving work of art that was his life.

*But what is real, anyway? The only way I have to judge the reality of that – that whatever it was is through myself, through my own thoughts and perceptions. For that matter, it is the only way I have of knowing anything. Cogito Ergo Sum and all that lot. But maybe my thoughts and perceptions are wrong, diseased somehow. Perhaps I've gone loony. How am I to know if it is real or not? And if it is real, then what? What does it all mean?*

Pondering this for several minutes, he decided that it would be much easier if he were to just assume he was going mad than to give credence to the implications of what he had just experienced.

*I must be mad... or drugged... That's it! Perhaps this is only some weird aftereffect of Aldo's drugged cigar.* But even as he thought it, he knew deep inside him that his denials were false.

He found himself reluctant to record the incident in his ever-vigilant journal, keeping the experience tight within him. Although this vision granted him the greatest moment of completeness that he had ever known, he felt that to write about it would somehow demean the loftiness of the experience, to bring it down to the level of language, which could be easily misconstrued. He also feared that if he examined it too closely, that experience would prove more mirage than vision. These topics were too hot for him to handle, yet he could not shed the lingering disquiet. He could never see himself and his life in the same way again.

# Chapter Thirteen

**30 December, 1872   Villa D'Amici   5:45 p.m.**

Sophia climbed to the surface, bathed in a lantern's glow. Making her way back up the dank stairs after spending the day in the villa's deep cellars, she found no comfort in the illumination of the kitchen as she reached the ground floor. Her thoughts were dark like the ancient shadows below, mired in unwanted revelations that begged her response.

Now in the well-lit kitchen, fragrant with the smell of roasting lamb and vegetables, she quelled her troubled thoughts with a deep sigh, and made arrangements with the plumber for his return after procuring supplies needed to repair the damaged pipes. She gave a quick acknowledgment to the kitchen staff and observed the arrangements for dinner, stealing a raw carrot to gnaw as the cook told her of new developments whilst she was down below.

Just when she thought she had conquered her unruly emotions, she learned that while she was below with the plumber, Colonel Haldane had finally come to call after three days' absence. At once, her stomach knotted at the news. The servants informed her that he was now in the library with her husband, and would join them for dinner. She had spent the greater part of the last three days wondering if she would ever see Haldane again, both hoping and dreading, confused by his uncanny resemblance to her dream lover, Alcibiades. Sophia decided to return to her rooms and dress for dinner early, to sort out her thoughts before she should have to withstand the overwhelming presence of the disturbingly attractive Englishman.

Passing the library she heard voices, so hard and firm that they caused her to pause in her tracks and listen.

"Oh, believe me, Haldane," Aldo said, agitation in his voice. "If I thought for one moment that you had anything to do with this unfortunate clerical error, well, let us just say you would not be staying for dinner."

"Signor Sergio," Haldane's rich baritone voice came through the library doors. "I assure you once again that the contracts were as you yourself had laid them out for the final signature. If you will recall, I was late to the proceedings. Late enough, in fact, to find the business already concluded and the contracts signed. Don't you remember?"

Haldane's voice seemed peculiarly emphatic to Sophia. She had never heard him use such force before, and yet, he had not raised his voice. It wasn't a difference in sound, exactly, but his words reverberated almost tangibly.

"Yes," Aldo's monotone voice replied, "all except for the final signature of yourself as witness..." Aldo's voice returned to its normal pitch and inflection. "Well, so the old Calendri gets a bit more profit than I intended. As long as the D'Amicis continues to have the same, there is then a balance."

"A balance that can easily be tipped in your favor," said Haldane, in a much lighter tone. With that, the voices of the two men exploded into laughter and insincere congratulations.

From her accustomed listening post, icy fingers gripped Sophia's heart.

*What is going on? Is Jordan plotting against me with Sergio?* Her heart screamed it wasn't so, yet she couldn't deny what she had just heard. Images from her haunting dream of months before of her Alcibiades' betrayal returned in full force.

"So, when will you be returning to merry ol' England?" asked Aldo. "Oh shit, we're out of brandy in here. Damned lazy servants. You'd think that at least they could keep the fucking spirits stocked up. I don't ask for much. There's some more brandy in the parlor – let's go there."

Outside in the hall, Sophia realized that the sound was drawing nearer to the door of the library.

"I should have already returned days ago, but couldn't get passage from Naples until New Year's Day," said Haldane, his voice closer to the door than Aldo.

With a shock, Sophia knew that her discovery was imminent.

She quickly ran several yards towards the kitchen, then spun on her carved Spanish heel and began back the way she had just come. She was casually walking at her usual pace when the first of the double doors of the library opened.

"Indeed, I hoped it was some tryst of yours in Milano that delayed your departure and not our business," Aldo was saying as Haldane opened the door for him. He turned in his wheelchair at the sound of falling steps in the hall. Sophia stopped with a feigned start.

"Oh, I didn't –," she broke off her words in convincing delivery of surprise. "Colonel Haldane," she continued, offering her hand in greeting, but avoiding his eyes. As his mustache and lips brushed the back of her hand, electric shocks thrilled through her, despite the suspicions aroused only moments ago. "I was just told we were to be honored with your presence at our table again so soon. I was on my way to my rooms to make myself presentable for company." Her hand went cold as he released it. Carefully schooling her features, she turned to her husband. "Sergio, I shall go immediately and dress to receive our guest. I'm a mess from climbing around in those muddy crawlspaces."

"Yes, my dear, you do that," Aldo told her. "Colonel Haldane and I had just concluded our business. Dress now, and join us for dinner." Sophia made her way down the hall. "We will be eating downstairs," he called to her as she reached the foot of the main staircase leading up to the family's private wing. She said nothing, stopping only for a quick glance at Haldane before darting up the stairs.

Haldane's quick eyes watched the married couple's exchange warily. He knew that he must be very careful with both of these two, though for very different reasons. Haldane had returned, almost drawn against his will, to the D'Amici Villa after three days of self-imposed isolation, while he absorbed and reflected upon the unaccustomed visions and feelings assaulting him. In the intervening days, he pondered his strange experiences, especially the infinite presence that seemed to encompass both him and Sophia in its vast creation. *Does she feel it too? No, this is my own madness.*

The more he had thought about his strange new vision-born connection to Sophia, the stronger it grew. He had to see her, even if it meant enduring more time with Aldo, risking the delicate balance he maintained. At last, unable to resist the insistent inner urgings, and against his better judgment, he hazarded the ride to the alpine castle.

Unfortunately, it was Aldo, and not Sophia, who first greeted him upon his arrival. Aldo had discovered that the "wrong" contract was signed on Christmas Eve, and was predictably enraged. Haldane managed to divert Aldo's anger for the moment, but it was Sophia who interested him. Now that he was in her presence again, he found he had to remind himself to breathe.

*Better watch your step, lad,* Haldane prompted himself, and forced his focus back to the moment at hand.

"Colonel Haldane, sir!"

The two men stopped and turned as Giovanni Zagriello, the plumber approached them.

"Might I have a few words with you, sir?" he asked, as he finished wiping mud from his cheek with a kerchief. "I heard you were here and have some questions about how to procure the supplies I need..."

"Of course," Haldane replied. "Please excuse me a few minutes, Sergio. You go on in without me, I will be right back."

Aldo eyed the plumber suspiciously, then grunted his assent and wheeled his chair through the door.

Haldane led the mud-smeared plumber back into the library and shut the doors.

"What have you found, Zagriello? Is the plumbing to the arbor repairable?"

"Oh yes, sir," Zagriello replied. "I should have it back up and running in a day or two. It's a magnificently designed system – absolutely brilliant! I've never seen anything like it. But I wanted to tell you that there's something mighty strange down there. I wasn't able to fully explore it, as Signor Aldo's men were swarming all over me. I remembered what you said about her husband, and didn't let on that anything was out of the ordinary."

"Good man," Haldane replied, nodding for the man to continue.

"The system looks like it started out as a typical Romanesque plumbing, but it's been modified within the last fifty years with highly efficient modern fittings," Zagriello told him. "It looks like the majority of the steam from the hot springs below is set up to be diverted somewhere else. Only about ten percent of the total amount of steam actually heats the garden and castle."

"Diverted?" Haldane echoed. His eyes flickered up to the fantastical painting of Sophia above the fireplace. "Could you tell to where?"

"I couldn't really investigate because of Aldo's men, but it looked like the pipes were going north, towards one of the towers," Zagriello said, rubbing his nose.

"I wonder what old Sandro D'Amici had going on here," Haldane said with a small smile. "Very well, Zagriello, you just continue working on the repairs. You are wise to be wary of Aldo's men. Get whatever supplies you need and bill me for them. And keep me informed if you happen upon any other discoveries." He offered the man a few bills. "But be cautious… and take care of yourself."

"Thankee, sir! I'll do just that," Zagriello agreed, taking the bills and stuffing the money in his pocket as they left the library.

"Annabella!" Aldo bellowed, much to Sophia's embarrassment and dismay. "Annabella! Get your lazy ass in here! I need more wine! Damn leg's hurting again."

Horrified, Sophia looked to Haldane in silent apology her husband's outrageous behavior at the dinner table. She was grateful that only the three of them were dining in the small family dining room, and that her siblings were not present to witness Aldo's abusive display.

"Here, I will fetch you some more wine," she placated as she rose from her seat.

"God's Balls! No, Sophia! You stupid bitch… That's what we have servants for!" Aldo spat at her. Stunned, Sophia sank back into her chair. "Annabella! There you are, you worthless piece of shit…"

The colorless maid appeared bearing a large cut glass cruet of one of the D'Amici's finest vintages. She rushed to Aldo's side and poured dark wine into his goblet. Aldo drank deeply, then held out his glass for more. When she hesitated to fill it again, Aldo slammed down his glass and snatched the cruet from her, spilling the wine onto his arm and the carpet below. Annabella knelt and began mopping up the mess with a cloth. Aldo again drank.

"Do you remember that pub in Berlin?" Haldane asked cheerfully. "I think we had both drunk well past our limits that day…"

Aldo looked up at Haldane with bloodshot eyes, then began chuckling at the memory evoked.

"Ah yes! I recall… and that pretty little barmaid," Aldo grinned, gesticulating broadly and sloshing his wine from its glass onto the white linen tablecloth. "And I remember what *you* did…" He wagged his finger in Haldane's face. "You're such a naughty boy… But in deference to my bride, I won't repeat it at the dinner table…" Aldo laughed heartily. "You've got machismo, Haldane, I'll grant you that!"

Sophia caught Haldane's eye, flashing him a look of gratitude for redirecting Aldo's hostility.

"Well, a gentleman must always be prepared to render service to a lady when necessary," Haldane replied with a nod to Sophia. "Donna Sophia, how goes that great glass arbor of yours? I saw that Zagriello the plumber was here today."

"Yes, he was," Sophia said carefully. "He's now gone for

supplies, but believes he can have it fixed right away. He also told me that you insisted on paying for all the repairs. I cannot tell you how grateful I am for all your help."

"Pah! Service to a lady…" Aldo interjected, his speech starting to slur. "Garibaldi's great lady, Anita, herself thanked me for my assistance in the swamps of Comacchio, back during the reunification wars. And Anita was no randy bar wench, let me tell you! Now *she* was a lady!"

"Indeed," Haldane encouraged, as he poured Aldo another glass of wine. "I am sure we would all enjoy hearing of your exploits during the reunification yet one more time. How old were you again, when you helped to lead Garibaldi and his troops?"

As Aldo wove his long, intricate war story, Haldane and Sophia exchange significant looks. Haldane refilled Aldo's glass twice more before Aldo finally passed out in his chair.

Once Haldane was certain Aldo was not likely to wake soon, he gestured to Sophia to withdraw. The two of them crept off and took the opportunity to inspect the recovery of Sophia's ruined garden.

"I think some of it will survive," said Sophia. "It is only due to your knowledge and endeavors that anything still lives at all."

"It will survive," said Haldane as he looked around the greenhouse. The smell of earth and peat now mingled with the oily smoke of kerosene. Outside the glass arbor, the cold dark night enveloped the mountains, but inside the late December chill was fought back with the glow of the pots and lanterns under the sheets, providing a warm, muted light for the ailing plants. But the warmth of Sophia by his side had its own tangible radiance. "I had an opportunity to speak briefly with Zagriello before he left for Milan. It is sad to think what has happened."

"You only know so far," said Sophia with a sigh. "I have heard from a very trusted source that Sergio deliberately allowed this to happen. One of the downstairs maids told me this morning that Sergio deliberately ordered the workmen to let the steam that heated the garden escape. She witnessed it with her own eyes. I can't fathom how Sergio could do it."

"Donna Sophia," he began levelly, "I know a great deal more about Signor Aldo than you do…" Here in her presence, his carefully rehearsed speech of explanation suddenly abandoned him, along with his discretion. As before, he wanted to bare his soul to Sophia, to confess all to her. He spoke without filter or forethought. "I have reason to believe Aldo may have attempted to drug me. He gave me cigars treated with a blend of substances that render the will open to suggestion, and could even cause death in some cases. It is an old trick of Garibaldi's cohorts from the days of clandestine meetings and political assassinations during Italy's unification. The dosage was not lethal, but it was sufficient to render me utterly helpless to his commands."

"Drug you...?" Sophia repeated in horror.

"Now," said Haldane quickly, "I do not know that for sure. I certainly can't prove it yet. I only know that I found interrogation drugs in the cigars he gave me. I feel I must warn you that your husband is a very dangerous man, capable of doing anything to gain his desires. I've known him to use means most unsavory – "

Sophia turned away and ran toward the arbor's exit in a flurry of ruffles and petticoats.

"Sophia, where are you going?" Haldane called after her as he started to follow.

"To my father's library," she said in a hoarse whisper as she reached the arbor door. "Follow, quietly."

Silently, they passed through the twisting halls to the library.

Once inside, Sophia shut the doors and locked the half-dark library. She went to the desk, sat down in the chair and opened the middle drawer on the left-hand side. Haldane checked the shadows, making sure they were alone in the vaulted room.

Sophia's portrait over the mantle caught his eye. Haldane filled a wordless longing so intense it hurt his chest. He muffled a gasp as he recognized what so attracted him to the painting was that somehow it captured an essence of the being in his vision, who encompassed both he and Sophia. He tore his attention away to behold the flesh and blood subject of the artwork, who seemed to him no less fantastic or magical than the Queen of the Night. Again, he felt himself bound to Sophia in ways he could not begin to fathom. And from her, the whiff of that vast being that encompassed them both intensified. He looked away, lest he become overwhelmed by the magnitude of implications.

Bending down, her hands searched the desk compartment. Haldane moved in to better observe her progress. She suddenly stopped and removed her hand from the drawer, retrieving two cigars and two slips of blue paper. She handed the cigars to Haldane who met her eyes with full understanding.

Taking the glass off a nearby oil lamp, he examined the cigars in its light. He carefully lit one and observed how the ash crumbled into a black powder and the bluish smoke curl up from the burning it. He nodded grimly and snuffed the cigar out, waving his hands to dispel the poisonous fumes.

When he returned his gaze to Sophia, he saw that she was standing with tear-filled eyes; one hand at her lips while the other held the two strips of blue paper she had found in the desk.

"Papa –" she said when she realized that Haldane was observing her, "My father had purchased tickets for 'The Barber of Seville.' He must have left them here for me to find. But, I never did... I never did." Her small form crumpled in tears as he caught her and gently guided her back to the nearby armchair.

"You didn't know, Sophia," Haldane consoled, as he knelt beside her. "You've found them, now."

"I'm sorry," she said, impatiently wiping the tears from her cheeks with the back of her hand. "It's foolish, really. A game my father and I played. He hid little gifts in the desk for me to find." She stiffened, becoming self-conscious under his hovering concern. Haldane moved back to allow her to regain her composure.

"What have you found, is it the same?" she asked, her voice still shaken.

"It is as I feared," Haldane said as he rose and returned to the ashtray in which he had conducted his experiments. "I can't be positive until I have a chemist's analysis, but it appears to be treated with much the same sort as Aldo used on me. The drug clouds thoughts and the judgment is clouded. The orders of others are obeyed without compunction. After repeated contact, the body becomes so conditioned that it must have the substance in order to function at all."

"I knew something wasn't right!" Sophia said in a stage whisper. "In those last few weeks, Papa wasn't himself. I knew that he was very worried about money – though of course, he would never speak of his fears to me. But there was something else about him that wasn't right. I knew something had to be wrong with Papa for him to trust a man like Sergio."

"In cases of respiratory problems or advanced age," Haldane continued, "the individual could suffer damage to the heart, lungs and constitution. If your father had any previous health concerns, Aldo's cigars could have –"

Haldane paused as Sophia motioned a finger to her lips.

"Lower your voice," she said in answer to his pause. "The library allows more sound to escape its doors than one might imagine." She motioned with a nod of her head.

"I see," Haldane said quietly, wondering if he had been too loud behind these doors on any other occasion. "Then you have had suspicions all along, and the means to confirm them."

"I have heard a great many things, Colonel Haldane." Her voice was smooth and steady as she rose from the desk chair. "What I need now is proof. I need proof that Sergio Aldo poisoned my father, that he has been bent all along towards the destruction of my family. If you can prove anything against him, I ask you now to tell me and I will drive that conniving murderer from my villa!" Her eyes were like black stars, burning and seething with barely controlled fury.

"Believe me, Donna Sophia," Haldane began, "I know how well he has covered his tracks. This is not something you can do alone. You have no idea of what level he has gone to - will go to, in order to obtain what he wants. Do not confront him with what you know. It is much too dangerous right now."

"Can you prove anything against him, or not," repeated Sophia.

To prove Aldo's guilt, Haldane would have to reveal his own dark dealings to public scrutiny. But there was no room left for equivocation and subterfuge. He started this, now he had to answer. He glanced up at the large painting of Sophia that dominated the mantle and then down into the living eyes of the painting's subject.

"Yes," he said, knowing that, henceforth, he was committed to honesty with Sophia, old Calendri, and his own family, not to mention the Milanese authorities.

A nightmare fantasy danced through his mind, as the possible consequences of his actions dawned on him. If any of Aldo's dirty dealings with the D'Amicis and the Calendris became public, then eventually, Haldane's own conduct would come up for review before the Royal Army, which would then entail the Diplomatic Corps and the Foreign Office, inevitably leading to the investigation from authorities in several nations scattered about Central and Western Europe, not to mention what hash the London tabloids would make of his brother's political career in the House of Lords if they caught wind of the scandal. Court Martial was only the beginning of his worries...

"Yes, I can prove many things against Signor Aldo. But, Sophia, now is not the right time. You must wait. I cannot even tell you why, but you must wait. Please know that I have done all I can protect you and your family. I have done so for very personal reasons. To tell you more will jeopardize the effectiveness of my strategies, and possibly your safety."

"I see," said Sophia coldly, as she turned away from him. "Then I have nothing but accusations, and acquaintances who will not help me substantiate them."

He caught her by the arm and spun her to meet his gaze.

"Believe me," he whispered intently, pulling her closer to him, "I am doing everything I can to help you. You must in turn do as I ask, to help me and to help yourself. You mustn't breathe a word of this to anyone…"

The intensity of the contact between the two of them electrified the room. Her breath tasted sweet on his tongue. The sweet-spicy scent of her filled his head. He resisted the temptation to take her in his arms, instead, searching her eyes, finding fear, confusion and trust.

*Trust…*

He wondered if he could trust this ferociously proud woman who stood before him, searching his eyes for the same level of commitment he sought in hers. He questioned, moreover, if he could trust himself. With a clean jerk, he broke away from her.

"I'll be in touch," he said as he released her.

"When," she called after him, as he started for the door.

"Soon… Trust me," Haldane said with a mischievous grin, as he unlocked the doors and exited the library.

Somewhere, something turned inside him. It had been given the promise of release for so very long, it now reveled in the possibility. Haldane flexed the muscles in his jaw. He hoped to God he hadn't already betrayed Sophia's trust.

## 30 December, 1872   Milan, Italy   10:35 p.m.

Delacroix warmed himself before the roaring fire in Calyx's spacious parlor.

"So, he just ignored my request for a meeting," cried the bearded Delacroix, from his winged armchair by the fire. "The cheek of it! I travel all the way to Italy on Christmas Eve, no less, and he doesn't even give me the decent courtesy of a response. I still have never heard anything from him."

"I heard this afternoon that he remains at the villa," Calyx replied. "For some reason he hasn't returned to Britain yet. I hope to God it's not because Aldo persuaded him to join their cause."

"Damn Aldo," Delacroix spat. "If Haldane has joined to the dark brothers, we'll have to kill him. But I'd sure like a shot at bringing him into our camp first, despite what the Matriarch says... But I can't unless the bloody whelp talks to me! And there's no one else in position to protect the library, is there?"

"Well, reports from the villa are that Aldo has torn up almost all of the flooring on the ground level and the basements, and still has not found anything. The D'Amici retainers are keeping an eye on things while they are working on the pipes. All we can do for now is to put our faith in our ancient brethren, the builders of Villa D'Amici and the loyalty of Don Alessandro's retainers, and hope Aldo's men don't find the entrance," said the Calyx. He removed his glasses and wiped them on his handkerchief. "Have you heard anything from Fra Diego in Spain?" Delacroix shook his head. "How about the Matriarch?"

"Not for days," the Frenchman replied. "I don't like this, Giuseppe. I don't like it one bit. Since they launched the offensive in Catalonia, the lines of communication are gone all to hell. We don't have enough men to deal with this properly. How are we supposed to recover the library now? I told Alessandro it was a bad idea, didn't I?" Calyx nodded wearily, as the fiery Delacroix raged on. "You say that Aldo has total control of the villa, and yet here we sit, unable to do anything because we are bound by superstitious old ways."

"There's no help for it, Anton," the Italian said, as he sank deeper into his armchair. "We know that Aldo does not have the keys to the secret library, or else he would not be tearing up the floors. Without the keys and the knowledge to use them, Aldo will never be able to find his way in. We must hope he will soon tire of his fruitless search and give up. Then, after he's let down his guard, we'll slip in through the catacombs and retake the villa."

"Are you content with that? " the Frenchman asked skeptically.

Calyx shrugged.

"I'm not," Delacroix continued. "There's no telling what Aldo might be able to do with the Illuminati's occult aid. And now, if Haldane is helping them – I hope to God he's not... I don't care what Mother Magda said. It is imperative we find out whose side Haldane is on. I'll take him out myself if he's joined Aldo."

"But what about the Oath? You are bound as much as I not to reveal ourselves to the uninitiated," the Italian objected. "If we break with our traditions, even if it is to save them, then we lose who we are."

"Damn the Oath of Silence!" exploded Delacroix. "What good will our all our secret traditions and ancient knowledge be, our careful preservation of the purity of the Bloodlines across the generations, if we are all extinct and Europe falls into the hands of the Dark Brotherhood?"

# Chapter Fourteen

## 30 December, 1872   Villa D'Amici   9:24 p.m.

Sophia watched Haldane's figure on horseback growing smaller from the parapet atop the family wing of the old castle, arms crossed tightly against the cold night. Long after he had receded through the gates, Sophia continued to gaze out over the darkened landscape, the biting wind whipping her dark curls loose from their accustomed braids and coils, not wanting to go in and face the reality of her life. She watched the heavy grey clouds fly south, propelled by the freezing north winds. The smell on the wind promised snow before dawn. Finally, the chill soaked her through, and she opened the door with shivering fingers.

Upon reaching her rooms, she gratefully prepared for bed in front of her roaring fireplace and crawled under the covers, her thoughts a jumbled chaos. *What a day!* she thought as she snuggled in to bed, savoring the warmth from the towel-wrapped crockery foot warmer on her cold feet.

Sophia trembled not from the cold as she recalled the morning's revelation by D'Amici household servants. She could not believe that anyone, much less her own husband, had purposefully destroyed her mother's garden. But several of Aldo's own hired workers confirmed Aldo's explicit orders to allow the steam to escape from the glass arbor's pipes. None had come forward for fear of Aldo's reprisals, but none denied it when confronted. But the evening's accusations overran the others, making them seem trivial in comparison.

*If Sergio is responsible for Papa's death, then he must be punished*, she thought as she wiggled down against her pillow. Anger, tinged with sadness swept through her. *I'll make that vile murderer pay for what he has done… Papa must be avenged! Surely, Jordan will assist me to free my house – and myself – from Aldo. That must be the reason God has sent Jordan to me. Why else would he so resemble Alcibiades…*

Unbidden, the haunting dream of her stone face exploding and Alcibiades' betrayal arose. She shook her head to dismiss the image and confusion. The conniving words she had overheard Jordan say to her husband behind closed doors now arose to haunt her.

*Was he speaking only for the benefit for Sergio or is that his true sentiments? And then, he asks me for my trust, promising to help me. But if Jordan truly is like the historical Alcibiades, the only cause he is truly loyal to is himself,* she thought with a tired sigh. *I can't solve this tonight.*

Sophia dimmed the oil lamp on her nightstand, watched the light from her bedchamber's fireplace flicker warmly about the rich furnishings of her room, before closing her eyes in bedtime prayer.

Suddenly, she heard a click, as a key turned in the lock of her door. She sat up, startled, aware that she alone had the only means of access to her own personal chambers.

Sophia turned up the lamp again, the flame flaring up from the not-quite-dead embers. Fear, coupled with a knowing dread, knotted her gut as the door slowly opened to reveal the standing figure of Sergio Aldo.

Aldo blundered into Sophia's bedchamber, drunken and stumbling. He dragged his injured leg across the room, balancing on an elegant black cane. His eyes were hotly fixed on Sophia, as she gathered the bedclothes around her like a shield.

"So sorry I was not awake for the departure of your guest, you little slut!"

His voice was dark and his eyes betrayed the purpose of his uninvited visit to her rooms.

"Sergio, you are drunk," she said as she slipped from her bed, poised for flight.

"Not too drunk!" He lunged at her, but stumbled against the bed as she slid past his reach.

"Leave here immediately," she ordered, assuming an imperial tone she did not feel. Her panicked eyes searched for escape.

"Leave here? Not very likely," he said, waving the key he had stolen and copied. "This is my home, you are my wife, and this is my bed." He returned the key to the pocket of his trousers.

"Sergio," she cajoled, taking a step towards him. "Please leave and get some rest, we will talk of this tomorrow when your head has cleared."

He weaved sharply, and she reached out a hand to steady him, fearing that he would pass out in her room and she would have to get the servants to carry him out. With one quick motion, he caught her arm and drew her to him.

"Now," he growled as he held her tightly to his chest, "Give me what is mine."

He forced her onto the bed under his weight. She struggled helplessly under his bulk as he succeeded in his first task of unbuttoning his trousers. Her nightgown offered no defense against his roaming, hot hands. As he fondled her breasts through its fabric, the delicate threads tore under the force of his grasping clutch.

"Stop! Please!" she cried. "Sergio, you are hurting me!"

Her pleas only hardened his lust, adding to the enjoyment of her powerless struggle against the inevitable. She gave several ineffectual blows against his sweaty back with her little hands. He laughed at her attempts at self-defense and easily pinned both her hands to the bed with one of his own.

"Stop it, Sergio! Stop!" she yelled, wondering if anyone was near enough to hear her cries.

Aldo began kissing and drooling down her neck, roughly grabbing and squeezing her body with his free hand. Repulsed, anger and frustration filled Sophia with a vigor that momentarily drove the panic of the attack from her mind.

"Don't touch me, you murderer!" she shrieked in his ear.

He stopped at her words.

"Murderer?" He glared into her face. "I'm no murderer."

"You are!" she cried. "Colonel Haldane says you killed my father! He told me all about you and your poison cigars! I 'd rather die than let you touch me!"

He held her roughly and studied her defiant face long enough to realize she was in earnest.

"Then, die you will, my proud and beautiful bride! Both you and your precious Colonel Haldane!" Aldo leered down at her, his sour breath polluting the room. "But not until I have what I want from the both of you!" He slapped her face again. "Now you'll give me all your secrets, you little bitch! Where's the entrance to the Archives? Eh?" He hit her again. "Tell me! Where are the Archives?"

Sophia twisted, trying to both free herself and block her face from his blows.

"C'mon bitch!" Aldo growled as he pulled her up by her hair. "Tell me where the damn Archives are hidden!"

Sophia gasped and tried to loosen his grip on her hair as she cried, "I don't know! I don't know what you are talking about... Please, let me go!"

He released her hair and backhanded her in the face, but Sophia was able to block his blow with her forearms, before Aldo shoved her back onto the bed, and covered her body with his own.

He redoubled his efforts against her with a forceful resolve. She almost escaped his grasp as he shifted his body while he drew down his trousers, exposing himself to the softness of her nightgown.

He caught her again, this time by her long, dark hair, and threw her against the bed. He began wrestling the white silk gown up her thighs, his hands burning and coarse against her delicate flesh. He placed himself triumphantly between her legs and prepared to force his way into her unexplored places.

Sophia screamed with all her might, praying that someone would hear through the thick walls and come to her rescue. Momentarily stunned by the piercing sound, Aldo stopped long enough to strike her savagely across the face with the back of his hand. The heavy gold ring Aldo claimed was given him by Garibaldi for his many years of service raked against her fragile flesh, leaving a scarlet crescent of blood near the corner of her eye.

Dazed by the blow, she gasped and struggled with her legs to free herself from his abhorrent clutches. He drew her head back by a length of her hair and slobbered kisses down the alabaster surface of her neck. The stench of his breath nauseated her as he closed his burning mouth over her attempted screams.

"Now," he breathed vehemently, "Let's see if my angel will bleed for me when I enter her paradise."

His expert technique had been honed along the many years of practice he had during the wars for unification. He spat into his hand and wiped the saliva between her legs, lubricating her for the anticipated assault. The touch of the slimy substance repulsed her and her stomach quaked as she felt her body start to submit to the forced titillation.

"Please.... don't..." she cried breathlessly, as tears mixed with the blood on her cheek. Her body desperately contorted and struggled against the unmovable weight he pressed against her.

He placed himself against the now moistened opening between her legs and started to rub his distended member against her surrendering flesh in an attempt to find access. With his other hand, he continued to pin her arms above her head. His teeth bit into the yielding white flesh of her bared breast, and he tasted her spicy sweat as his tongue danced across the burgundy nipple.

"No please...."

Her voice was trembling as he pressed against the resistance of her untried womanhood. In one last desperate attempt, she spread her legs.

His eyes narrowed and he smiled an ugly grin. Thinking that she was surrendering, he allowed her legs to stretch open and reduced the force with which he held them with his own. The sweat from both their bodies washed over her legs and made them slick enough for her to slide one between his.

Instinctively, she kicked upwards with all her remaining strength as she slipped from beneath his oppressive weight.

Aldo gasped as the lucky blow squarely met the center of his vicious manhood. He rolled back, while her other leg racked across his burns as she accomplished her struggle for freedom.

Sophia leapt from the bed and ran through the forced doors of her chamber. Here she met Aldo's maidservant, Annabella. Sophia's eyes met Annabella's, instantly communicating all she had suffered. Annabella lowered her eyes and clasped her hands behind her back in submission and silence. Seeing no help, Sophia hurled on in her desperate flight of escape.

"Catch her, you fool!" commanded Aldo, rising from the bed.

As he reached for his trousers, he knocked Sophia's scrapbook from its resting place on her nightstand. The heavy book struck his bandaged leg with all its weight. Howling, Aldo tossed the book into the blazing fireplace.

Sophia fled down the staircase, around the great hall, through the glass arbor and out onto the grounds. Though her thoughts were bent on escape, she had presence of mind enough to grab a thick dark cloak from a peg as she passed out the arbor doors, but did not stop to look for shoes.

She threw the cloak about her as the chill of the night cut through her sweat soaked gown. She ran towards the carriage house, no destination in mind but *away*. The cold stones of the path bruised and cut her bare feet, but she paid them no mind.

Carlo, one of the family's most trusted bondsmen was just returning from his nightly survey of the grounds and was replacing a small open carriage when she burst into the carriage house.

"Carlo!" she cried, as she ran towards him. "Sergio is mad! He has said he would kill me! He attacked me in my room! Oh Carlo! Help me!"

Though often dramatic, Donna Sophia was not a lady known to be given to hysterics. The sincerity of her panic and the state of her disarray moved Carlo into instant activity.

In a moment, he hitched up the strongest horse to a small, open buggy and lifted Sophia gently into the ready carriage. Then, he turned only to find Aldo careening towards them.

"Signor Aldo is coming this way," Carlo said as he climbed into the carriage. "I believe I saw a gun in his hand. Get down, Donna." His voice was calm and level as he gently pushed Sophia to the floor of the carriage.

"Oh God," whispered Sophia, as a new and terrible fear drew its inky shroud over her hopes of escape.

"Stay down now. I'm going to make a run for it."

With a flick of the reins and a loud cry from the horse, the carriage burst from its enclosure.

From her hiding place on the floor of the open carriage, Sophia peeked up and saw Aldo's upraised hand as the carriage approached him on the road to the castle gates. She heard the shot and smelled the acrid smoke from the weapon on the sharp wind. Simultaneously, Carlo swerved the carriage towards Aldo.

The bullet whizzed by the carriage harmlessly, as the wheels of the carriage found their target and cut Aldo down and away from their route of escape. As Aldo's body crunched beneath the wheels, the bondsman glanced at Sophia in triumph.

"You killed him," she gasped as she looked back at the crumpled heap on the path behind them.

"If only I had," Carlo said. "Listen, Donna Sophia. Those are not the cries of a dying man, only a drunken fool."

Sophia listened as the curses of Aldo faded into the distance. The sound of her attacker's suffering gave no comfort to her ravaged soul as she placed her hands over her ears in a vain attempt to shut out the disquiet.

When they reached the main gates, Carlo swung out to open them, led the carriage through, and closed them again.

"Where do you wish me to take you, Donna?" he asked. The clouds hung low and heavy, lighting the mountainous terrain with an eerie pale glow. The cold wind smelled of snow at higher elevations.

"Where..." she echoed, rubbing her hands together for warmth. "I can't go to Gemma's – that would be the first place Sergio will look for me. I do not wish to bring down Sergio's wrath on my own sister and her husband. And any hotel would grant my husband entrance at his request." She paused to think. "Do you know where the old hunting cabin is, the one that borders the lands of D'Amici and Calendri?"

"The one where Colonel Haldane is staying," Carlo asked

grimly. All the staff had marked the Donna's response to the dashing Englishman with raised eyebrows.

"Yes, if he is still there," she said. "He'll be able to help me. Take me to the cabin, Carlo. And if Colonel Haldane is no longer there, we can spend the night and then go on to Milan in the morning."

As the manservant turned the carriage to comply, Sophia felt something dry and crusty on her cheek. Touching it, she found dried blood from the wound Aldo had inflicted with his ring. Her examinations caused a trickle to slide down her cheek. She trembled with the memories of what she had too recently endured, and drew away from Carlo.

"He struck you," Carlo said quietly.

"Yes," she sighed, as her attempts to quelch the bleeding failed.

"Then I truly wish I had killed him," came Carlo's reply, heavy with emotions.

"Carlo, you mean no such thing," she said in surprise.

"I do, Donna," he said. "My family has served yours for as long as any of us can remember. I have devoted my life in service to the D'Amicis... But even if that were not so, I would risk all for you, Donna. I know that I should never be more to you than just a faithful retainer, but I am resolved to that. If I can save you from that villain, even if it means delivering you to another man, I shall not fail you."

Sophia sat in stunned silence, her mind reeling. Carlo's declaration robbed her of speech. Shame stung her for asking this honest man, who had pledged his life to hers seeking nothing in return, to take her to Haldane. Her fears about Alcibiades and Colonel Haldane resurfaced, as panic arose anew. Yet she could not find words to tell Carlo to change the direction of the speeding carriage. She had nowhere else to turn.

All the way back to his lodgings, Haldane mentally kicked himself for committing to help Sophia, thereby potentially ruining himself. The cold night air sobered his ambitious perceptions. Surely pursuing this mania that had overcome him would be certain destruction. Although he wasn't exactly an atheist, this whole thing with Sophia and that other vast being that contained them both smacked to him of religious heresy at best, with the options getting worse from there.

*My best stratagem would be a polite note, ensuring her that I am doing all I possibly can for her, and get the hell out of Italy without further distractions from the curiously tempting Donna Sophia.*

He longed to protect her, to take her far away from Aldo's threat, to explore this strange other reality he felt they somehow both belonged to. He wanted to save her, like he wished he had been able to do for that poor Spanish girl, during his last mission. But he had not been able to help the Spanish traditionalists, and he could not now help Sophia.

*Perhaps I could return next spring, give me some time to get Lizzy calmed down from missing her blasted New Year's Masque and allow this whole drug-induced madness of mine to clear. I imagine I can find some valid excuse to come back to the region, come April. I hear Lake Lario is beautiful in the spring. That will also give me sufficient time to design my revenge. And if I still have such mad thoughts then, I'll better be able to assess and deal with them. Best to table this for now. Quite right. Good thinking.*

He arrived at the one room cabin with his usual speed of horse. He walked the animal to cool it, as there were no servants at the cabin. He relished the time it gave him to breathe in the chilling mountain air and the musky scent of the gallant steed he brushed with care, warm in his caped greatcoat.

As he stroked the thick brown coat of the animal, his thoughts turned to the shining image of Sophia's hair. He lingered on the memory of how it fell in curling dark cascades, like a lively ebony fountain surrounding the perfect sculpture of her ivory skin.

The image of Sophia became alive in his mind. In a single instant he watched her move, and speak and laugh. She came towards him out of a sea of darkness, so real to his senses that he believed he could catch her in some impossible embrace. For a fragment of a moment, he sensed the two of them together, contained within that larger entity that was himself, and his heart leapt. And then it was gone.

"Haldane, old boy," he chided himself aloud, shaking his head. "You do have it rather badly indeed, don't you?"

He led the horse into the small shed stall that served as a stable for the cabin. The details of bedding down the horse for the night became his chief concern, and he welcomed the relief they gave from other cares. He provided the gelding with fresh water and barley oats, and made sure the animal had settled before he ventured towards the cabin to serve his own needs.

As he walked towards the cabin, his mind once more became unsettled with images of Sophia. Haldane paused to unlock the cabin door as his imagination stretched out a panoramic presentation that begged his participation. He envisioned an encounter between Aldo and Sophia, one in which his own fears and self-doubts had reign as director.

*If she confronted Aldo*, Haldane wondered silently, *what would be his response?*

His mind reached deep into its own shadow where it kept the

darkest and most sinister secrets. There, it wrought such vile and frightful imagery of Aldo's potential revenge on Sophia that Haldane turned and ran with all his speed back to the dozing animal.

The horse snorted indignantly at being saddled again so soon after settling for the night. Haldane did not have time for a temperamental beast, resenting the resistance the creature displayed. He gathered his saddle and tack with quick precision, all the while feeling clumsy and slow.

He led the animal out of the shed and placed the riding blanket on its twitching back. Haldane pressed his knee deep into the brown steed's ribs as he cinched the saddle straps against its breath filled sides. The horse snorted and released the air it was holding in an attempt at preventing being mounted.

"Sorry, friend," he said to the horse as he placed one foot in the stirrup and swung into the saddle. "Duty calls."

As he hurried the horse down the trail from the cabin, Haldane wondered where the extent of that duty might end tonight. He rode on, driving the horse to take the dark mountain path faster than was prudent. He contemplated turning off to try and save time by cutting across rough land, but his recent unfortunate experience with the thrown horseshoe suggested to his better judgment that he should stay on the main road to Villa D'Amici.

He cursed himself several times during the thunderous ride for believing in his own imagined disaster. Just as often, he considered turning back to the cabin and allowing events to take place as they would. He had promised himself that he would write in his journal this evening, exploring his strange new perceptions and feelings. The neglected promise now joined with his skepticism. But each time the doubts of his mission arose, they were overshadowed by the image of a cowering Sophia, hardening his resolve and fixing it on his goal.

Sophia watched the shadowy figure of a man on horseback barreling towards them. At first sight of the rider she had cried out in alarm, fearing that somehow Aldo had sent someone to intercept them. Sophia wrapped herself tightly in the dark cloak and clutched tightly to Carlo's strong left arm as he continued to drive the carriage.

She knew that on this next hill, the man on the horse would encounter them. Carlo whispered to get down low in the carriage. She ducked down into the foot of the buggy, trying to make herself as small as possible. Her mouth was dry, her hands clammy and cold. As the sound of the rider slowed in approach, Sophia hid her face in the folds of the hood and prayed with all her might for deliverance.

# Chapter Fifteen

"Ho! Carlo!" The clear and familiar baritone of Colonel Haldane called out of the darkness. "Where is La Donna Sophia?"

"Here! I am here," came the answer from the shrouded figure on the floor of the carriage.

Sophia pulled back the hood of the cape to reveal her features glowing in the pale-clouded moonlight. She reached out to Haldane from the carriage, as he lifted her with one hand into the cradling comfort of his arms. She nestled across his lap and drew her cape around her torn and bloodstained gown. The icy breeze whipped at her dark hair and cloak.

"Jordan, oh Jordan," sobbed Sophia. This was all she could manage as the panic of the night caught up with her. Her head swam, her ears roared and her vision narrowed to a small tunnel. She clutched at him before slipping into blackness, falling limp in his arms.

"What happened?" Haldane called to Carlo as he shifted Sophia's crumpled body in his arms. He saw the blood lacing the edges of the torn white fabric of her gown. He turned her small face in his hands and located the source of the crimson stains.

His gut grew tight. With a tone in that would have frozen Lucifer on his throne, Haldane called again to Carlo.

"What has happened to your lady? Speak man." But Haldane feared he already knew the answer.

"Signor Aldo, sir," came Carlo's steady voice across the road from the carriage. "He attacked Mia Donna in her chamber and tried to shoot us when we fled in this carriage. Please, Colonel Haldane, she asked me to deliver her into your care. And I have done as she asked. I shall go on and lead a false trail towards Milan. If Signor Aldo has recovered, he may follow after."

"Recovered? From what?"

"From my running the Signor over with this fine little buggy," said Carlo.

The two men exchanged appreciative glances regarding one another's character. There existed between them a bond of fellowship and service to the delicate woman Haldane held in his arms.

"Here's money for you, friend," Haldane said as he reached into his pocket and produced several bills, which he pressed into Carlo's hands. "There's a man in Milan, his name is Master Benvolio Armento. You will find him on the street of goldsmiths. Tell him you are my friend, and he will help get you out of the country."

Carlo looked at the cash and then to the limp childlike form in Haldane's arms. With one last rallying of heroics, he demanded, "You will take good care of her and see she comes to no harm?"

"As you yourself have," vowed Haldane earnestly, as Carlo took the cash. Haldane wrapped his arm around Sophia, drawing her closer to his chest. He pulled the cloak closer about her as freezing rain and light snow dry began to fall, driven by the wind in tiny hard pellets. Her soft face rested against him, her mouth was slightly open and her very breathing seemed delicate and fragile.

"I trust you to your word, as Donna Sophia does," said Carlo as he twitched the reins.

Haldane's horse made an unexpected start as the carriage drove past, and he had to shift Sophia's slight weight as he sought to control the startled animal. He watched the carriage take off down the road in the long shadows of night. Then he looked down again at the unconscious face of the woman in his arms. She seemed so peaceful in the grave surroundings, overcome by the horror of her ordeal. He drew her close to him and started the horse towards the cabin.

"Oh bloody hell," he murmured. "What have I gotten myself into now?"

As he looked to guiding the horse, he thought of the final words Carlo had spoken to him. Was it trust that had driven Sophia to him, or desperate need of dire circumstance? He wondered as he rode through the night what he would do with her in the days to come. His thoughts turned to England, and to his neglected family, his responsibilities and duties. He knew he must return home soon, preferably while he still had a home to return to. His passage back home sailed in two days… And he could not take Sophia home with him. The burden of practicalities weighed heavily upon him.

"Jordan...." The soft voice of Sophia cut through his disturbed thoughts.

"Yes?" he replied, with a glance down at her.

She had not stirred when she had spoken his name. When she did not speak again he slowed the horse and focused his attention once more on her face. She was obviously still unconscious.

*What is she doing to me? I should have left days ago. Why have I allowed myself to get caught up in her misfortune, when I have my own problems? All because of some crazed hallucination? Yet it was real – as real as now... only more so.*

He looked down at her profile; ivory nestled against the blackness of his breast. *How can I leave her to Aldo's tender mercies? I can't. God help me, even if it destroys me, I can't simply abandon her. She is my other self.*

The snow picked up, falling harder and thicker, making the night sky unusually light. The wind died down as the snow fell faster. Large white flakes dotted the thick black wool of his greatcoat. Haldane urged the gelding to hasten its pace back up the narrow mountain road. When they arrived at the cabin, he carefully dismounted with the rag doll form of Sophia in his arms.

Remembering that he had forgotten to lock the cabin door, he cautiously pushed open the door with his foot and searched the one-room cabin for signs of intruders. Seeing none, he placed Sophia in the only bed the cabin offered. He set pillows under her head and made sure that she was covered and warm. He then returned to the horse and repeated the cooling and bedding procedures in the small shed.

His tasks complete, he entered the cabin and hurried to Sophia's side. Her breathing was steady and even, though her hands were in tight fists near her bruised and bloodied face. With a wet cloth, he washed as much blood from her face as he dared without disturbing her, trying to ascertain the extent of her injuries. After satisfying himself that the wound was superficial, he finally removed his greatcoat, and saw to his own physical needs.

"Rest now, my dear," he said as he lightly stroked her ebony hair, now wild and tangled. He pulled a chair next to the bed and watched over her sleep, a loaded black iron service revolver in hand.

The snowy dawn of the final day of 1872 found Haldane out scouting the perimeter of the cabin. Several inches of snow had fallen overnight, and loose flakes periodically blew down from the tall pines surrounding the hunting lodge. The air smelled fresh and crisp. Heavy clouds foretold more snowfall at the higher elevations.

From its lofty perch on the side of a mountain, he could observe the coming of any intruder in time to prepare for necessary action. The fresh snow revealed no human tracks except his. Since there had been no sign of Aldo, Haldane hazarded a guess that either Carlo had been successful in leading him away, or had so injured Aldo in his flight with Sophia that Aldo was unable to follow.

After taking the time to fully satisfy his military conscience that no one was on the road from the villa, nor hiding in the woods beyond the cabin, he hurried back and found Sophia still sleeping where he had left her.

"Good. Take the medicine of sleep, my dearest Sophia," said Haldane as he pulled the faded comforter over her shoulder, "and forget."

He looked at her her torn cheek. Anger brought the familiar tension to Haldane's jaw, it ached and he ran his hand over its surface. The stubble on his face and down his neck felt sweaty and rough. The high collar of his tunic had rubbed against it during the night making his neck chafed and raw. He went to the little iron stove and added several sticks of wood to its fire, and put a kettle of water on to boil.

When the water in the kettle came to a boil, he took it into the curtained area in the corner and mixed it with cooler water in the porcelain basin. He stripped to the waist and bathed his upper torso, leaving the curtain partially open so that he might keep an eye on her rest.

Sophia's eyes slowly fluttered open at the soft splashing of water in the basin. She remained motionless in the unfamiliar surroundings, unsure of where, or even who, she was. Apprehension filled her as she realized she was not alone. She froze and focused her eyes, trying to ascertain her situation. The smell of wood smoke and tea assailed her nostrils. Her eyes were drawn to the curtained area and she watched the figure across the room with silent awe.

Slowly she recognized from the glimpses between that Haldane was the moving figure who washed at the meager facilities behind the curtains, and the knowledge gave her comfort. She stretched her neck to follow his motions and found her muscles sore and bruised. She relaxed against the pain and continued to silently observe.

His lean upper torso was powerfully built and the lines of his body were clean and even in the morning light. She watched through the sliver of the curtains as Haldane poured hot water into a shaving cup and worked up a lather with the brush. As he applied the lather to his face, she admired the sinewy muscles of his arms and shoulders.

*How like Alcibiades he is!* she thought with a warm quiver running through her. *So sure of himself, so strong...*

Haldane's strength seemed far removed from that of Carlo's, whose body was knotted with hard muscles, overdeveloped in the chest and arms from lifelong service to the forge and winepress. She next considered how different this handsome English gentleman was from the insidious, pudgy Aldo.

Thoughts of Aldo flooded in, along with the memories of the terrifying attack and her narrow escape of the night before. As the events invaded her mind, she gave a start and sat up in the bed.

Haldane heard her gasp, quickly parting the curtains and moving towards her.

"How are you, Donna Sophia? Are you in pain? Is there anything you need?" he solicited, as he wiped the remaining lather from his face with a towel.

"N-no, I'm all right," she whispered with trembling breath, avoiding looking at his bare torso directly. "I've just realized what's happened..."

"I'm so sorry, Sophia. I should have never told you of my suspicions –" Haldane began.

"No, I am glad you told me..." she hastened to say. "I don't think it would have made any difference if you had kept silent." She sighed heavily. "I think Sergio was intent on having his way regardless of anything I may have said."

She met his eyes and then, suddenly self-conscious, she glanced down at the open front of her gown. With honest modesty, she drew the remnants of the torn white fabric over her exposed breastbone, then gazed up at him in wordless appeal.

He rushed to her side still shirtless, commencing the now longed for tightening inside Sophia. She attempted to raise her eyes from the patch of dark curly hair that traced the outlines of his chest. Instead, she found herself deliberately following its narrowing lines downward to the point where it disappeared into his military trousers. She shook slightly as she imagined where the dark hair of his chest must reach its hidden conclusion. Suddenly horrified that she should feel aroused so soon after Aldo's attack, yet resistance was the last thing on her mind.

"Jordan..." she whispered softly and reached out her arms to him as he rushed to fill them.

She felt her nipples harden inside the tatters of her nightgown as she impacted on his chest. Though the sensations brought back more memories of Aldo's attack, she held Haldane even closer, hiding her face in his neck, breathing in his musky scent. Haldane closed his eyes as he held Sophia and sat on the bed.

"Oh Jordan! I was so weak, so helpless! He tried to force me. Force me against my will!" Her voice was at once filled with a combination of indignation, self-loathing, fear and hatred. "I should have listened to you. You were right, so very right," she continued, her small form trembling in the warm comfort of his arms. "Don't leave me! Dear God, Jordan, never leave me again."

His eyes stung and a hard lump filled his throat as he kissed the top of her head.

"I'm here, and I'm never going to let him harm you again." Her urgency solicited his unconsidered but sincere promises to Sophia. "I shall do anything I must to insure your safety, even if it means my own destruction."

The compact had been made and Haldane felt complete in its honest offering. She pushed off from his chest at these words and bore into his eyes. Her breathing was fast and uneven as she fought back her own emotions to ponder his words. Her wide eyes quickly traveled from one to the other of his.

"I'll not allow you to be harmed any further by my own stupidity," she began as she attempted to wipe the tears from her eyes.

"Sophia, I am wise enough to encounter Aldo without tipping my hand." Haldane reached to embrace her again, but her self-contempt forced her to withdraw from his offered solace.

"Don't you understand?" she said as tears started to well up again, "I told him everything I knew, everything you told me. God, I'm such a fool! Such a stupid, stupid fool!" She beat upon her head with her small fists. "He knows all we suspect of him. I have undone you and myself with my foolish pride." She flung herself lengthwise across the bed and sobbed more heartily than before.

"Sophia," Haldane's voice was soft as he gently stroked her hair. "You have set things into motion sooner than anticipated, that's all. When I told you what I had discovered about the cigars, I thought I did so for your protection. It was wrong for me to fill your mind with accusations and fears. I had hoped to warn you to be careful. You haven't ruined anything. I am the one to blame, not you."

He reached for her arm again, this time she allowed his help and rose to sit.

She sniffled softly, and he wiped tears from her uninjured cheek. His fingers softly reached around the side of her face as she allowed his gentle touch to draw her closer. Their eyes fixed deep on one another. They sat transfixed, staring into one anther's eyes for several moments before closing them simultaneously as their lips met in a trembling and delicate kiss.

The twisting sensations were replaced with a sudden raging fire in Sophia's bosom. Surprised at the rush of her own passion, she drew back from the heat and once again gathered the dilapidated gown over her bosom.

"I'm a frightful sight," she half-laughed, half-sobbed. "I see you have a few amenities," she said as she indicated the place where she had observed Haldane shaving. "Might I be so bold as to share them?"

"Certainly," said Haldane as he rose. He wiped the final remains of the lather from behind his ear, hiding the wounded look in his eyes. "I – had finished with shaving when you awoke. Give me a moment to warm some more water and lay out some clean clothing for you.... I only have a shirt and some trousers." He stopped and surveyed her small size and feminine curves. "I fear they will fit you rather poorly. I shall have to go to Milan and obtain clothing for you before we can - "

"No!" Sophia shrieked and threw her arms around his waist, "*Please* do not leave me! Sergio will come and kill me, or worse, he will find you in Milano and kill you. No, I will not allow it! I simply will not!"

The panic in her voice was matched only by the strength with which she clung to him. He turned within her arms and allowed her to pull him down into the bed with her once more.

"Sophia," he said gently, both terrified and thrilled that she wished him to stay. "I have no fear that Aldo will be able to harm me. I can handle myself. As for you, I believe you will be safe here at the cabin until I return."

He paused and placed a long finger softly on her lips to still her protests. "Carlo told me last night when we met on the road that he had run Aldo down with the carriage during your flight. If Sergio is in Milan, he is probably in no condition to be much of a threat. Besides, Carlo took the carriage on into Milan to lead a false trail away from the cabin."

""Oh, please, Jordan, stay here," Sophia cried. "It's too dangerous. Sergio has allies everywhere."

"Look, we're accomplishing nothing, carrying on like this," he said. "I should at least go scout around the grounds again. If I see any sign of trespassers I will immediately return and stay here to protect you. In the meantime, I want you to wash and dress. You will feel better once you have done. We'll then have a bit to eat and discuss our next course of action. Fair?"

"Fair," she finally agreed as she allowed him to rise and prepare water for her bath.

He laid out soap, towels, and a clean change of his own clothing for her to use as best she might. He dressed in the clothes he had been wearing the previous evening, giving her the shirt and trousers he was planning to change into after his own bath.

She watched him, amazed that a gentleman such as he could manage so well without servants. She recognized that she herself was helplessly lost without them. Yet, Haldane seemed to her to be totally self-sufficient and self-sustaining. Exactly as she imagined her Alcibiades to be.

As Haldane closed the cabin door behind him, Sophia rose from the bed and ventured to the corner where the pitcher and washbasin had been readied. She took up Haldane's shaving mirror and examined the scarlet crescent on her cheek near her left eye.

She winced painfully as she touched the surrounding bruise, which smeared purple and brown under her eye. *He has marked me for life, the beast.* As she laid the objectionable reflection face down on the counter, she took up the pitcher and leaned over the basin to wash the dried blood from her face and hair.

She allowed her mind to become blankly focused on cleaning herself up. She did not toy with the events of the preceding evening. They were too new, too painful and too hot to touch.

Instead, she escaped in a childish fantasy that she was a princess, preparing for some longed-for ball or night at the opera. There would be no turmoil outside her door to frighten or alarm her, no vengeful man bent on destroying her and her family. There would be only those she cherished and loved most dear to comfort and embrace her with affection. She would be safe and at home in the elegance of family and tradition. She would find strong and loving arms to enfold her and carry her off to exciting, wonderful realms.

As she finished her toilet, she reached for the beautiful silken gown, only to find it had been transformed into a man's attire. As she gathered it up, so too came all the horrible memories of last night. Vulnerable to their pressing reality, she could not stop the trickle of tears.

# Chapter Sixteen

## 31 December, 1872   Calendri Cabin   11:40 a.m.

Haldane circled the cabin twice, not so much making sure there were no travelers, as he had already reconnoitered the area less than an hour before. He left the cabin more to allow Sophia some private time to collect herself. The snow-covered road itself seemed clear of all traffic, but he still took time now to check the trails leading to higher vantage points in the mountains.

The icy wind whipped against his freshly shaven face and played havoc with his hair. He brushed the unruly locks from his eyes as he traveled back to the cabin. Stopping briefly at the stable shed, he checked on the horse and the state in which he had hastily placed his tack the night before. As he hung it in its proper place, his thoughts went to Milan and what he might find. He must go into the city and find out word of Aldo. He must also obtain suitable traveling attire for Sophia, before he could take her anywhere. He grimaced most at this task, knowing his distaste for accompanying his wife shopping.

Images of Elizabeth immediately filled his mind. *She must have reached an almost intolerable state by now*, he thought as he remembered his last communication with her. *Tonight is Lord Northampton's Ball. Lizzy will never forgive me for missing it again.*

"Enough of that, old boy," he mused out loud to himself.

His thoughts returned to Sophia and what to do with her – a much more pleasant conundrum than placating an outraged wife.

Thankfully, his plague of visions seemed to have abated in the light of day, allowing him to continue the deceit that they were just a wild fantasy, as long as he did not probe too deeply. He turned willingly back towards the cabin. When he reached the door he identified himself and entered.

Sophia stood in his shirt and trousers, a pitiful sight. The long sleeves of the fine cotton shirt were rolled back to where his elbows would have been exposed, yet still hung too long over her tiny fingers. She had tucked the tail of the shirt into the trousers that ballooned around her, masking her shapely legs with bulky dark wool. The uniform pants fairly swallowed her narrow waist. Unable to use the closures, she had taken a length of curtain cord from the window to use as a belt. The tops of the trousers flopped over the makeshift belt as she relinquished her attempts to lift them.

Haldane could not help but grin at her. She returned it with an embarrassed smile of her own.

"I must speak to your tailor," he chuckled, "I've wanted an outfit exactly like that one for some time."

They exchanged good-natured laughter as he took her hand to assist her walking in the cumbersome pants, whose rolled-up legs extended some length beyond her own feet.

He sat her down at a small wooden table near the iron stove and prepared a simple breakfast of eggs, bacon and toast on the cast iron stove. Again, she marveled at his self-reliance.

For several minutes, they ate in a tense silence, neither one wanting to speak of the circumstances that brought them together and shatter their semblance of a peaceful morning. As they finished eating, Haldane broached the subject of travel.

"I must go to Milan," he insisted once again, after taking the last bite of his meal.

"Take me with you," she parried, as she reached for the last piece of toast and buttered it.

"Dressed like that? Not a chance. You would attract far too much attention. Taking you into town is out of the question," he tried not to sound harsh. He sat quietly contemplating the serious consequences of what he was prepared to offer her as a consolation for several moments before speaking.

"Sophia," he began evenly, "have you ever fired a weapon?"

She stopped chewing, her eyes wide, as she solemnly and slowly shook her head. Haldane drew the small derringer from its secret place in his tunic.

Sophia swallowed loudly before saying, "No," when she saw the weapon in his hand. "I want no part of that – that thing."

"That thing," Haldane said, "is the only thing that can truly protect you and comfort you while I am gone to Milan to buy you clothes and gather information." The tone of his voice and the flash of tension in his jaw told Sophia she had lost this battle of will.

"Very well," she said, straightening in her chair. "Do you have enough ammunition to teach me how to fire it and still leave me enough to defend myself when you abandon me?"

She fixed him with an intensity in her voice that matched his own. He watched as the muscles of Sophia's jaw tighten in mimicry of his own habits, and smiled.

"It's not for holding off regiments, you know," he quipped. She missed the intended humor of his comment, and he cleared his throat before venturing to speak again. "Yes, there is plenty of ammunition."

He took her outside, she completely enveloped in his greatcoat, and he braving the cold in just his uniform. He explained the workings of the weapon and impressed upon her that the derringer had a very limited range of accuracy and the kick of the firing must be prepared for in the aiming. Her attention was fully fixed on every word, every detail of his explanation.

After firing two shots into a wooden post, he gave the tiny pistol over into her hands to do the same. She repeated his own motions of loading and preparing to aim with such exacting detail, her shots hit almost directly on his own.

"There now, you're a sharpshooter already," he said with growing pride.

Once back inside, he handed her a full box of ammunition for the derringer and started to take his leave, knowing that if anyone were foolish enough to enter the cabin unannounced it would be their last such action. Sophia remained cold and distant as he made his farewells. The details settled upon, Haldane took to horse and rode towards Milan, relieved to escape the paradoxical tension in which La Donna Sophia engulfed him.

It was late afternoon when Haldane finally arrived in the ancient city of Milan. He had departed much later than he wished, but it couldn't be helped. He sought out word concerning Aldo. He discovered from his own sources that Aldo had indeed come to Milan, early this morning. But first, Aldo had stopped his carriage at his offices and ordered his maidservant, Annabella, to attend to some pressing legal business. Aldo had then gone to the hospital where a team of surgeons was now trying to save his leg.

The secretary in Aldo's office informed Haldane that some mad servant in the D'Amici household had attacked Donna Sophia. The eager young man told him that Signor Aldo interrupted the servant's attack on his beloved bride, and had been cut down by the criminal's escape in a carriage. The servant-turned-kidnapper had taken Sophia with him at gunpoint as he fled. Haldane expressed the expected degree of horror at the story, shaking his head and clucking at the outrage.

The servant, Carlo was sought now for rape, kidnapping and attempted murder, so the gossip went. No one knew where the monster had taken La Donna Sophia. Aldo had so feared for her life, that he stopped at his own offices on the way to the hospital to do all in his power to insure her safe return to him and punishment for the criminal.

Though the fantastic story imparted to him slightly resembled the truth, Haldane gained the information he needed.

Knowledge of Aldo's whereabouts eased Haldane's apprehensions. He went to the hospital where Aldo had been taken, and checked on his condition. Although still unconscious, Aldo had survived the surgery, but lost his leg. He wasn't going to be concerned with anyone else for at least a few days – sufficient time to get Sophia securely taken care of and himself away to England.

Haldane's next chief concern was to discover any information concerning Carlo, and to protect him from wrongful prosecution, if possible. Haldane had no doubt that the business Aldo had ordered Annabella to attend to was immediately related to capturing and eliminating Carlo and Sophia.

*How absurdly easy it is for men like Aldo, self-proclaimed hero of the United Kingdom of Italy, to hang an honest and true man in place of punishment for his own crimes,* thought Haldane as his emotions plunged into the shadow of his soul. He rode on in his state of inner gloom, seeking assistance from his own dark past.

The place he visited was not some dingy and avoided corner of the city, but rather the finest and most anciently respected craftsmen's' square in old Mediolamum. He asked after Master Benvolio Armento, a goldsmith of highest quality that Haldane had helped out some years ago and who still owed Haldane a favor or two. He had instructed Carlo on the road to seek out Armento, knowing the goldsmith's underground affiliates would be able to safely whisk Carlo out of Italy.

Armento's assistants told Haldane that Carlo had indeed come there this morning, but the Master was away on family business, forcing Carlo to look to other help. With Armento's absence, Carlo had also been left to his own resources, without the promised aid.

Haldane had no choice but to resort to less savory means to gain information of Carlo's whereabouts. He knew from working with Carlo in the rescue of the glass arbor that the D'Amici retainer was a clever and resourceful fellow, but Haldane still worried about the extent of Aldo's reach exceeding Carlo's clever resources.

At a certain tavern he knew of, Haldane let it be known, through a somewhat clandestine network of rough characters, that a reward would be paid for any information concerning the scion of the D'Amici house known as Carlo. Haldane ordered a pint of ale and settled into a booth in the back to wait.

As he waited, Haldane nursed his drink, the alcohol burning in his knotted stomach. As time ticked by, the ale and a small band of musicians who played folk songs succeeded in untying that knot. He allowed himself to drift away into the lively yet simple music, rather than invoke thoughts of the yawning chaos that awaited him as soon as he left the tavern. He was grateful for the respite, however brief, while he waited to know the faithful servant's fate.

Haldane had been cooling his heel for a couple of hours, enjoying the rustic entertainment, eying all new arrivals. As he returned from the necessary room, a tall, bearded man in non-descript clothes accosted him in the narrow wood paneled hallway.

"Excuse, sir, would your name happen to be Haldane?" the man asked in French-accented Italian.

Haldane regarded the man warily, then glanced around the tavern to ascertain their privacy. "Do you have some business with me, sir?" he asked, neither confirming nor denying his identity.

"That rather depends on you," the Frenchman countered, and moved closer, lowering his voice. "I understand you are a business associate of Sergio Aldo's. Is that true?"

Haldane bristled at the mention of the name.

"Who are you?" he demanded. "What do you want from me?"

"I must speak with you about your business with the D'Amici's and Calendri's," the stranger replied.

Haldane's eyes narrowed in the dimly lit hall, halfway between the main room of the tavern and the men's water closet, strategically assessing the tight quarters.

"Identify yourself."

The bearded man stared into Haldane's eyes, scanning his face intently for longer than Haldane was comfortable with.

"My name's Delacroix. I tried to reach you once before," he began. Delacroix glanced around uncomfortably. "I must speak with you on a matter of some urgency… But this is not the place to do it. Will you come with me to my room?"

Haldane emitted a dry humorless laugh, and crossed his arms, readying himself for action.

"And why should I be interested in doing a thing like that?" he queried. "Why should I trust you, some bloke I've never seen before, who comes up to me unintroduced in some random tavern?"

Delacroix gave Haldane another measuring gaze before responding.

"Because your life might depend on it," he replied.

As Haldane opened his mouth to respond, the barkeeper approached.

"Sir, I hate to be interrupting, but you said you wanted to be notified immediately if…" the barkeep trailed off suggestively.

"Yes, immediately. I'll be right with you," Haldane called to the barkeep. He turned back to Delacroix. "Look, friend, I don't know who you are or what you want with me, but I find it difficult to believe you have my best interests at heart. For all I know, you're some sort of cutthroat or blackmailer or other scourge. Another day, I might have had time enough to be curious about whatever game you are playing and play along. But today, I simply haven't the leisure."

He walked away from the flabbergasted Frenchman and approached the street urchin indicated by the barkeeper.

His news of Carlo in hand, he left the tavern and assailed the dressmaker Sophia had recommended just before closing. Within twenty minutes, he had procured a day dress and all the requisite unmentionables. He even enticed a shop girl to sell him her shoes to save the time of visiting a cobbler, weaving a romantic story of a surprise gift to his wife back home.

Once again, the thought of sending a wire to his wife struck him. He didn't see how he could leave Sophia in time to catch the train to Naples before his ship sailed tomorrow afternoon unless he left early in the morning. He thought he should telegram Elizabeth to let her know that his return was going to be even further delayed. But if he missed this ship, he might not be able to book passage again until next week sometime. The thought of her response re-energized the knot in his stomach.

He looked about the dusky, windswept street lined with shops closed for the New Year. Small piles of dirty snow lined both sides of the muddy street and frost crept up the glass windowpanes of the storefronts. The public wire offices would be closed at this time of evening and Haldane had no wish to enter the British Embassy and use their wire service.

*I shall just have to brass it out once I get home… whenever that should be,* he decided as he reached his horse. He fumbled with the myriad packages filled with food and Sophia's gear attaching them to his saddle, the cold breeze making his task all the more difficult.

Haldane finally secured the packages to the saddle of his horse and mounted the animal. He started back to the hunting cabin, where he imagined Sophia sat frantically counting the minutes until his return. In spite of himself, a soft smile curled his mustache at the thought of her waiting for him. He considered hiring a carriage, knowing he would eventually need one to transport Sophia. He finally ruled against it, deciding that he did not yet know where he was going to take her.

Gemma and Roberto lived in Milan, but their home would offer too high a profile for Sophia to stay with them. He could put Sophia on a train and send her to Florence where he had superior resources, unknown to Aldo and his company of cutthroats. He knew his friends in Florence would be honored to receive her and protect her until Haldane could sort out the details.

The idea of Sophia traveling alone struck Haldane as absurd. She had never been alone, without family and a small army of servants to rely upon, in all her pampered life. Sophia was a grand lady in the tradition of the old school. He simply could not imagine her being able to deal with the effort involved.

He pictured her confused and frightened in a sea of bustling strangers as she attempted to change trains without proper assistance. Her stubborn pride, coupled with her present state of suspicion, would enforce upon her trust a damaging trepidation. In such a state, Sophia would likely mistrust people who could help her and fall into the hands of those sent to destroy her.

Haldane relented, that for the present at least, the safety of La Donna Sophia was his responsibility alone. With Aldo at least temporarily out of commission, it seemed the bulwark fortress of Villa D'Amici was her best sanctuary – *if* he could dislodge the rest of Aldo's men from the fine estate… single-handedly. His thoughts became once again obsessed with wondering how to best provide for Sophia's future security, not allowing himself to dwell on the prospect of a long evening ahead alone with her, or the haunting mystery that drew him on.

As he rode the horse out of Milan with its brightly colored array of packages bouncing and tousling against the saddle behind him, he failed to notice the shadowy pair who followed with ominous intent.

# Chapter Seventeen

For the first three hours after Haldane left, Sophia sat quietly with the derringer tightly clasped in her hand. The small weapon and her fear of the necessity of it were her constant companions, until boredom overcame her anxiety.

She had wearied of holding the small pistol and had eventually stuck it into the cord she wore around her waist. For the last few hours, she amused herself by exploring the personal belongings of Lieutenant Colonel Christopher Jordan Haldane.

Her first discovery was Haldane's journal, which she had been drawn to due to its overstuffed resemblance to her own scrapbook. When she opened it and saw that the large, black book contained a child's handwriting in a foreign tongue, which gradually reduced in size and clarity to the hand of a master calligrapher, she shut it, carefully placing it back where she had discovered it.

"This is what Jordan spoke of at Christmas when I gave Eduardo the scrapbook," Sophia said aloud, wondering if some day Eduardo's book would be as full of exciting adventures as Haldane's own must be.

Sophia then turned her attentions to the dime novels that lay next to the journal. She thumbed through the pages, scrutinizing the words of a language she did not well understand. She stopped at the engraved illustration of a hero on horseback, valiantly engaged in shooting it out with some desperadoes, as a beautiful dark haired damsel looked on in distress.

Sophia fantasized that the pages of the novels contained her own story of anguish at the hands of a base and evil villain, and her rescue in the arms of a handsome and noble deliverer, embodied by Lieutenant Colonel Christopher Jordan Haldane. Sophia looked at Haldane's thick black journal again, musing that, if not for the lack of illustrations, would Haldane's writing prove just as action-filled as the novels she closed and placed on top of it.

The threatened violence of the current adventure made her touch the derringer for reassurance. She decided to focus instead on more mundane arts, and busied herself with washing out a few of Haldane's soiled shirts and linens, hanging them to dry near the cast-iron stove. She enjoyed the novelty of the unaccustomed work.

As she tidied up after her laundering, she dropped a towel she was using. Bending down to pick it up, she discovered a large pistol strapped under the washbasin table. The gun was easily four times the size of the derringer tucked in the cord about her waist. Cautiously, she backed away from the sight of it, on hands and knees.

Another pistol revealed itself when she drew back the curtain to look out at the setting sun through the frosted window at the front of the cabin. This weapon was smaller than the one under the washbasin, but still sizable. It swung on a hook behind the curtain, cold metal brushing her face when she looked out the window. The swinging barrel of destruction so near frightened and disturbed her. She stumbled back from the window.

When she happened upon a long thin stiletto, tucked neatly in the seam of the stuffed leather divan, she realized that Colonel Haldane was an arsenal of prepared readiness in any surroundings. The thoughts of Haldane being attacked in route to or from Milan returned with a new heaviness, as she once again looked at the clock. It told her the time was now after nine o'clock.

*It's been over six hours now since he left*, Sophia noted as she looked at his small travel clock for what seemed the thousandth time. *How long does it take to ask a few questions and buy a frock?* She knew the ride to Milan was around an hour and a half away at full gallop, but she was still anxious for his swift return.

"Hurry home safe, my Jordan… my Alcibiades," Sophia whispered as she sat down and listened for his approach.

Haldane slowed his horse and prepared to dismount while the steed still ran at a steady gallop. The full moon shone intermittently through patches in the clouds, making the ground a moving mosaic of depths. He knew he would have to time his leap to the speed of the horse and his legs' own ability to match it instantly, while not slipping in the ice and snow.

*Lovely opportunity to break a leg,* he noted. But he pushed his pessimism aside. He squeezed his eyes shut for a moment, steeling himself for the jump, will overriding fear. He took a deep breath, consciously relaxing the tight-gripped muscles in his stomach and chest. Opening his eyes, he began looking for a level spot to land.

He had noticed the pair of desperate characters following him about a kilometer outside of the city. He tested the theory that they were indeed in pursuit of him by turning a few times, traversing some bridges and connecting roads that lay slightly out of a direct path of return to the cabin. The men followed him at every change in course, except for the last. Haldane deliberately gave his shadows the quicker, lower road through the windy, pine-filled canyon, while he, in turn, took the winding upper road, giving them the opportunity to ride ahead.

He timed his leap from the running horse with expert rhythm. His feet ran at the exact speed of the horse as he stepped out of the stirrup and onto the road. He slowed his gait, boots crunching on crusty snow and ice. He allowed the horse to run on ahead, knowing that at this close proximity the animal would go directly to the stable it knew to exist at the nearby hunting lodge.

He slipped easily into the tree line with feline grace, and drew a long black military stiletto from a secret scabbard in his riding boot. The coal black instrument of death gave no hint of its presence in the patchy moonlight.

Silently cutting through the woods, Haldane approached the place he reckoned most likely for an ambush, faster than his abandoned horse could traverse the road. He waited for his horse on the road to draw nigh. When the sound of the galloping steed came closer, one of the cutthroats lifted his head from their place of concealment. Haldane smiled at the predictability of his opponents and circled around their position without a sound. He took up guard at their rear, waiting with his own assailants for the final approach of his horse. When the riderless animal rounded the bend and trotted past the hopeful attackers, they stood up in wonder and looked blankly at one another.

Haldane was suddenly in their midst, dropping one man into with a swift chopping blow to his neck.

As the other tried to lift his ancient two-barreled blunderbuss and fire, Haldane's left leg gracefully pirouetted and landed a kick into the second adversary's chest. The thunderously loud blunderbuss discharged its first load harmlessly as Haldane completed his ballet-like move, driving the cold ebony stiletto deep into the criminal's heart at its finale.

While retrieving his blade, Haldane was struck from behind and sent sprawling to the ground. The other cutthroat had recovered and hit Haldane with a tree limb.

Haldane quickly turned his fall into a somersault and landed facing his opponent in a crouched position, the stiletto poised for attack. In the silvery moonlight, as his adversary dropped the makeshift club and retrieved the discarded blunderbuss of his late companion. The man now leveled the huge old gun at Haldane's chest at point blank range. Haldane stared up its long wide barrel, a cold sweat breaking out on his forehead and palms.

"Say arriva derchi, comrade," the man said, his oily grin flashing in the moonlight. He readied the weapon and a shot rang out in the chilling air.

Haldane flinched as he realized that the shot had not hit him, though he seemed doomed that it should.

The murderer's expression turned from one of filthy enjoyment to one of deep concern and surprise. As the astonished man fell face forward, the blunderbuss he was holding discharged its final deadly load of lead shot and brimstone flame into the earth between them.

Still crouched, Haldane looked in disbelief at the dead man before him, then raised his eyes to behold the diminutive figure of Sophia, who stood several yards away holding a large smoking pistol in her steady white hands, her dark curls wafting in the cold breeze.

## 31 December, 1872   Calendri Cabin   10:05 p.m.

Sophia lowered the smoking pistol, releasing the spring and carefully returning the hammer to its safe position to prevent accidental discharge, as Haldane had instructed her. She then ran to the clearing as quickly as the thorns and roots of the woods would allow her delicate feet to travel.

When she reached Haldane's side, he was turning over the man she had shot to confirm he was dead, and to examine the contents of his pockets. The face of the dead man startled her and she spoke aloud with a mixture of fear and disappointment.

"I thought he was Sergio," she said.

Haldane recognized the short fat man as one he had purchased a drink for at the tavern where he obtained news of Carlo and food for Sophia and himself.

"Easy enough to mistake the servant for his master these days," Haldane said as he started to remove items from his assailant's coat pockets. "I hear that even our friend Carlo has taken to dressing like a gentleman."

At the mention of her trusted servant and friend's name, Sophia became excited.

"Carlo," she said, "you heard news of Carlo? Is he safe, is he here?" She quickly scanned the trees for sign of the servant.

"He is fine, if price is proof," Haldane said as he stood with the collection of personal effects he had taken from the still figure on the ground. "I received some information, and proof of passage, from reasonably reliable sources, who told me Carlo purchased a gentlemen's wardrobe and took a train into Rome. I gave Carlo more than enough money to execute such a plan last night." He paused, seeing her continued expression of concern. "Oh, he's a bright fellow, Sophia," Haldane assured her, "I am sure he will fare quite brilliantly. I'm afraid I can't say the same for these poor fellows." He pointed at the men that they had dispatched together. Sophia's eyes widened as the reality of the havoc she had participated in revealed its casualties.

"Who are they?" she asked breathlessly.

"Two unfortunate sots hired to follow me out of Milan and finish me off, it would seem." He stopped his search of the dead man for a moment, and looked up at her. "Thank you, Sophia. I thought I was done for, for a moment there," he said quietly.

She nodded in response, not trusting her voice to get past the lump in her throat, as the wind whipped at her unbound hair.

Haldane gave Sophia his caped overcoat against the cold night air, ignoring the freezing cold of his sweat-soaked clothes. He then turned and looked through the other attacker's pockets, taking a few relevant items for later.

Dealing with the Italian authorities could be dicey, as one of the pair was shot in the back. Even though he was not in Italy on assignment, he was reasonably sure he could avoid any punishment for the two deaths with his diplomatic immunity, should the plea of self-defense prove insufficient. But the unwanted bodies added a layer of complication Haldane did not have the time or patience to deal with. He figured no one would come looking for these two any time soon. At present, he had other concerns more pressing. He handed the blunderbuss to Sophia, who resisted taking the large, heavy weapon.

"Sophia, it's empty now. It only holds two rounds. It won't fire again," he explained to her reluctance, showing her the vacant chamber before she would take it. "See, it is nothing but a harmless and somewhat decorative antique."

She relented and took the weapon from him. The heavily armed Sophia stood like some fantastic statue of Minerva in the full light of the moon. She cradled the two-barreled blunderbuss in one arm, the other clutched the naval pistol she had recently fired with deadly accuracy. Haldane mused that perhaps his earlier assessment of her was mistaken. If he sent her alone by rail to Florence thus accessorized, it would be the assassins sent to follow her that would be in danger.

As she watched, he prepared a hasty grave of piled stones over the two bodies in a shallow ditch. When finished, he approached her. Sophia's eyes were closed and her lips moved in soft prayer. She crossed herself through the arsenal of weapons she bore. The act made her seem a crusading mercenary praying after a victorious battle. But the tear that trickled down her cheek betrayed her true emotions at taking a human life. Her sincere act of faithful repentance both fascinated and appalled Haldane, for he felt no remorse at the life he had taken, only relief. Once more, he wondered at the mystery that drew them together.

Haldane carried her back to the cabin to avoid further damaging her already torn feet. Wrapping her arms about his neck, she held him closely in the cold moonlight of New Year's Eve, inhaling his masculine scent. The clanking of the various weapons she clutched accompanied them with a martial rhythm for their retreat to safety.

When they reached the cabin, Haldane put Sophia down on the small porch and saw her safely inside. Retrieving his overcoat, he then went looking for the horse. He found the beast milling around the shed, awaiting food and water. He unstrapped the packages from the saddle and brought them inside to Sophia, who received each one with delight.

Giving her the feminine attire seemed to lift her spirits, as he had hoped. He also handed her the package of food he had purchased at the tavern, telling her not to bother with preparing it. He promised that after he bedded the horse for the night, he would return and fix supper for the two of them.

After tending to the animal, and satisfying himself that no one had trailed his attackers, Haldane returned to the cabin to find that Sophia had wasted no time to dress in the new outfit he had purchased for her. The green and gold silk shone in the lamplight, the height of current Milanese fashion, with a multitude of layers of flounces and lace.

"I trust everything fits," Haldane said as he looked at the smartly dressed lady before him.

"Yes, perfectly. You must do this sort of thing often, to be so skilled," she coquetted. Sophia preened and turned for Haldane to observe the perfection of her figure. The exact angles of her every surface were not wasted on him. Haldane looked away to disguise his abashment.

"But of course," he retorted with a soft choke. "Dreadfully sorry about the shoes, but they were the best available."

"They are fine. They are a mite too big, but I am glad for that, after walking over all those rocks and roots in the woods," Sophia said as she lifted her skirt for Haldane to see how neatly the simple shop girl's shoes fit her own dainty foot.

He observed that she lifted her skirt somewhat higher than absolutely necessary to show him her shoe, displaying the delicately patterned silken hose on her shapely shin. She peered coyly at him over the top of her sleeve, then, released the skirts and let them fall.

"Thank you, Jordan," she said with simple sincerity, dropping her coquetting as easily as she dropped her skirt. "They are all quite beautiful. You must have gone to great trouble and expense for me. Thank you, they are very lovely." She curtsied politely and said, "I am sure you would like to bathe and dress in clean clothing yourself. Please do so while I see what it is you have brought for our supper."

Sophia showed him the garments that she had readied for him on a chair near the curtained washing corner. Haldane raised an eyebrow at her initiative and took the clean clothing she had provided.

"That was most thoughtful of you, Sophia. Thank *you*," he responded, and stepped into the corner of the cabin where the basin had been prepared with freshly heated water. Drawing the curtain made him uneasily aware that he could no longer see the contents of the room.

Sheepishly, he stripped down to his waist to wash and change into the fresh clothing, knowing that Sophia was a mere two or three meters away on the other side of the thin green curtain. Her shadow was occasionally cast on the gossamer barrier between them, distorted by the lamplight.

Sophia began to hum the tune of "In diesen heil'gen Hallen." He listened as Sophia's well-trained voice easily mastered the famous aria with passion and a deep understanding of the Germanic music she wordlessly hummed.

Haldane just finished closing the last button on his sleeve as Sophia reached the end of the aria. He parted the curtain of soft green fabric that had separated them during the impromptu rendition of Mozart's music, and beheld the beautiful creature who had filled the very air with splendid song.

"I had no idea how lovely your voice is," said Haldane. "Sophia, have you ever considered singing professionally?" His admiration was genuine, as was his suggestion. Haldane had numerous contacts in the cultured class of opera. As he thought of them a new plan for Sophia's possible future emerged in his mind.

"Professionally?" she said with a laugh. "Me? Surely you jest, sir... However," she gave a little pause. "When I was a girl I did dream of being a diva, traveling from city to city, singing the great music of the masters.... But, such a thing was not to be for me." She ended with a sad little smile and turned away.

"And whyever not," asked Haldane as he came up behind her.

"I'm the eldest daughter of a Grand Marquis and Marquessa. Opera is to be participated in by attending, not performing." Her words sounded as if she were reciting a rehearsed speech.

"If that is what you truly want to do with your life. If that is who you wish to be," said Haldane against the onslaught of self-restriction in her voice and manner.

"No, I am too old now to even consider such an idea. It takes years to properly train for the stage, a lifetime. You speak of fulfilling the dreams of a foolish little child. She no longer exists, I fear." She started to move away from him, only to be caught by his strong hands to face his insistence.

"How old are you, Sophia?" he asked.

"Twenty-six," she replied.

"You are certainly not too old," he encouraged. "It is obvious that you have already trained your voice to a point where with further a bit of work you could prove successful. Sophia, I can help you. I know people who could train you and establish you in a fine company. It might be difficult at first, but you could have the resources to support yourself. Be who *you* design *yourself* to be," he said emphatically, as he held her hand. "Do not follow blindly in the easy mold cast for you by title and estate. I know too well how confining nobility can be, how limiting to the unfolding of dreams and personal ambitions. But, you are no longer a child and this dream has never been foolish, for I can see that it comes from the depth of your own heart. Dream this dream with me, Sophia. Allow this to happen for yourself, you deserve it. Let me help you make your dreams come true."

Sophia's eyes widened in surprise, as Haldane held her hand captive. Electric shocks ran through her body at his touch. She looked away self-consciously.

"You have already helped me more than enough for one life time. You have saved my arbor *and* saved me from Sergio. That's quite sufficient," she said softly, as she extricated her hand and broke away to turn back to the table where she had set their dinner. "Come, let us dine."

"Yes, and you have saved my life, this very evening, for which I am eternally grateful, and in your debt," said Haldane. As she stopped and turned to face him, lingering silence fell between them. His eyes bore into hers once more. "Well, if you should ever change your mind," he finally continued, "the public eagerly awaits the delight of your voice, as do I."

During the meal, Haldane imparted his plan to return Sophia to her villa, now that Aldo was gone. She readily agreed, her preference being to go home, rather than go into hiding, possibly endangering whomever should shelter her. She trusted the stalwart defenses of Villa D'Amici far more than any safehouse Haldane could provide.

Later, they sat together on the worn leather divan, which Haldane had drawn near the iron stove. They agreed not to speak further of the dire circumstances that brought them to the cabin, nor the ensuing ambush. Instead, they talked of opera, botany, London and Milan. Haldane did his best to describe the differences between the two ancient cities, their politics, markets, and arts. Sophia listened with intelligence, drawing profound conclusions on her own. He delighted in talking to her, and listening as she explained her often-startling point of view, gleaned from her studies.

Engaged in conversation, Sophia's stubbornness faded. She became attentive and talkative, yet never shallow or false. Throughout the evening, Haldane often fought off the urge to take Sophia in his arms and make her forget about everything except him. Yet, he resisted this impulse resolutely, without knowing or caring why.

He knew that under similar circumstances in the past he rarely resisted temptation, but this time was different. He enjoyed being so tantalizingly close to Sophia, without actually touching or making advances. He discovered, to his surprise, that he would rather listen to her lovely voice and share her perceptions and feelings. From time to time, every now and then, Sophia would look at him a certain way, and his heart was ravished anew by the memory of their mysterious unity. Madness or not, he did not want it to end.

Many times during their lively conversation, a hush would come over them, when they would sit quietly, without need of words to understand the other's meaning.

Sophia was relieved, confused and slightly hurt that Haldane had not made any advances on her. She knew that her honor was in a precarious position.

*He is a true gentleman. He is nothing like Sergio. And he has given so generously to me, without trying to claim repayment,* Sophia thought, even as she secretly wished he would demand his pound of flesh. *He is too honorable, he would probably be horrified to know I had such unworthy thoughts of him,* she scolded internally. *Even these base thoughts condemn me. I am glad they do not seem to burden him, too.*

155

They welcomed in the New Year at midnight, toasting one another with champagne he had bought in Milan, both of them pretending not to notice the electric shocks running through their bodies when their fingers happened to touch. They turned their words to the dialogues of Plato, and the battles of Caesar and Alexander, instead.

"So tell me about your travels," Sophia encouraged, as she nibbled on a piece of pannetone, curled up on the divan, while Haldane sat nearby in the cabin's only battered armchair. "Where all have you been?"

He smiled and rubbed his jaw. "Where haven't I been... All over Europe... Moscow... India... Egypt..."

"Oh, I'd love to go to Egypt and see the pyramids!" she exclaimed. "It must be wonderful to get to travel so much! I've been to Naples and Florence and Assisi, but I have never left Italy. So what is it, exactly, that you do in the British Army, that keeps you travelling so?"

"My official title is Strategic Analyst and Negotiator. I am sent into various nations to assess the military situations and determine what actions are in my kingdom's best interests. And I also help to negotiate treaties, ransoms and what-not," he replied.

"Oh my!" she said. "That sounds like a great deal of responsibility."

"It can be," he said, as images of the dead Spanish girl arose in his memory. "Sometimes, it can be hard to separate my personal sentiments from the requirements of my position... But I have certainly had opportunity to see the world."

"So how is it that you ended up working with Sergio?" Sophia asked, without looking at him.

Haldane flinched and looked away.

"I'm afraid my family's story is not much different from your own, you see. I borrowed some money from Aldo to keep them out of bankruptcy, but he also prevailed upon my negotiation skills as payment, just as he maneuvered you into marriage. I have almost repaid him – this was to be the last contract I negotiate for him." He gave a dry little laugh. "I thought myself almost free."

Sophia sighed. "I fear I shall never be free now."

"Nonsense," Haldane said, leaning forward and taking her hand. At once, her whole body tingled with his touch. "I should think your first order of business would be to find yourself a good legal counsel and see if you can seek an annulment."

"Annulment," she echoed. "Oh, do you think it is possible?"

"Well, you have been married only a couple of weeks, it could be," he said reassuringly, as he released her hand. "But you need to find out from someone knowledgeable of Italian law. At the very least, perhaps you could arrange a legal separation."

"Yes, I suppose so," she said dully, as the enormity of her dilemma threatened to overwhelm her. "Well, my godfather is a judge in Milano. He has been gone for some time, but I shall speak to him of it as soon as he returns."

"Excellent," Haldane replied. He pulled out his pocketwatch and checked the time. "Well, it's almost one-thirty. Perhaps we should think about getting some rest, eh?"

The idea of sleeping arrangements had been broached several times during their conversation, and had just as many times been interrupted by another topic. At two in the morning, they finally decided that perhaps they should discuss it again seriously.

"I insist. You take the bed, Sophia. I will sleep on the couch. I don't mind. I want you to be well rested when you go back home in the morning," Haldane told Sophia while stifling a yawn. "I'm so tired, I could sleep anywhere."

"But, how well can you rest, cramped on this small divan? I am much smaller. I could be quite comfortable here. You need not give up your bed a second night."

"No. I shouldn't be able to rest. I will not allow it. No more arguments. It is decided. You shall sleep in the bed and I shall take the couch," Haldane said with good-natured finality.

Sophia longed to tell him that he need not sleep on the couch at all, that they could share the single bed.

*Oh, what wicked thoughts!*

She was horrified by the insistent feelings that refused banishment. Never before had her emotions taken such precedence over her principles. But instead, she accepted his offer of sleeping arrangements and began to prepare for bed. She went behind the green curtain of the washing corner. There, she wriggled out of her gown and into the luxurious pink satin nightgown that Haldane had so thoughtfully provided.

Haldane nervously took off his shirt and boots, while he listened to the rustling that was coming from the curtained corner.

*I'm not going to try to boff her, after all,* he decided. *I can't use her to hurt Aldo. She deserves much better treatment than that, even if he doesn't.* The concept that sex could be other than manipulation never crossed his mind. *I'll take her back to the Villa D'Amici first thing in the morning, and catch the noon train to Naples in time to board the ship for London with the outgoing tide. It's best for everyone that I get the hell out of here at the soonest possibility.*

When Sophia parted the curtain, she found Haldane already resting on the small divan, his wool greatcoat draped over him. She quickly made her way to the bed and slipped under the covers with a shy little glance in his direction.

She had hoped that he would sleep bare-chested so she could once again follow the outlines of his torso. She wondered what it would be like to run her fingers over his chest, following the line of curling little hairs down his flat belly... Shocked at her own thought, she pulled the covers up closer to her face.

After numerous exchanges of "goodnight and sleep well," Sophia heard the change in Haldane's breathing and knew he had spoken his last to her for the night. She thought of the fact that they had purposefully stayed up together to toast the New Year, aware of the traditional folk beliefs that whomever one spent New Years Eve with past the stroke of midnight would prove their close companion for the coming year. Sophia closed her eyes to dream of such a possibility.

# Chapter Eighteen

The nightmare that trapped her offered little resemblance to the sweet dream of her expectations.

Sophia ran through dark woods where some monstrous pursuer followed with sinister intent. She called Jordan's name frantically as she stumbled and fell, cutting her hands and feet on the stones and thorns. As she lifted herself from the biting earth, she looked back at the villain who relentlessly followed her. She could only see the shadow of his fearsome and foreboding hulk. She pushed herself up from the ground and took flight again, calling the name of her new champion as she sought escape. Her eyes searched in frenzied desperation for any sign of Jordan in the hellish surroundings.

Suddenly, she saw him standing by the side of a deserted road, wearing a gentleman's frockcoat, not his accustomed uniform. Sophia's heart jumped with alarm at what the nightmarish panorama now presented to her. Her monstrous assailant loomed over him, threatening Jordan with violent death.

She watched in defenseless horror as the phantom demon destroyed her hopes and dreams of life with a fiery blast of iron and brimstone, emitted from the sinister figure's diabolical mouth. Jordan's body collapsed and fell into the mud. The hideous creature turned once again towards Sophia, the fires of hatred and revenge burned in its eyes.

"Jordan!" she screamed, as the nightmare turned on her. She awoke suddenly, only to find herself safe and looking up at the very man she feared dead.

"I'm here," Haldane said as he took her into his arms. The throes of her nightmare had awakened him and before he even knew what he was doing, he had moved towards her in the flickering light of the open stove. He stroked her hair and continued to soothe her with gentle words and caresses.

"There, there, my Sophia. I am here. Feel my arms around you, my dear, I'm right here with you," he murmured into her fragrant hair. She smelled so good.

She lifted her face from his wide chest. With gentle fingertips, Haldane wiped away Sophia's tears, careful not to touch her healing cuts and bruises from the night before. Looking into the dark pools of her eyes, he longed to answer their unuttered invitation, and bent his face towards hers.

She first offered her lips to his softly, with small whimpering sounds each time they lightly brushed together. Her rapidly beating heart, driven into panic with nightmare of his demise, longed for the security of his embrace. His lips gently touched and fondled hers, while his eyes held Sophia's, his mustache tickling her face. As she slowly stretched her slim white arms around his neck, the vengeful shadows of the monstrous phantom villain of her dream faded and fled.

A myriad of emotions played through his being. This exquisite and delicate woman was inducing equally exquisite and delicate responses in him. Tingling fingers traced Sophia's warm white jaw and throat, as his lips gently fondled hers with a small smile.

Her pink satin gown slipped down to reveal one smooth ivory shoulder to his caress. His warm hand rolled over its surface, enlivening her spirits with his appreciation of its beauty. The more she surrendered to his touch, the more empowered her soul became. Her head fell gently back against the pillow, basking in his adoration. He gently shifted their combined weight onto the bed, gazing into her dark eyes before bending towards her face once more.

Abandoning his earlier resolution to keep their relationship chaste in the face of his rising emotions, Haldane realized, on some level, that he was making a choice at this moment that would forever change the course of his life. Once more, the double awareness assailed him, as he felt Sophia's body and his in the dark cabin, but also in the other knowing, he and Sophia were not separate, but joined in the peculiar aether of the vast being. Never had anything felt so true, so real. The completeness and perfection of the moment made a pale mummery of everything that had come before. He saw the pattern of his life laid before him, and eagerly answered the call of his soul as he again avowed his fate to hers.

Their kisses became deeper, more lovingly familiar with each encounter of their lips, while their eyes remained locked in each other's embrace. Sophia's lips parted under Haldane's insistent pressure. Her eyes widened as she felt his tongue slip sensuously into her mouth and gently tantalize her own response. Surprised at her body's reaction, Sophia's fears were replaced with a bold yearning that blossomed upon her sensibilities. She returned his passionate kisses, searching his mouth with hers.

Her hands explored the texture of his face as her thoughts centered on his potent effect upon her life. He had come to her like a heroic champion out of her long forgotten dreams, giving freely all his resources and skills in loving service to her needs, willing to risk life and limb to see to her well-being and protect her. She wanted now to please him, to show him what his efforts meant to her.

Haldane received her increased ardor with a delighted little chuckle. His hand glided over Sophia's satin covered breasts, caressing and exciting her. She smelled his virile scent as his warm kisses moved down her creamy throat, towards the deep crevasse of her bosom. When Sophia cradled his head to her heart, Haldane knew with a shock that he had been creeping up on this one moment his whole life. His entire existence was merely the prelude to this time… this choice, the sweet taste of which was sufficient to justify his past and his future.

Her desire was bolstered by his smile when she slipped her hands under his knit silk undershirt, as she bit her lower lip mischievously. The feel of his warm flesh sent delicious thrills throughout her whole body. Haldane half sat up on his side, and with Sophia's help, yanked the shirt over his head. He sat up and discarded the garment, tossing it to the floor. She reached a shy hand to him and touched his bare shoulder. His encouraging eyes invited her spirit of adventure to proceed.

A slow grin broke out on Sophia's face as her hands began fearless exploration of Haldane's chest, now living the earlier fantasy of the sensations she would find there. But how much more there was to it than she could have imagined! She ran her hands over the taunt muscles of his body, exploring his smooth skin and curling hair, noting how dark his skin seemed next to hers in the flickering firelight.

Sophia soon began to explore with her lips what her curious hands had discovered, moving into Haldane's welcoming arms. He rolled over, pulling Sophia on top of him. Haldane reached up to kiss her as she allowed herself to be drawn down onto his chest.

She stretched out her body on his, feeling the hard strength of him through her nightgown. She felt the growing pressure of his ardor against her thigh with mounting excitement. She had never seen an aroused man before, except for horrifying glimpses during Aldo's attempt at her, yet she knew in theory what to expect. She reveled in the delicious fear of that expectation. She longed to know Haldane's body as well as he seemed to know hers.

His hands slid over the surface of her body, and his kisses hot down her neck. Arching her back, Sophia raised up from Haldane's chest enough to allow him to curl his face towards her breasts.

With one hand, Haldane pulled the ribbons holding her gown closed at the breastbone. Tenderly, he swept it out of his way so he could cover her bosom with his lingering kisses. She gasped as honeyed lightening struck through her when he took her nipple into his mouth. A fierce hunger was now ignited in her. She again cradled his head to her heart as he continued to fondle and inflame her.

Haldane could feel the heat from between her legs upon his thigh, straddled between her own. He ran his hand down her side and on top of her backside. Gently, he pushed her derriere down towards his own hips, which he raised to meet hers. Sophia released a soft sigh as her hips began to pick up the rhythm that Haldane was teaching them. Wrapping his arms about her, he gently rolled Sophia onto her back, coming to rest between her legs.

Every sensation of her sent his mind to higher levels of attention. Every moment was saturated in poignancy, lasting a thousand years. Every curve, look, smell, touch and taste of her revealed a whole new universe both within and without him. He was enraptured in an immortal joy that begged fulfillment. Never had anything felt so right to him as having Sophia in his arms – the perfection of the moment was complete. Even the horrors of the past two days seemed an integral part of the whole, contributing to the cosmic symmetry. In the double awareness, the embodied part of him feared he was losing his mind, yet the other part that abided in eternal vastness knew he was merely discovering it. His heart refused to heed the objections of his intellect. He drowned his doubts in the sweat mead of Sophia's mouth.

Sophia's lips slid off of Haldane's and down his neck, as he hovered over her. Her lips touched metal. She pulled back to look at a fine gold chain around his neck, bearing a small cross and religious medal. Pulling these out of her way, she kissed and nibbled her way down his chest. Following in his treatment of her, she took his nipple into her own mouth.

She smiled with satisfaction when she felt Haldane's body involuntarily jerk on top of her own in response to her attentions. She slid her hand down his ribs, past his waist, until the fabric of his uniform breeches stopped them. Mimicking his earlier motion, she reached and pressed his hips into her. Sophia opened her legs as much as her long gown would allow, as Haldane slid between them. He kissed her mouth with deep, lingering kisses, gently teasing and probing.

Carefully balancing so as not to crush her, Haldane leaned to one side, propping himself on one elbow. Now that his weight was removed from on top of her, she once more began her explorations of him. This time her search was the terra incognito of his trousers. She ran her hands over his firm buttocks, over his narrow hips and the growing bulge between his legs. Haldane half-closed his eyes in pleasure as he pressed himself into the palm of Sophia's hand.

Watching his face in growing amazement, Sophia grew more intrepid. Her nimble fingers began fumbling at the fly to his breeches, forbidden excitement making her fingers clumsy. Surprised and pleased by Sophia's boldness, Haldane rose to his knees, straddling her soft thighs between his knees.

She reached up with trembling fingers and unfastened the buttons of his trousers, steeped in the deliciously dangerous responsibility of her own actions.

*This is really happening! He wants me as much as I want him!*

She hesitated a brief moment as the thought, *I am a Murderess-an Adulteress, leading Jordan into sin with me,* flashed across her mind. But she chose to listen instead to the passion of the moment, which swept her away in its growing demands on her senses.

He drew off the uniform pants and dropped them to the floor. He lay down on the bed and embraced her again, wearing only his silken jersey shorts to conceal the heights of passion she had stirred in him. He wanted her so, yet he allowed Sophia to make all the advances, not wanting to risk frightening her after the ordeal she had endured only the night before at the hands of Aldo. When she gently tugged at the waistband of his shorts, his hand slid gently over her own.

"Are you sure?" he whispered as he studied her face half hidden in the flickering shadows.

"Are you?" Sophia challenged playfully.

Haldane's briefs soon lay next to his uniform trousers on the floor. As he slipped under the bedclothes, Sophia greeted him with a loving embrace. She kissed his fiery mouth while his hand traced the luscious curves of her inviting hips. Her pink gown slowly rolled up her full round thighs as Haldane's hand explored their smooth surface. She thrilled to the discovery of her own skin's silken beauty, experienced vicariously in the appreciation of his gentle and instructive hands. When his warm palm came to rest on top of the mound of dark curls between her cushiony hips, she quivered with anticipation.

He kissed her as his fingers tugged masterfully at the silken bed surrounding her feminine secrets. Her body rose forward with delicious desire, inviting his fingers to slip into her. His eyes searched hers as his touch lightly traced the outlines of her warm wet opening. She pushed against his hand and moaned deeply in her chest, on the verge of discovering the long-denied mysteries she sought. Her mouth found his with an eager wanting as he moved himself between her soft enfolding thighs.

Sophia trembled in reaction to the wave of passion that flooded over her senses, as Haldane rubbed against her, without actually entering her. She drifted in timeless ecstasy, allowing her body to become more familiar with the strange sensations that engulfed her.

Sophia's pulse united itself with Haldane's heartbeat, as his masculinity unfolded her feminine awakening. Suddenly, lightning surged through her body, as Sophia's hips strained towards Haldane's in the throes of rapture. The ecstasy of her first orgasm embraced her soul with release, and Sophia's passion yearned for completeness.

"Give yourself to me," Sophia breathed in a dark, husky voice, "As I give myself to you, forever." As she spoke, her scorching hands grasped his waist, suddenly pulling Haldane down into her aching depths.

The chaste temple of her body gave up its token resistance. Sophia's eyes widened, she gave a surprised little cry as the feminine door of her recesses broke open and bathed Haldane with her virgin blood. She had not expected this burning, stinging pain after the liberating sensations of her climax only a moment before. Fearing she had done some injurious wrong, she slowed her impassioned movements.

"Oh, Sophia," Haldane cried, his surprise at taking her virginity was matched only by the surge of his own passion.

She was opened and filled with the length of him, at once alarming and enticing her. The stinging pain vanished as quickly as it had made itself known. It was now replaced with wonderful new sensations at every stroke of his body against her, faster, deeper he moved within her. Her heart pounded, sweat glazed her body, making it easy for Haldane to slide across her skin.

Haldane gasped and closed his eyes. Then, with a soft, low moan, he raised up onto his hands, thrusting into her again and again.

Sophia trembled anew with the knowledge that she had truly given herself to Jordan. She felt the force of him deep within, as she delivered him to the heights of ecstasy. A tear trickled from her eyes, mixing with her spicy sweat. She grasped his hips, raised her knees, making possible for him to plunge even deeper.

Sophia quivered again, as energy pulsed from between her legs, as she reached for another peak of fulfillment under Jordan's tutelage. This time she rode the crest of her mounting passion. Every nerve and fiber of her being was on fire, taking her higher and farther into the mysteries of love. Every muscle in her body strained with the effort as her breath came in harsh gulps.

The darkness of the room was suddenly illumined with a thousand suns, and for one brief, eternal moment, the twin souls of Jordan and Sophia joined together in an ageless rapture. His double vision resolved into one whole awarenss of endless light and limitless love. The yearnings of a thousand lifetimes tasted fulfillment. Liquid lightning flew up Jordan's spine as the balance tipped, and his body jerked again in climax. His soul seemed to rush into her receptive body, along with his seed.

Sophia fancied she heard Jordan's secret thoughts, communicated through the mystical and holy aether, which seemed to permeate their passion. The voice was the same she had always equated with Alcibiades, having a quality that seemed to emanate from all places. The masculine inner-voice asked her to take the offered soul of a child into her body.

Seeking out the loftiest places of her noble character, Sophia felt Jordan's spirit bond with hers in an unabashed ceremony of willing capitulation and commitment. As her passion reached its surging peak, Sophia looked deeply into the living eyes of the father of this new mystery of her soul, gasping for breath before sweet spasms blotted out all thought. As Jordan pushed to his final depth inside her, Sophia knew she would bear him a son.

Jordan rested inside Sophia's warmth, as the trembling in both their bodies began to quell, the brilliance to fade into the shadows. Tenderly, he nuzzled her neck and throat, murmuring endearments, more at peace than he had ever known. He wondered at this incredible woman he now held.

The tugging sensation in his chest bid him whisper in her ear, "I love you, Sophia. I always will, no matter what. You must believe me, no matter what happens, I shall always love you... I feel as if I always have done, but only known it just now."

Sophia looked into her lover's face with tears clouding her eyes. "Oh, Jordan... I love you! I feel it, too. It's as if I had always known you would find me. I'm so sorry I didn't wait any longer for you. I should have known you would come for me when I needed you most. I was afraid you were only a foolish girl's dream. I should have had more faith," she cried with tears staining her cheeks. She looked into his eyes, ignoring her tears. In a fierce voice, she said, "I love you, Jordan... I don't care what happens now. We've found each other, and that's all that matters."

"Sophia... There's much I should tell you. I don't know what the future holds—"

"– Ssshhh!" Sophia interrupted, stopping his words with a finger to his lips. "No one knows what tricks fortune might play upon us in the future. Let's not spoil this moment by talking about tomorrow. I only want to enjoy this time now, so I can remember it for the rest of my life. I want to have you now, and not think about the consequences tomorrow brings. We may not have tomorrow, but we do have tonight."

With that, Sophia raised her head to kiss him once more. Their lips touched and the passion flared again, and once more they gave in to the wild ecstasy that engulfed them.

# Nineteen

Count Otto Wittgenstein stood in the sunlit ward of the whitewashed hospital, gazing down at Aldo's unconscious form. Aldo lay prone, the gory stump of his left leg propped up on pillows to slow the bleeding from the fresh amputation.

A reptilian smile played across Wittgenstein's handsome features as he stood with arms folded across his chest, his golden ponytail spilling about his black-coated shoulders. He reached into his pocket drew out a small ebony enamel sphere about the size of a small apple, which he held up and admired from different angles.

"So much for your superior Italian planning," he smirked. "Now, it is my turn. We shall soon see which is the Master Race. Heal well, comrade… heal well."

# SPRING 2014

*It is always the darkest before the dawn...*

At the bottom of the night, in the aftermath of their forbidden affair, Lieutenant Colonel Christopher Jordan Haldane and Marquessa Sophia D'Amici must confront who they have allowed themselves to be, and who they wish to become. On the run from the dark forces they have evoked, Haldane and Sophia face the mysteries of blood, love and identity. Don't miss any of the sexy, mind-expanding action!

*"The nature of things is in the habit of concealing itself."*
*-Heraclitus*

**Herald of the Dawn is Book II of the GrailChase Chronicles, the mind-boggling series of expanding consciousness and strange technology. Written by philosopher and best-selling author, Dara Fogel, the GrailChase Chronicles challenges traditional beliefs and definitions of reality.**

**Website:** www.province-of-the-mind.com
**Facebook:** Dara Fogel's Author Page

## Bonus Chapter

# HERALD OF THE DAWN: BOOK II OF THE GRAILCHASECHRONICLES

### 1 January, 1873  Calyx Residence, Milan, Italy   9:06 a.m.

Judge Giuseppe Calyx rushed into the workshop attached to the back of his fine townhouse, holding a letter. The cold room smelled of sawdust and gunpowder.

"Anton! Where the devil did you – ah! There you are!" he said, as he saw Delacroix seated at the workbench, bent over his project. "I just got word from Villa D'Amici!"

Delacroix looked up at the excited Calyx with wary eyes. "Yes?" he asked.

"Aldo is gone! It seems that somehow, Haldane has managed to get rid us of Aldo and his minions," Calyx said.

"What?!" Delacroix cried, dropping the revolver he was cleaning onto the rough wooden workbench. "What's that you say?"

"Haldane has gotten Aldo out of the villa," Calyx repeated. "The details are somewhat unclear, but it seems that Aldo was badly wounded last night while attacking Sophia. He was taken to hospital here in Milan last night in very bad shape. Sophia escaped, and this morning, Haldane showed up at the villa and turned out the rest of Aldo's men."

"How?" Delacroix demanded incredulously.

"I don't know," Calyx replied. "All I know is that the Archives and Sandro's workshop are safe! Whoever's side Haldane is on, it certainly does not seem to be Aldo's."

"This is very welcome news," Delacroix said, and looked down at the weapon he had been preparing with a sigh of relief. "I suppose I won't be needing this today, after all," he said.

"A good omen for the New Year," Calyx rejoined with a broad smile.

## 1 January, 1873   Calendri Cabin   9:27 a.m.

Insistent pounding invaded Sophia's sweet dreams. Resisting the call to awaken, she moaned and rolled over, pulling a pillow over her face to muffle the unwanted intrusion.

A sharp crinkling poked into her ear. Surprised by the unexpected sensation, Sophia opened her eyes to a world quite different from the sweet one she had just left.

*Damn those workmen!* Sophia thought with sharp resentment. *I thought I told Sergio to...* Horror overtook Sophia as her eyes revealed the spartan interior of the mountain cabin rather than the luxuriant bedchamber she expected to behold.

*Where??? How??* Her mind struggled to catch up to the present, but kept getting snagged on the tumult of recent events. She sat upright in bed.

"Donna Sophia! Are you alright?" a vaguely familiar voice cried through the pounding.

Sophia rubbed her eyes, pushed the hair from her face and began to take her bearings. Suddenly chill, she realized she was naked, her nightgown on the floor where it had been discarded the night before.

"Yes, I believe so," she replied shivering, as she began to gather the bedclothes about her.

"Thank God! We were terrified for your life, Donna! We came as soon as Colonel Haldane told us where to find you," the gruff voice continued from behind the door.

Sophia glanced about the cold room, the fire in the stove down to dying embers.

*And just where is the Colonel?* Sophia wondered as Haldane's absence sunk in. She pulled herself out of bed, swathed in the faded comforter, and padded to the heavy wooden door and opened the latch enough for her to barely make out the face of Lucio, one of her father's few remaining aged retainers. Sophia flung open the door to greet him.

"Oh, Lucio! I can't tell you how happy I am to see you," she cried as she looked to the carriage beyond him. "Have you come to take me to Colonel Haldane?"

The old man took in his mistress' disheveled state cautiously.

"No, Donna," he told her, averting his eyes from her sudden self-conscious blush. "Signor Colonel charged us to bring you home. Signor Sergio has been taken to a hospital in Milan near death, and all his men have left to attend him, at the Colonel's insistence. Colonel Haldane ordered us to close the gate and lock it after them. Then he sent Julio and I to come bring you home."

"He's gone," Sophia whispered in awe. "Oh, you said you would and now you have...." She realized the servant was watching with growing concern for his lady's mental state. "Colonel Haldane promised he would help me to free myself from Signor Sergio... never mind that now... Tell me, where is Colonel Haldane? H-he left last night, I think, while I slept..."

"I do not know where he is, Donna," he replied uncomfortably. "All I know is what I've told you. Colonel Haldane told us to bring you home as quickly as possible."

"Yes, of course, Lucio," Sophia answered. "I'm sorry. Give me a few moments and I shall be ready to travel."

She closed the door and looked about the spare room. Not only was Haldane missing, so were all his belongings. Thinking it odd, she found her clothes, dressed, and arranged her hair as best she could. She pushed her questions away and focused at the task at hand, trusting that Haldane had provided for her best interests and would soon reappear. She wished to acquit herself well for his inspection, in echo of his display of noble self-sufficiency that had so impressed her the evening before.

She gathered up the last of her few belongings and started to leave, yet, casting a glance back, she saw something on the unmade bed which had escaped her earlier notice: a note pinned to one of the pillows. Breaking into a relieved smile, Sophia dropped her things and ran to snatch up the folded piece of paper.

*See, he didn't just leave without a word,* she thought, finally giving form to her unspoken fear.

Tenderly, she unfolded the paper and read its contents with growing reassurance.

*My Darling Sophia,*
*I regret leaving without speaking with you first, but I couldn't risk damaging your honor if I were to be discovered with you,*

*and if I were to stay, my devotion would be too obvious to all. If you are to secure an annulment from Signor Aldo, your name must not be in question.*

*Therefore, as much as it pains my heart, I must be away. I shall do my utmost to see you home safely. Perhaps someday, but, no, I can't even hope for that, my dearest Sophia, for my regard for you is too high to bring stain upon you further than I already have. I offer my apology in no expectation of forgiveness, but know that I only want what is best for you. Please remember me kindly, as I shall you.*

*With Greatest Affection,*
*Jordan*

Sophia's eyes stung with tears as she finished reading the note.

How like her Alcibiades to sacrifice his own happiness to protect a lady's reputation. The combination of passionate abandon and ancient chivalry that Haldane seemed to be enchanted her and endeared him all the more to her.

*He is so noble, so thoughtful. How wonderful he is...* Her eyes glanced back over a few lines of the note, "Perhaps someday..." *Maybe someday, I'll be free from the mess I've made by marrying Sergio, and you can claim me as your own, my Jordan, my Alcibiades... But I've waited all my life for someday. How much longer do I have to wait? No... Now that I've found you, how can I let you pass so soon?*

Sophia tucked the note into her bosom, wiped her moist eyes and picked up her gear and strode out of the cabin into a new life.

Sophia swung up onto the step of the carriage and paused.

"Lucio, I have decided that instead of going home, you will take me to Milan," she commanded.

"Donna, Colonel Haldane told us to bring you straight home, and lock the gate behind us," Lucio objected.

"I don't care what you were told, Lucio," Sophia insisted. "Plans have changed, and I am telling you different. Now, I must try to catch Colonel Haldane. I have something of great importance to tell him."

The two servants looked at one another in resignation. Although it was against the better judgment of both men, they knew not to contradict their lady when she used that tone.

"Very well, Donna. To Milano it is."

In Milan, at the British Embassy, Sophia was informed that Colonel Haldane had taken a train south for Naples and was scheduled to return to Britain on the next ship.

Sophia sat in her carriage outside the railway station, trying to decide how to proceed. Her resources were meager at best, as was her experience. Yet, how could she let the man of her dreams walk out of her life without response?

Summoning all her resolve, she drew the elegant diamond ring from where her now betrayed and ailing husband had placed it, but a few weeks before. She handed the ring to Lucio.

"Take this to that jeweler's across the street. Tell them who you are and that I wish to sell this ring."

The old servant accepted his mistress' charge.

"I'll get the best price I can for you, Donna," he promised as he took his leave.

An hour later found Sophia perched in the bench of a train bound to depart for Naples. She was both amazed and surprised at her own audacity. Pride thrilled through her when she imagined Jordan's shocked delight when she would eventually catch up with him.

She had never traveled alone before, and her two trusty old servants were very reluctant to return to the villa without her. But Sophia thrilled to a new level of experience as she began to realize the radical freedom she had only imagined before.

*I should have done something like this years ago, and not just waited for some man to get me to try my wings,* she thought with growing enthusiasm. *Of course, Papa would have never let me...* The thought of her father left her feeling alone and frightened, suddenly small in the big world.

Second thoughts about pursuing this adventure plagued Sophia, snuffing out her flickering resolve. She rose to leave when the train began to lurch forward. Thrust back into her seat by the acceleration, Sophia realized the depth of her commitment as the trained pulled out for Naples.

Six hours later, as the train pulled into the Naples station, Sophia was still at war with herself. While her heart told her to find her beloved at any cost, reason spoke of responsibilities to home and family, and the lurking danger which still hung over her head by the slenderest of threads.

Sophia disembarked into the confusing bustle of the train station. She had been there several times before, but always accompanied by her father, who had made all arrangements and comforts easy. She now wished she had paid more attention on those outings to how the arrangements were made and where. Bewildered, she cast about for any familiar landmarks by which she could take her bearings.

Unable to remember the way, she decided to follow other passengers in the hopes of eventually finding something she recognized. She picked out an older gentleman who reminded her of her own father and followed him out of the huge building. At the front curb, the man hailed a waiting handsome cab, entered and rolled away. This seemed a reasonable course to Sophia. She hailed her own cab and instructed him to take her to the port.

Once at the wharf, the immensity of the task that she had set herself again threatened to overwhelm her. Thousands of people, coming and going, streamed past her without a second glance in her direction. There were hundreds of ships of every imaginable type and size, and dozens of docks. How could she find one single man in this tangle of humanity and iron?

Sophia had always prided herself on her intelligence and resilience, but now she felt stupid and weak as tears threatened to flow. Yet, her love urged her on. She ignored the long looks of the snickering men as she wandered along the wharfs, seeking out a midnight blue tunic festooned with gold braid. Relying on her previous tactic of following those who looked to her like they knew where they were going, she eventually found the docks from which British ships sailed.

She located a British officer who directed her to a central office for coordination of all British Military transport from these shores. Relief spread through Sophia, as she entered the office, sure she would now find her beloved.

"Pardon me," she smiled coyly at the young officer at the desk. "I am trying to find the whereabouts of a certain British Colonel. I understand you would know which boat he is on."

The smile had its intended effect upon the green young lieutenant.

"Yes, milady. Indeed, that would be me. How can I help you?"

"Where can I find Colonel Haldane, please?"

"Colonel Haldane?" the lieutenant repeated. "I'm sorry, milady. The only Colonel I've had come through here today sailed for London three hours ago."

"Oh," Sophia breathed, all her dreams unraveling before her eyes. She had never thought he would find passage so quickly from Italy. "How can I get a seat to Britain?"

The lieutenant took her measure.

"Milady, these are military transports. I'm afraid it's not possible to get you onto one of our ships, but I am sure that you could find passage on one of the passenger ships at the South Docks," he offered helpfully.

"The South Docks, yes. Thank you," she replied numbly. None of this was going as she had expected.

She found her way to the South Docks and spoke with a purchasing agent about the price of a ticket to London. The sum required exceeded the proceeds left from the sale of her wedding ring. She would either have to sell more of her jewelry in order to buy the ticket or return back to the villa. The ticket agent looked at her expectantly as she tried to decide what to do next. Unable to come to a snap conclusion, she thanked the man for his help and told him she would return.

Uncertainty permeated Sophia. Never had she felt at such a loss to meet her circumstance. Even her darkest moments had always been ensconced with familiarity and the underlying security of her family and home. But now, leagues from home and truly alone for the first time in her life, Sophia became acutely aware of the limits of her education and experience.

A low rumbling in her belly reminded her of the practicalities of life: she had not eaten since the evening before. She decided the first order of business was to get herself a decent meal and then to sit and plot out her next move.

She found a likely cafe and self-consciously indulged her appetite – the first meal she had ever eaten alone in public. It took her a few minutes to become accustomed to the wondering looks a woman sitting alone attracted. But after the initial discomfort wore off, she found that she actually enjoyed being able to concentrate all her attention to her meal, instead of dividing her focus between eating and maintaining an interesting conversation. Afterwards, she sat, sipping her coffee and thinking about how her life had turned upside down.

*Why did Papa never teach me how to get about a city?* she wondered. *He could have prepared me, taught me how to take care of myself. But no, I am a woman, so no matter what my own abilities indicate, I must be helpless.* Resentment began to bubble forth. *Papa, why did you teach me of honor and history, but not give me the means to take part? Why did you give me wings but not teach me to fly?*

Hating the role thrust upon her gender by her culture, Sophia was caught – she knew too much to ever be satisfied in the role society demanded of her, yet, she did not know enough to break free from those constraints. Her extensive readings in classics and philosophy did nothing to prepare her for the reality she now faced. Women were but a footnote to the on-going narrative of history. Study of history might serve to keep an intelligent daughter passive, but never should young girls be encouraged to adventure like their brothers. Everything in her life, even to the restriction of her very breaths taken within corseted ribs, was determined by her sex.

*In the past month and a half, I have been passed as possession through the hands of three men,* Sophia mused. *First was Papa. Sweet and adorable as he was, he still treated me like child. He never really had any faith in me.*

*Then after Papa died, I married Sergio, damn me, because I didn't think I could deal with the estate alone. I should have known better.*

*And then there's Jordan... my Alcibiades.* Tears welled up in her eyes. She struggled to keep her composure as a waiter approached her table and freshened her coffee.

After the waiter left, her thoughts took a new direction.

*Alcibiades... And just who is Alcibiades?* she wondered. *Is he just someone I made up, or is there more? Is Jordan really he? But how? Yet, I was so sure, it felt so right. And he felt it too... Didn't he? He seemed to...*

She dug into her bosom to retrieve his note. She reread the lines, trying to see behind the words to her lover's intention. But this time, instead of seeing the nobility and self-sacrifice, she saw a polite dismissal of a master to a servant after services rendered. Indignation stung through her, as cynicism crept into her heart.

*He used me... He got what he wanted from me and then he left. He's no better than Sergio...*

She thought again about her phantom lover and his resemblance to this roguish Englishman. *And yet, this is exactly this is the sort of thing that Alcibiades would do – not the Alcibiades I made up, but rather the historical Alcibiades. After all, he did betray both his home in Athens and his enemy Sparta. Why should I be surprised if my Alcibiades takes after the historical one? Now, I too have felt the sting of his betrayal.*

Rueful in her self-condemnation, Sophia smiled at her own folly. *I have undone myself. I should have known better. But why is it that the interesting ones are always such rogues?*

Sophia could not deny that Jordan had touched her soul as no other man ever had. In spite of her hurt and humiliation, she could not bring herself to hate him, for even in leaving as he did, he still seemed faithful to her archetype.

*Well, it seems there's nothing left for me to do but to return home and straighten things out there. I must get rid of Sergio for good and teach myself how to take care of the House's business.* She swallowed the last of her coffee, and looked ahead with new resolve.

# Special Exclusive Bonus!
## Only in the paperback edition

## Suggested Reading List

For those who would like to delve deeper into the topics and inspiration in The GrailChase Chronicles.

**Fiction**
*Dune*, by Frank Herbert
*Dune Messiah*, by Frank Herbert
*Children of Dune*, by Frank Herbert
*The Mists of Avalon*, by Marion Zimmer Bradley
*Stardust*, by Neil Gaiman
*Time Enough for Love*, by Robert Heinlein
*Raise High the Roofbeams Carpenters*, by J.D. Salinger
*The Earthsea Trilogy*, by Ursula K. LeGuin
*Beelzebub's Tales to His Grandson*, by G.I. Gurdjieff

**Non-Fiction**
*Holy Blood, Holy Grail*, by Biagent, Lincoln & Lincoln
*The Gnostic Gospels*, by Elaine Pagels
*The Nag Hammadi Library*
*Up From Eden*, by Ken Wilbur
*The Time Falling Bodies Take to Light*, by William Irwin Thompson
*The Republic,* by Plato
*The Nicomachean Ethics*, by Aristotle
*The Book: On the Taboo Against Knowing Who You Are*, by Alan Watts
*"The Self"* by William James
*Timetables of History*, by Bernard Grun

**Music Playlist**
"Carribean Blue" by Enya
"Tonight and the Rest of My Life" by Nina Gordon
"A Poem for Byzantium" by Delirium
"Sanveen" by Dead Can Dance
"Enjoy the Silence" by Depeche Mode

# ABOUT THE AUTHOR

Dara Fogel is an author, philosopher and educator in the American Southwest, where she lives with her husband, son, mother, two cats, a dog and a fish.


## OTHER BOOKS BY DARA FOGEL

### Before The Chase: A Short Anthology
A collection of three short and sassy stories, focusing on three characters at pivotal moments from the GrailChase Chronicles series.

### Herald of the Dawn
(spring 2014)
At the bottom of the night, in the aftermath of their forbidden affair, Lieutenant Colonel Christopher Jordan Haldane and Marquessa Sophia D'Amici must confront who they have allowed themselves to be, and who they wish to become. On the run from the dark forces they have evoked, Haldane and Sophia face the mysteries of blood, love and identity.

### Subjective Reality: Are You In or Out?
(spring/summer 2014)
Nonfiction. A non-technical consideration of the true nature of reality and what to do about it.


## CONNECT WITH DARA
Website: www.provinceofthemind.com
Blog: www.province-of-the-mind.com/personal-development.xml
Twitter: @aferalgod
Also on Facebook